YOU WILL KNOW ME

YOU WILL KNOW ME

MEGAN ABBOTT

PICADOR

First published 2016 by by Little, Brown and Company,
Hachette Book Group, New York

First published in the UK in 2016 by Picador
an imprint of Pan Macmillan
20 New Wharf Road, London N1 9RR
Associated companies throughout the world
www.panmacmillan.com

ISBN 978-1-4472-2635-2

Printed and bound by CPI Group (UK) Ltd, Croydon, CR0 4YY

Visit **www.picador.com** to read more about all our books
and to buy them. You will also find features, author interviews and
news of any author events, and you can sign up for e-newsletters
so that you're always first to hear about our new releases.

For Alison Quinn

YOU WILL KNOW ME

The Party

**GO DEVON! KNOX ROX! NEXT STOP: ELITE QUALIFIERS!
BELSTARS 4-EVER! REGIONAL CHAMPS!**

The vinyl banners rippled from the air vent, the restaurant roiling with parents, the bobbing of gymnast heads, music gushing from the weighty speakers keeled on the window ledges.

Slung around Devon's neck were three medals, two silver and one gold, her first regional-champion title on the vault.

"I'm so proud of you, sweetie," Katie whispered in her daughter's ear. "You can do anything."

Later, Katie would come to think of that night as the key to everything that came after, the secret code.

But at the time, it was just another party, a celebration like dozens of others, all to honor their exceptional fifteen-year-old daughter.

In six months, Devon would compete in Elite Qualifiers and, after years of bruising toil and hamstring tears and twenty-five thousand dollars in credit-card debt and one fateful misstep at her last qualifier, would at last assume the mantle of Senior Elite. From there, anything felt possible.

Everything was glowing: the disco ball spinning above, and the Sterno lights flickering under the kebabs and lomi-lomi atop long tables skirted with raffia, candles in coconut shells and pineapples that Katie had helped hollow out with ice cream scoopers.

Everyone was wearing a lei in honor of the booster club's Polynesian theme, and Katie spotted Devon smelling hers, the only one made with real orchids, purple and green, the exalted Coach T. having draped it over her head as she walked under the thatched arch to great applause. *Hail our Devon*, he'd intoned, that big voice of his, *for the future of BelStars rests on these powerful shoulders!*

It was the giddiest Katie had ever seen her daughter. Maybe it was the night, or the plastic cup of rum-spiked punch Eric let her have, offering some small release from the tight pincers that held her constantly.

In a corner, her son, Drew, sat with two other quiet fourth-grade boys, eating frozen bananas dipped in chocolate, their heads craned over handheld games. He was quieter than usual, scolded earlier for spilling, or pouring, chocolate milk all over Devon's perfectly softened good-luck grips.

"But Devon never gets in trouble," he'd said. "Not for sassing, or doing the treadmill when she's supposed to rest her knee. Not even for sneaking out at night."

"I never snuck out," Devon had insisted.

"You were dreaming," Katie had reminded him. He was always dreaming about his sister, saying he'd heard her, seen her doing things impossible and forbidden. *Mom, Devon was on the roof, flying. Her bed was on fire, Dad.* When he was little, he used to dream she had claws for feet.

"Buddy," Eric had said. "Let your sister have her night."

But Katie had whispered a promise to him: all the coconut cake and pineapple kebabs he wanted as long as he behaved.

By her second cocktail, fabric petals tickling her cheek, Katie had forgotten about Drew's misdeed, forgotten even about the uncomfortable moment, hours before at the stadium, a dozen rows ahead of them in the stands, that beet-faced dad in the GymDreamz cap, upset over his daughter's ranking, who'd shouted that disgusting thing (*Devon Knox! Devon sucks c—*), only stopping, midsentence, at his wife's glare.

But Eric had heard it. She could tell by the way his back stiffened, his jaw tightened.

She'd grabbed for his hand. Held it firmly.

But the moment passed, and now Eric stood at one of the banquet tables, carving the glistening ham, pink as a newborn.

Coach Teddy, a parasol'd mai tai impossibly dainty in his bear-paw hand, pulled Katie aside and said he was counting every second until July's qualifiers, when Devon would gain Senior Elite status and everyone would finally see.

"Because look at her," he said. "Just look at our once-and-future champ."

And Katie did, peering through the candy-colored crowd at the poppy and cobalt of Devon's jacket, its sparkling BelStars logo.

Less than five feet tall, a hard, smooth shell of a body. Hipless, breastless still, but the way she'd transformed her body in the last two years, thighs like trunks, shoulders and biceps straining her tank-top straps, staggered Katie.

"The world is hers now. Is yours. Is ours," Teddy said, then diving in for a loud rummy smack of a kiss flush on Katie's lips. "Just like I promised, Katie-did!"

Had that really happened?

It had, and it all made sense that night, the holy consummation of everything.

"I wish I could do what you do," Kirsten Siefert kept saying to Katie. "I want it for Jordan. I want to know everything you did. If it's not too late. Have you seen Jordan's breasts? But Tansy's only seven . . ."

The music boomed louder, and soon enough the adults started dancing, taking over the playlist from the endless thump and squeal of teen pop and club music, playing every song they'd loved fifteen years before, every opening chord releasing a chorus of *Yeahs* and *Oh God, remember?*

And there was that remarkable conversation with the booster vice president, Molly Chu.

In front of the ladies' room, capri-panted, soft-shouldered Molly—who rarely talked about anything but gymnastics and carpooling—leaned close and told Katie how, when she was a little girl, all she wanted was to be a majorette, like Erica Neubauer, the prettiest girl at Shelby West High.

"I used to watch her in all the parades, marching in those red-tassel booties, hurling her batons up to heaven," she said, giggling like a girl. "I remember watching her and thinking: *That is all I want.*"

And she told Katie how she'd stolen a piece of pipe from her father's tool bench, sprayed it silver, and jabbed a cork on one end.

"I'd twirl in the front yard for hours," she said. "It looked like a pinwheel in the sun."

She glanced at Katie, her eyes filling.

"Remember that kind of wanting? That kind that's just for yourself? And you don't even have to feel guilty about it? You wouldn't know you should."

Katie nodded and nodded and nodded, because it felt true even if she couldn't name the thing she'd wanted. But something. Looking around, she wondered, *Was it this?*

In front of them, a group of the littlest girls, still in their leotards—they never liked to take them off—started dancing in a circle together, chins lifted high and faces pink like ice cream.

"It's free then," Molly said, watching the girls, tilting her head and blinking fast. "It's never free again."

"What?" Katie said, because she'd lost the thread, if she'd ever had it. "What?"

But the music swallowed them, and then someone brought out a tray of shots, flaming.

Later, she found herself dancing with Eric (which hadn't happened in years, since that night they'd snuck to the hotel bar after a TOPs meet, Devon and Drew asleep upstairs, that lounge singer inexplicably crooning "Smells Like Teen Spirit").

Eric had always been a terrific dancer, and the championship and the lanterned loveliness of the old catering hall—they all enlivened him, his smile and his fingers moving so delicately, his arm grabbing her so firmly, and didn't everyone in the hall look at them?

A thought came to her rum-soaked head: *He's never loved me more than this. Because of Devon. Because of Devon. Something else I owe Devon.*

But they were changing partners, and Molly, who would later pass out in the wrong car, wiggled over, lassoed Eric, while Katie, who was tired anyway, ambled toward the ladies' room looking for Devon or Drew.

When she returned, there was Coach T. spinning his wife, Tina, around, a splotch of maraschino on her immaculate white shirt.

And the starry new arrivals: Coach's niece Hailey, yanking at the hand of that boyfriend of hers, Ryan Beck, both of them so tanned and love-blissed.

This would be the piece that mattered most later, months later when Ryan was gone. She would think of their arrival and wonder why she hadn't seen it all coming. But who could have seen anything at all that night but their bright-spangled beauty?

Hailey, the favored junior tumbling coach, blond and magnificent, a towering five feet seven, was beloved by her eight- and nine-year-olds (*Kiss those knees, sweetheart!* she'd tell them as they did their back hip circles), all of whom stared at her now from the corner, gaping at her lanky prettiness as if it were an achievement to strive for—after nailing the front tuck, before the back layout.

And Ryan, whose appearance sent all the girls into satellites of whispered frenzy.

"The only one here more handsome than your husband," said Becca Plonski, laughing.

And suddenly there was Molly Chu again.

Improbably, she was tossing a tiki pole into the air like it was a baton, like she was still the star twirler of Shelby West High.

My, Katie thought, *it is like a pinwheel.*

The music kept getting louder, the Forbidden Tiki playlist spinning, and Greg Siefert corralled Katie, pitcher of blue Hawaiians in one hand, reaching for hers with the other, and he was telling a story about Eric shouting at some man in the parking lot.

"It was great, it was great. That one who'd been talking trash

about our Devon. And Eric just let him have it. Hell, I was glad
to see it."

...But Katie was drunk, and it didn't register, the music loud
in a way that reminded her of when loud music was an urgent
necessity, a full-body sensation, and the next thing she knew she
was back at the punch bowl and Greg was limboing with Hailey,
freckled and game.

Then came the part that seemed like nothing at the time.
Months later, after Ryan was gone, its meaning would change, as
if by magic, every time Katie thought about it:

Ryan, dark-haired and grinning, took Katie's hand, spun her
once, twice, three times, to a power ballad she remembered from
age fourteen, an art-class infatuation, a fumbled encounter behind the shop room, then another girl and her heart breaking.

Before she knew it, though, Hailey was grabbing him back, a
wink and a gleam in her eye like, *Don't you dare, he's mine!*

At some point, she lost Devon, but there was Eric talking to
Gwen Weaver on the chilly loading dock, sharing a purloined
cigarette and laughing like they'd been shouting for hours.

Everyone was smoking, it turned out. She'd even caught
Ryan sneaking a puff in the hallway, the back door propped
open, the cold air giving her goose bumps.

Ryan, who smelled like soap and had the nicked, brambled
hands of a cook.

And she'd ended up in some long conversation with someone
about something, and she never could remember anything about
it after except the feeling of sticky, pineapple-streaked wall
against her back.

Finally, she and Eric shared one last dance before everything
broke, and pressing against his shirt she smelled candle wax and

a dozen perfumes; he was teasing her about the coconut husk furred onto her chest from the dance with Greg Siefert, or Bobby, or Ryan, who'd since been charged with making something called a momtini, carrying a tray for all the ladies.

"He *is* a momtini," whispered Kirsten Siefert, nearly rubbing her hands.

Crushed cocktail parasols gathered on the sills and crumpled leis collected in the corners like parade remnants catching on her feet, heels too high, too narrow, and she found Devon in the restroom, washing her face, washing all the performance makeup away.

Turning to her mother, she looked oddly blank.

For a second, Katie wondered about that look, but the second passed, and then there was more dancing, and more visits to the punch bowl, and the next morning she would puzzle over when she'd even been outside, finding grass blades between her toes, dried mud on the pad of her foot.

The ride home, Devon covered her head and wouldn't speak, and they thought she'd probably had more than one glass of punch but left her to it.

And then Drew, gorged on coconut cake, threw up into Katie's hands.

But none of it mattered, everything felt wonderful and she and Eric laughed and laughed.

Back in the bedroom, Eric standing over her, his face hidden in the dark.

"Wait, wait," she asked, remembering what Greg had told her, "did you get into an argument with that dad after the meet? The creep who called Devon that name? In the parking lot, did you—"

"Who told you that?" he said, laughing, his hands hooked around her legs, throwing her back on the bed. It reminded her of when they first met, that laugh. She'd sold him cotton candy at the Kiwanis fair.

That was more than sixteen years ago, and now, sometimes, they didn't see each other for days other than in the blue hours of late night and predawn. They knew each other most deeply through body-warmed sheets and the tangle of half dreams.

You might think it would doom the marriage, unless you pondered it for one more beat. Consider the prospect that your spouse could forever remain slightly other from you, his body never too familiar, his hands on you almost wholly to seduce you. You were mysterious to him and he was mysterious to you.

Other moms, in the confidences of long huddles in the stands, waiting in line for the restroom during a meet, would confess sexless stretches lasting for months, barren and mutual. Katie could only nod kindly and say nothing because Eric still felt like her secret lover, furtive and surprising, a bristly mouth on her neck, half-asleep murmurs and, in the morning, the soft welt on her shoulder, the lingering shiver of her legs.

They had been together so long, and a part of it was this. They had shared it long past when all the other couples they knew had stopped sharing anything other than credit-card debt and casual, or focused, resentment.

Strangely, in part it was because of Devon. They shared so much in sharing her, her endeavor. She held them together, tightly.

The morning after the party, Katie turned over and saw a violet smear on her pillowcase.

It took her a while to remember. After midnight, trundling

Drew across the ice-ribbed parking lot and into the car, Eric still inside, trying to find Devon, saying final good-byes.

A tap on the shoulder and it was Ryan Beck again. Smiling that chipped-front-tooth smile.

"Devon's?" he asked. Dangling from his open palm was a familiar lei, purple and green orchids, petals shredded. "I found it over by the dumpsters."

"What a shame," Katie said, feeling it more sharply than she should, blaming it on the rum. "Thanks."

He draped it over her head, its dampness tickling her, his sneakers nearly slipping on the rimy concrete. A squeak, a skid. Later, she would wonder if he'd slipped like that on Ash Road seconds before he died, his sneakers on the sandy gravel as the headlights came.

"Careful," Katie said, a catch in her voice. "It's not safe."

"Nothing ever is," he said, winking, his white tee glowing under the lights, backing away, into the dark of the emptying lot. "Good night, Mrs. Knox. Good night."

I.

"The eyes of a young girl can tell everything. And I always look in their eyes. There I can see if I will have a champion."

—Neshka Robeva, gymnast and coach

Chapter One

If she ever had to talk about it, which she never would, Katie would have to go back, back years before it happened. Before Coach T. and Hailey and Ryan Beck. Back before Devon was born, when there were only two Knoxes, neither of whom knew a tuck from a salto or what you called that glossy egg-shaped platform in the center of the room, the vault that would change their lives.

And Katie would tell it in three parts.

The Foot.

The Fall.

The Pit.

You could only begin to understand what happened, and why, if you understood these three things.

And Devon's talent. Because that had been there from the beginning, maybe even before the beginning.

In proud-parent moments, of which there were too many to count, she and Eric would talk about feeling Devon in the womb, her body arching and minnowing and promising itself to them both.

Soon, it turned to kicking. Kicking with such vigor that, one night, Katie woke to a popping sound and, breathless, keeled over in pain. Eric stared helplessly as her stomach seemed to spasm with alien horrors.

What was inside her? they wondered, her rib poking over her sternum, dislocated while she slept.

It was no alien, but it was something extraordinary.

It was Devon, a marvel, a girl wonder, a prodigy, a star.

Devon, kicking her way out. Out, out, out.

And they had made her.

And, in some ways, she had made them.

For years, Katie would touch the spot the rib had poked, as if she could still feel the tender lump. It was reassuring somehow. It reminded her that it had always been there, that force in Devon, that fire.

Like that line in that poem, the one she'd read in school, a lifetime ago. Back when life felt so cramped and small, when she never thought anything so grand could ever happen.

The force that through the green fuse drives the flower.

"She's been doing it since she was three? How is that even possible?"

That's what other people, never gym people, always said. Making private judgments, unspoken charges of helicopter parenting, unmet maternal, or paternal, ambitions, Olympic dreams. No one ever believed that Katie and Eric never cared about sports, or even competition. Eric had played high-school baseball, indifferently. Katie had never been athletic at all, devoting her adolescence to art class and boys and sneaking off to see bands, the vestige of which was the *Fight Like a Grrrl* tattoo snaking around her left thigh.

"My three-year-old just wanted to play," they'd say smugly. "We just let her play."

As if it had ever been a choice, or a decision.

"It started as play," Eric always told people. "It started with the trampoline."

Then he'd tell them how, one long Sunday, he'd installed it in the yard, leaning over the auger rented from the hardware store, a pile of chicken wire, empty beer bottles at his feet.

The trampoline was the better story, an easier one, but it wasn't the truth.

Because the trampoline came after the accident, came after the Foot. And the accident was how it truly began. How that force found its fuse.

Three-year-old Devon, barefoot, running across the lawn to Daddy.

Her foot sliding on a grass mound, she stumbled into the rust-eaten lawn mower Eric had left idling, her foot so tiny it slipped behind the blade guard, the steel shearing off two toes and a squeak of soft foot flesh.

A few feet away, face white with panic, Eric slid to his knees beside her and somehow managed to pluck both toes from the grass.

Packed in ice, they looked like pink peas and Katie held them in her hands as Eric drove with careering ferocity the six miles to the hospital where doctors tried (but failed) to reattach them, like stringing beads, Devon's face blue and wet.

"It could have been worse," their pediatrician, Dr. Yossarian, told them later. "With the riding mowers, sometimes the whole foot pops off." And he made an appalling pucker sound with his mouth.

"But what can we do?" Eric asked, even as Dr. Yossarian assured them Devon would be fine. "There must be something."

So Dr. Yossarian suggested kiddie soccer, or ice-skating, or tumbling.

"It'll help with balance," he said.

In years to come, this would feel like a moment of shimmering predestiny, in the same way everything about Devon's life eventually came to feel mythic within the family. Fate, destiny, retroactivated by a Sears Craftsman.

That fall, Katie drove Devon to the Tumbleangels Gym on Old Taylor Road and signed them both up for Mommy & Me Movers & Shakers.

"At first, she'll be overly cautious," Dr. Yossarian warned, "but try to push her."

Except it was just the opposite. Within a few weeks, Devon was forward- and backward-rolling. Next came chin-ups, handstands, cartwheels as accomplished as those of girls twice her age.

The Human Rubber Band, Katie called her.

Supergirl, Eric called her. *Monkey-bar superstar!*

And, in some mysterious way, it was as if the foot were helping her.

Frankenfoot, Katie dubbed it. Making it their private joke. *Show Mommy how you work that Frankenfoot.*

By the end of her first month, Devon had graduated to Tiny Tumblerz, and within a year, Devon was the gym's VIP, her cubbyhole sprayed silver and festooned with sticker stars.

Watching her on the practice beam, Katie would think, *This piece of wood is four inches wide, two feet in the air. Four inches. And I'm going to let my daughter plant her dimpled feet on that and do kicks and dips?*

"Do the O," the other girls would say, cheering as Devon arched her back from a handstand until her tiny bottom touched the top of her head. Every now and then, Eric would lift her up in the air to see if her backbone was really there.

Prodigy, Katie whispered in her most private thoughts but never said aloud. Eric said it. He said it a lot.

And so Eric installed the trampoline.

Hours, days devoted to making the yard ready for her talent, laying thick mats like dominoes. Just as he would eventually do in the basement, hanging a pull-up bar, scraping the concrete bumps off the floor, covering it with panel mats and carpet remnants, wrapping foam around the ceiling posts. For Devon.

And so gymnastics became the center, the mighty spine of everything for them.

Devon turning five, six, seven, thousands of hours driving to and from the gym, to and from the meets, a half a dozen emergency-room visits for the broken toe, knee sprain, elbow popping on the mat, seven stitches after Devon fell from the bars and bit through her tongue.

And the money. Gym tuition, meet fees, equipment, travel, booster fees. She and Eric had stopped counting, gradually becoming used to swelling credit-card debt.

Then, when Drew came along, their delicate, thoughtful son, nothing changed. Quiet, easy, he fit so perfectly—in temperament, in disposition—with everything that was already happening. Devon was happening.

After one meet, Devon medaling in three of four events, in the car on the way home, their fingers stiff from cold, Eric asked Devon, age nine, how it was, how it felt.

"I beat everybody," she said, solemnly. "I was better than everybody."

Her eyelashes blinking slowly, like she was surprised.

And Katie and Eric had laughed and laughed, even though Katie felt sorry, always did, for all those other girls who just weren't as good, didn't have that magical something that made Devon Devon.

"You gotta get her out of there," a competition judge confided to Eric the following day. "Ditch that strip-mall gym. Get her to BelStars. Get her to Coach T.

"You keep her here, it'll all go to waste."

And that very night Eric began researching second mortgages.

It was, Katie had to admit, exciting.

Coach Teddy Belfour watched Devon's tryout, rapt.

"Let me offer you a big, mouth-filling oath," he told Katie and Eric, never taking his eyes from her. "Bring her to BelStars and she'll find the extent of her power. We'll find it together."

That was how he talked, how he was.

The next day, Devon was on the BelStars beam, under the tutelage of the exalted Coach T., the most decorated coach in the state, the silver-maned lion, the gymnast whisperer, the salto Svengali, molder and shaper of fourteen national champions at the Junior Olympic and Elite levels.

That night, Eric told Katie how he and Devon had walked past the long rows of beams and bars, the fearsome BelStars girls whippeting around with faces grim as Soviets'.

He thought she would be terrified by the time they finished the gauntlet. But instead she'd looked up at him, her eyes dark and blazing, and said, "I'm ready."

And overnight BelStars became their whole world.

Twelve thousand square feet, a virtual bunker, it had everything that jolly Tumbleangels, run by two sweet women both named Emily, didn't. The color-coordinated foam wedges and cartwheel mats were replaced by mammoth spring floors, a forty-foot tumbling track, a parent lounge with vending machines. All of it gray, severe, powerful.

And BelStars had Coach T., nearly all his energies devoted to Devon, beneath her on the beam, the bars, spotting her at the vault. Barking orders at everyone but Devon. ("She doesn't need it," he said. "She just needs our faith.")

This was the place Devon began spending twenty-five hours a week, before school, after school, weekends. And, because it was thirty minutes from their house and Eric's work schedule was unreliable, it was often the place Katie and thus little Drew spent four, five, seven hours a day, Katie's default office, her laptop open, trying to do her freelance design jobs.

But it was impossible not to watch Devon. Everyone watched her.

Katie and Eric tried never to say the word *Olympics*. But it was hard not to think about. Because it was all anyone at BelStars thought about.

"Once in a generation," one of the other parents said, watching Devon

You never think you'll hear a phrase that big in real life, much less find yourself believing it.

You never think your life will be that big.

Just after Devon's tenth birthday, Coach T. pulled Katie aside.

"Let's meet tonight. You and Eric and me," he whispered so no other parent could hear. "To talk about our girl's future. Because I see things bright and bountiful."

And so it was, that night, sitting at the grand dining-room

table of his grand home, Coach T. pulled out a large easel pad and showed Katie and Eric the flow chart, punctuated by fluorescent arrows, Sharpied hieroglyphics. It was titled "The Track."

"My friends, this is a decision point," he said, perpetually bloodshot eyes staring over at them. "Are you ready?"

"We are," Eric said.

"Yes," Katie said. "Ready for what?"

Teddy laughed buoyantly, and then they all did. Then, turning the easel paper toward her, he waved his pen, magician-like, and explained.

"Devon's on the brink of becoming a Level Ten gymnast," he said. "The highest level."

THE TRACK

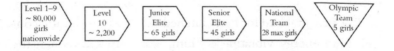

"And she can top out at Ten," he said, shrugging a little. "And be proud of herself. Compete in big events across the country. Attract recruiters for a college scholarship."

He looked at them, that forever-ruddy face, the dampness of his bloodhound eyes.

"Or she can take the other path, the narrow one. The challenging one. The one for the very few indeed. The Elite path."

E-lite. It was all anyone talked about in the gym. *Elite-Elite-Elite.* A constant purr under their tongues. The trip of the *l*, the cut of the *t*.

"Going Elite means going from competing nationally to competing internationally," Teddy said. "If this is the desired track, she needs to qualify as an Elite gymnast. First, Junior Elite, and she's not even close to ready yet. I'm shooting for her thirteenth birthday. Then Senior Elite, the year she turns sixteen."

All three were silent for a moment. Eric looked at Katie, who looked back at him, trying not to smile.

"An Elite career lasts five or six years, max. But each year, the hundred, hundred and twenty Elites compete to land spots on the national team. From the national team, you are only one step away from..."

Teddy paused, briefly, watching Katie and Eric, letting the moment sit with them.

Then, with his thickest Sharpie, he underlined the words *Olympic Team* and circled it, and starred it.

The words themselves like magic, an incantation.

Katie felt for Eric's arm and then began to pull back, embarrassed.

But Eric grabbed for her, clutched her hand. And Katie could feel it, an energy vibrating off him, like sometimes when they watched the meets together, their bodies humming beside each other, so alive.

"Then, God willing, Devon makes the world championship team. And, every four years," he said (and the way Katie remembered it, they all held their breath), "the torch."

Eric exhaled, looking down at the rug. "So," he said, "you see it?"

Teddy nodded once, slowly.

"But you need to commit. Both of you." He paused. "It takes a family to make this happen. And it takes action. Devon needs to be here at least thirty hours a week, maybe more. We need to get her before she changes."

"Changes?" Katie asked.

"Changes," he said, nodding again, grimly this time. Then, in a flash, turning a smile on. "They all change. Become women. Glorious women."

"Well, you can't stop that," Katie said, smiling too.

"No," Teddy said, laughing with sudden loudness. "Of course not."

And it happened, just like he said it would. Just as the Track foretold.

First came constant, vein-pulsing work, more five-hour practices, more out-of-town meets, countless jammed fingers and torn palms and two weather-beaten cars with blistered tires and dent-pocked doors, Eric's in the shop half the time, and the debt ticking up, and a gym that cost almost as much as one of their two mortgage payments.

But it happened. That spring, Devon reached Level 10. One of only ninety-six in the state.

"There's no telling how far we can go now," said Coach T., watching Devon dive, flip, stick.

A few months later, after placing sixth on beam and bars in the Level 10 Junior Nationals in sunstruck Orlando, she was ranked first among all Level 10s in their home state.

"The greatest day of our life," Devon said, and everyone laughed at the *our*, except it was true, wasn't it?

"A star is born," announced Coach T., rocking back on his heels, beaming, holding up that dazzling photo of Devon in the local paper—stoic and grand in her snow-white leotard, her dark eyes, Eric's eyes. Alongside, there was that crackling interview with Coach T., and the next day, BelStars was flooded with new recruits, its coffers swelling.

"Nothing can stop her now," Coach T. assured Katie and Eric

over a celebratory dinner for Devon at Shell Shuckers, the best restaurant in town.

They took up the largest table: all four Knoxes, kindergartner Drew, the shrimp cocktail bigger than his little head, alongside Coach T. and his wife, Tina, and a young woman whom Katie had never met, with hair like Rapunzel's—that's what Drew would say later.

"I'd like you all to meet my niece," Teddy said. "Well, she's like a daughter to me."

And that was how they came to know Hailey, whom Coach had taken care of since she was thirteen and going down what Tina euphemistically called "the wrong path."

"I couldn't deal with my mom," Hailey confided, leaning close to Katie. "And she couldn't deal with me. We were both being brats."

With Teddy's help, Hailey had thrived, starting gymnastics, joining the swim team, winning a scholarship, and now soon to graduate from State. Which just showed the kind of man Teddy was, why Devon was in such able, loving hands.

"I was always good on the beam, but I wasn't anything like Devon," Hailey added. "And my mom was nothing like you."

And Katie, maybe a little tipsy, found herself tearing up.

"One more toast to our Devon—the Invincible!" Teddy hurrahed, and Tina hear-heared, jumping in, "So long as she doesn't grow three inches or get hips," with a wink.

And everyone laughed, and all eyes turned to Devon, taking her first sip of champagne, a pinched nose, a sly blush, ponytail bobbing, just like before a routine. She drew her index finger across her front teeth, as if it were too sweet.

"Why are you all looking at Devon?" little Drew asked, head darting from one to the next.

And Coach T. laughed.

They all did.

Later that night, their minds racing, their hearts thumping too wildly to sleep, she and Eric sat at the kitchen table and drank dusty bourbon from juice glasses and tried to calm themselves.

It felt as it did after big competitions, when together they'd break it all down, everything that had happened, tell it and retell it until the kitchen table hummed with warmth and achievement.

But this time it took a turn, and here was Eric, his eyes bleary, pained, talking about something a judge had said, and about Devon's "cross to bear."

"I'm telling you, he was talking about her foot. That she'd never get that balance perfect, not without two fewer toes on her left foot to even it out."

Despite countless conversations about Devon's body, her development, her strength, her preternatural calm and focus, she and Eric almost never talked about her foot. About the accident.

"Oh, Eric," Katie said, wrapping her hands around his forearms. "Like Coach T. says, she figured out long ago how to compensate and—"

"I think about it sometimes, Katie," he said, nudging closer toward her.

For a second, Katie thought he might say something, an admission. *I can't believe I didn't see her. I can't believe I was so careless—*

In all marriages, there are questions you never ask. Instead, Katie could only wonder, less and less as the years went by, how Eric could have left unattended, even for a moment, that relic of a mower, hustled from a garage sale, when he knew it didn't shut off like it was supposed to. Why he'd taken that chance in spite of the way Devon followed him everywhere, all the time, scurrying after him like an eager, pink-tongued puppy.

"I think about what we did," he continued.

His words landing fully.

"What *we* did," she began, head tilting. "We—"

"She was different before," Eric said. "Devon was. Before the accident."

And the *we* drifted away, forgotten. Bourbon-obscured.

She knew he meant *different* in ways that went beyond the peculiar maceration at the top of her foot, the places two angel-ear toes had once wiggled.

She wished she weren't so drunk, could stop a million tiny, pushed-away thoughts from scurrying across her brain. About Devon, about the lonesomeness of her daughter's life, about—

So she spoke instead, to stop the thoughts.

"She was only three when it happened," she insisted. "There was no Devon before."

Feeling the bourbon whirl inside her, a heat under her eyes, she said it once, then said it again.

"There was no Devon before."

In bed that night, her throat scraped dry from drinking, her head muddied and hot, Katie remembered something that had happened not that long ago. She'd walked into the TV room, laden with trophies and the tilting ribbon rack, and saw Devon, her feet propped up on the sofa, her shins aching, rubbing Zim's Crack Creme on those ragged gymnast feet, the white of the lotion making her foot bright, conspicuous, a white worm wriggling.

Walking by, Katie had plucked at her daughter's greased toes, saying, cooing even, "Take care of my girl's magical Frankenfoot."

A week later, Eric had confided to Katie that Devon had come to him to ask if she could start wearing Dance Paws at the gym so it would be harder for people to see. Because even Mom thought her foot made her look like a monster.

Hearing it was like a punch in the stomach.

"Why didn't she say something to me?" she asked Eric, and he said she was probably embarrassed.

She always assumed Devon never really thought about it, the telltale white rings of scar tissue banding her forefoot. *It just doesn't feel as much*, she confided once. She had less sensation there, and could hold the beam longer without pain. But she never felt pain anyway. Not like the other girls. Besides, her feet, both of them, were, more than anything else, the feet of all gymnasts. Ripped and peeling from the beam. Deformed, clawed, just like that nightmare Drew once had (*Devon was a chicken hawk, Mom. With needles instead of feet*).

"I'm the worst mother ever," Katie said, and Eric shook his head, reassured her.

That's what parenthood was about, wasn't it? Slowly understanding your child less and less until she wasn't yours anymore but herself. Especially Devon, who kept so much inside.

"She's a thinker, a worrier," Eric sometimes said. "She never stops."

A serious girl, that's what all her teachers said. An intense one. *Old beyond her years;* they said that too.

That was what gymnastics did, though. It aged girls and kept them young forever at the same time.

And the face Devon wore at three years old, full of stiff determination and a native opacity, was the same one she wore at BelStars today, her nimble body spearing over the vault.

Ice Eyes, the other girls called her. Staring at her from the sidelines. They all wanted to be like that.

Look at Devon, Coach T. always said. *She doesn't give away any of her secrets.*

Chapter Two

First the Foot, then the Fall. Katie would always wonder if the first begot the second, but she was certain both begot what came next.

"Whatever happens today," Katie assured her, Devon's face drawn and ancient-looking, the oldest thirteen-year-old in the world, "we're so proud of you."

"But I don't know if I'm good enough, Mom," Devon whispered in the muffled dark of the garage, waiting for Eric and Drew. "I really don't."

It was the day of Junior Elite Qualifiers.

At last, Devon Knox would compete and become a Junior Elite gymnast, as the Track had prophesized, set in Sharpie.

And so what if it was happening a year later than they all wanted? That hamstring injury, which Devon concealed from them for months until after one long practice, the back of her leg turning an angry violet. *It looks like grape jelly*, Drew had said. *Or a smooshed beetle*. But now the hamstring was long healed, and this was Devon, after all. She would make up for lost time. She was still on the Track.

"You can do anything," Katie promised as Devon finally slid into the backseat.

"That's what Dad said," she whispered. "You guys always say the same thing."

The four Knoxes, Drew swinging from his parents' hands, entered the building, a conference center, a hundred girls and their twitchy, caffeine-palsied parents hiving everywhere.

TODAY: ELITE QUALIFIERS. REGISTRATION TO LEFT. The banner so modest, like it had been rushed off at the copy center moments before.

This next step was a big one, but they were all big. Everything with Devon was big.

"Bye," Devon said, waving as she walked backward, slight as a grass blade, into the Gymnasts Only area.

Next up, Devon Knox!

High in the stands, Eric clasped Katie's hand.

There Devon stood, on the competition floor. Four feet ten inches tall, nary a curve on her, but her dark eyes heavy with history, struggle. Squinting down, body pressing forward, Katie wondered at those eyes, that face. It was as if this weren't her teenage daughter but a woman deepened by experience, a war-battered refugee, a KGB spy.

She has a sense of mystery, she'd heard a judge say once about Devon. *Like a sphinx.*

And it was true. Where did it come from?

A nearly fourteen-year-old girl but with a voice like Minnie Mouse who still slept with her good-luck stuffed animal, the same plush tiger she used to hold, age eight, between her knees on the horizontal bars, trying to keep her legs together.

Except out there on the competition floor, her eyes like hawk slits, that little girl was gone.

Beam, floor, bars. She was achieving.

Yes, there were a few stumbles, which were surprising but nothing that couldn't be overcome. Katie could barely breathe, Eric kneading his jean legs with red hands. More than ever, watching Devon had become a profound experience for them. Taking in each routine with their whole bodies, every nerve on high, their hearts jammering against each other. Because she was theirs, but now she was also so much bigger than they were.

"She's got this," Eric said now, knocking the bench as he said it.

But then it happened.

Devon's final routine, the vault.

Eric's fingers laced in hers, Katie watched their daughter stand at the foot of the runway.

Watched her gaze fasten on the vault table, four feet long, three feet wide, its white spring top like a shiny orb, a womb.

Watched her jump up once and explode into her sprint.

Catapulting into the air.

Glorious height, strong landing.

And then, in a heartbeat, it happened.

On the stick, her feet safely on the mat, Devon's right ankle rolled slightly, and one foot landed just outside the corridor. Only an inch, maybe. (The judges would say it was a shoulder's width.) And, yes, maybe there was the slightest of wobbles. A minuscule ankle cave.

But Devon lifted her chin high, her face showing no sign that anything had gone wrong.

When the final scores came, however, Devon was out. By seven-tenths of a point.

*　　*　　*

Down on the floor, Katie wanted to sweep her daughter into her arms, but you weren't allowed, and all she could do was reach for her shoulder, squeeze it.

"It's all over. My life's over," Devon said, looking up at Katie, her hand shaking slightly as she pushed back a stray strand from her ponytail. "You know it is."

Words every adolescent says—grounded, a humiliation at school, first crush.

But Katie secretly felt its partial truth. No Junior Elite meant no Senior Elite, which meant—she could see the black marker skating across Coach T.'s flow chart—no national team, no international. No Olympics.

Devon's life wasn't over, but her life, their lives, had changed, in a foot bobble.

"Everything's gone," Devon said, eyes shut and face twisted. "Now there's nothing."

"Honey," Katie began. Then, the words slipping from her mouth, the words that would haunt her for years to come, "You'll compete in college, the best programs in the country will want you. Gymnastics aren't everything. The Olympics were a long shot anyway."

The look Devon gave her in return was so savage Katie flinched.

She knew at once she'd been wrong to say it, at least so soon, in the teary heat of everything. But it was too late.

There was an awful quiet second, Katie stuttering, before Eric seized Devon's shoulders, making her face him, look into his eyes.

"Hey," Eric said, "we're coming back. This was just the first shot. Next qualifiers, we'll be here. You'll nail it."

This is why I married him, Katie thought. Why hadn't those words come out of her mouth?

Instead, the shameful thought whirring in her head was *You've fallen off the Track. You'll never make the next Olympics now. By the one after that, you'll have pendulous breasts and dragging hips. You'll be too old, an ancient nineteen.*

"I don't want to do it again," Devon said. "Ever."

In the weeks following the Disappointment, everything seemed to shift, perceptibly.

Before, they'd all stay at the dinner table long after the plates were cleared, talking about new recruits, about Devon's hand rips, about the gym's aging equipment, and about the need for an inground pit and a new spring floor.

But now, Devon spent dinnertime in her room, over her homework, headphones never leaving her ears. Which is what teenagers did, but Devon wasn't a teenager, really. Not like other teenagers.

"I just wish she'd talk about it," Katie said.

But Devon had always held her feelings so tightly, as if balling them up in her clenched fists. Even when she got a staph infection from the torn flaps on her hands and they had to drain fluid from incisions on her palms, she would not cry. She refused to.

Her brother, Drew, always slipping around corners in the house, small and invisible, told Katie he'd peered through Devon's half-open door and seen something.

"She made a mess," Drew said, shaking his head. And he told her how Devon had pulled a milk crate of old stuffed animals out of her closet and dumped them all over her bed, teddy bears and Beanie Babies, so many monkeys in leotards, and the bright, blazing stuffed tiger she'd so loved.

Katie looked in later and found Devon buried under them, sound asleep, surrounded.

"What matters is that she doesn't let this shake her," Teddy told them, having summoned them to his home for the postmortem. "You can't let her see your disappointment."

"We're just disappointed *for her*," Eric clarified. "She wanted it so much."

"Well, don't be," he said sharply, eyes on them both, chin lifted. "Because she's not like us. She's better than all of us."

On the car ride home, Katie put her hand over her face.

"I made it worse. I shouldn't have said that ▨▨▨▨▨ ut the Olympics. About—"

"No," Eric said, eyes on the road, "you shouldn't have."

In the weeks that followed, Katie decided to give Devon her space. She spent more time with Drew, their little stalwart, just starting first grade, pullet head perpetually bent over his science projects, the ant farm, the earthworm composter, the tree-bark samples lit over a can of Sterno, stopwatch ticking in his hand. There was so much going on in his head that she hadn't known before.

Each night, however, Eric sat beside her in bed and watched the footage from the qualifiers over and over. Studying it, rubbing his face, trying to make sense of it. It was all he talked about, his eyes twitching from the screen.

"Eric," Katie finally said one night, "stop."

But the next day, he came home with a thick catalog from Champeen Athletics.

"I've been thinking a lot about this," he told Katie, nearly bouncing on his toes. "We all know it. The equipment's been holding Devon back. We need to push Teddy. We need that in-ground pit."

"A landing pit?" Katie said. "She doesn't need a pit. Teddy always spots her and he's never missed."

"Katie," he said, his eyes glittering with energy, his hand pressed on her wrist, "I've been reading about it all day. There's so much I didn't know. Gymnasts who practice their vaults with a pit to cushion the impact have fewer injuries and perform better in competition. It's easier on their joints."

And then, more quietly, he added, "And it helps control the fear."

"But Devon has no fear," she said, and he wouldn't look at her. For the first time, it felt like he knew something she didn't about Devon. Or thought he did. Watching the video from qualifiers again and again, he thought he'd figured something out.

But Katie had her own theory. After all, the foot that had bobbled—why, it was the same foot that had been caught in that mower blade. Part of her wondered if that slim bit of flesh where the skin-graft tissue sealed over might have played some small role.

Sometimes, she caught Devon looking at her foot, examining it very closely, and wondered if she was pondering the same question.

"The landing pit is the solution, Katie," he said, his hand on her arm, eyes fixed on her. "I'm telling you."

It was so hard not to believe him, his palm pressed on the catalog's glossy page, the photo of the enormous pit dug deep into a gym floor, filled to the brink with bright foam cubes like casino dice.

*   *   *

"I want to support this, Eric," Teddy told them, "but I ran the numbers." He jabbed the catalog page, his butcher's thumb over the price. "That dog won't hunt."

"Teddy—" Eric began.

"It's gonna have to come from the boosters," Teddy said. The BelStars Booster Club, a barely functioning klatch of four parents who held an occasional bake sale to buy competition tees, preshrunk.

"Tell you what," Teddy said, "why don't you show them the Eric Knox charm?"

And Eric did, inviting them to the house for dinner, making his famous (only) dish, Cajun gumbo, extra hot sauce, and drawing each of them out with earnest questions, lavishing them with attention. Within days, an election was called just for him. Four votes were cast and Eric was the new president of the BelStars Boosters.

"We've always hoped Eric would get involved," Kirsten Siefert, the booster secretary, said, adding snidely, "I guess this is what it took."

Within days of the election, the BelStars Boosters issued a calendar of revenue generators: summer camp, free gym days for the community, party-room rentals, a car wash, smoothie days, a pro shop carved out of the parent lounge. And Eric recruited sponsors, a local dry cleaner, a tanning salon, their logos splashed over leotards, water bottles, tracksuits.

But most important of all, he got Gwen.

Gwen Weaver, the owner of a fleet of parking lots and of Weaver's Wagons, a mini-chain of family-style restaurants that would prove perfect for cost-free pizza parties, fund-raisers, booster meeting sites. The woman who had single-handedly funded a new junior-high gym floor when her daughter was still in elementary school. Her daughter, Lacey, happened to be an aspiring gymnast.

"She's the one we want," Eric had said, pointing Gwen out to Katie at a town meet.

The serious-looking woman with the ash-blond bob and the cat's-eye sunglasses. When she removed them, scanning the gym, Katie was reminded of something Drew had told her: Never make eye contact with a wolf. The wolf will take it as a challenge.

"First we poach the daughter," Teddy said, joining them, nearly rubbing his hands. "Then we make the mama treasurer. After that, nature takes its course."

And so, a dinner was arranged.

Shaking her head in wonder, Katie watched as Eric put on his crispest white shirt, his sole tie (later, Gwen gifted him a second, a woven silk one that came in a long green box, when he was honored with State Booster of the Year). He even polished his best shoes with his dad's old shine box.

When he came home a few hours later, a little drunk, his face bright, nearly pumping his fist like he never did, even at big competitions, Katie had to laugh a little.

"She's in," he shouted, spinning Katie around the bedroom, her head knocking the lamp, the lamp rolling across the floor and sparking as if in joint celebration.

Her husband, like a military general, fortifying the flanks. Or, in this case, after a few more wine-soaked dinners with Gwen, maybe more like an ace salesman. A confidence man. A gigolo. Because the long meals always turned, at some point, to talk of the poor state of the tumbling mats, the spring floor, the vault table, and, most of all, of the need for a landing pit.

So Gwen emptied those deep, silk-lined pockets, and they got a new elite spring floor, new mats, new fiberglass bars to replace the wooden ones, new everything.

All that was left was the pit.

There was a dinner party at Gwen's home, a cherry-walled wonder so grand that Katie felt as if the hushed click of her modest heels on the floor was in bad taste.

She hadn't even wanted to go. She dreaded leaving Devon alone these days, her daughter emerging from her dark bedroom only to take showers, her shoulders hunched, hair covering her face, as if she were no longer a gymnast at all.

"Gwen," Eric said, training those gray eyes on her, "look what BelStars has done for Devon. She's on track to compete nationally. Your daughter can bloom here. We can do this, together. We can make BelStars a place all our girls feel challenged and supported, motivated and inspired. There's only one thing stopping us. One investment we need to make, together."

"And what is that, Eric?" Gwen said, eyes narrowing.

"What else?" he said, smiling lightly. "A pit. We need a pit."

And, remarkably, Gwen nodded. "Of course we do."

"Gwen likes the soft sell," Coach T. whispered to Katie, shaking his head in wonder. "And no one sells softer than Eric."

And that very night, all of them flush from old wine and something called drunken prawns, they walked into Gwen's study and watched as she flipped open her massive white-leather checkbook binder and, fountain pen in hand, signed in her swirling script.

All for that inground landing pit, which, Katie calculated, cost more than a year of their mortgage payments.

"It's a must for Elite training," Gwen told Katie, as if Katie didn't know. As if these very words hadn't come directly from Eric himself. "We shouldn't skimp on our children's dreams."

"No," Katie said, "we shouldn't."

"It's a disgrace," she added, handing over the check, "that we've waited this long."

All of this, Eric managed. As if he were born to it.

It was an Eric Katie hadn't seen in years and years, maybe even since their first, frenzied dates, those seven-, eight-hour adventures of shots and pool and soul-sharing and Katie hanging over the edge of a mattress, breathless with wonder over him. Nineteen-year-old Eric, who wanted so many things he couldn't begin to name them all. Or any of them.

More than a dozen years later, two kids, a creaking split-level with water stains but strong beams, loose shingles but copper pipes, both working in jobs they wouldn't have chosen but wouldn't have fled, and where had all that energy, that exuberance, that sense of limitless possibility gone?

For Eric, for both of them, it went to this.

After all, who wouldn't do anything for one's child?

Especially when that child worked harder and wanted something more than either of them ever had? Who wanted in ways they'd long forgotten how to want or had never known at all?

"This is just the beginning," Eric said, unscrolling the design plan for Coach T.'s approval, Gwen flanking him, smelling strongly of perfume. Katie, behind everyone, unable to see.

"We'll have to go dark," Coach T. said, reading glasses slipping down his nose. "And find another place to practice. But hell, I'm grateful."

During practice, high up in the family viewing section, all the parents could talk about was the pit.

"Teddy's been dragging his feet on this for years," Molly Chu said to Gwen. "And you and Eric, it's all because of you two. Our pit at last!"

Gwen twitched a smile. "It's simply required for a competitive gym," she said. "And why Teddy hasn't installed one is a major concern for me."

"The building owners wouldn't allow it," Molly said. "That's what he told me."

"He told me good spotting means you don't need one," Kirsten Siefert said.

But there were whispers among the boosters that Teddy's true reasons were more personal. Rumors of financial strain—two sons at expensive colleges and one in law school, a house renovation, a new deck. It was his gym, of course, but given the high fees he charged, couldn't he invest more in BelStars? And when Eric filled out the booster club's tax forms and saw how much Teddy paid himself, he had to admit to Katie that it was frustrating.

"Well, now we have everything," Katie said, looking down at Eric on the gym floor, hands on Devon's shoulders, talking and talking and talking.

Construction took place during the Summer Olympics, the BelStars buzzing with Olympic fever, holding viewing parties and even, among the boosters, a small betting pool.

Practice was relocated to the nearby middle school, an arrangement made possible, of course, by Gwen, though no one knew how.

Meanwhile, under Gwen's vigilant watch, a crew of men of Portuguese descent worked seemingly around the clock to dig the pit, splitting the floorboards like matchsticks, pouring concrete all day.

When one of them fell ill, a substitute worker arrived in the form of Coach T.'s pool boy, a lean-hipped young man named Ryan Beck.

This was how Ryan came into their world.

Chapter Three

The Foot might have been an end. Instead, it turned out to be the beginning. The Fall might have been an end too, were it not for the Pit, which offered a second chance.

But the Pit brought Ryan Beck. And Ryan Beck, that sweet, chipped-tooth, handsome young man—well, he ruined everything in his own way.

Walking into BelStars with Drew, Katie caught her first glimpse of Ryan, with his long, tanned arms swinging a piece of rebar like a baton, laughing at something one of the workers had said Ryan was always laughing.

Over the next two weeks, everyone came to watch the construction of the pit. And to see Ryan.

Each morning, he stripped down to his undershirt, jeans hanging low on his waist, and climbed down into the pit, eight feet beneath the gym floor. And then it began, all the gymnasts, ages seven to seventeen, making excuses to visit, taking turns peeking over the pit edge, hoping for one of his smiles. And many of the booster moms too.

But it turned out Ryan was already taken, by Hailey, everyone's new favorite tumbling coach, who tended with such care to the younger girls, hands on their curling spines, their sprigged thighs, somersaulting them. The pair had been spotted sharing French fries at the Sundae House, their foreheads nearly pressed together, like Archie and Veronica.

"I'm glad for Hailey," Gwen said, and all the mothers agreed. Because Hailey was adored, and no one knew why she had so much trouble keeping a boyfriend.

Soon enough, Hailey started coming to the gym too, arriving in her sprightly purple car and sitting in the center of the bleachers as Ryan worked and leaving only when practice required her to. Finally the other girls got the hint and stayed away.

Only little Drew remained.

He was supposed to be in the game room, but Katie and Eric found him hovering a few feet from all the activity, watching the concrete mixer spin and whir.

Inside the pit, Katie could see the back of Ryan's head, the delicate curve of his neck. Earbuds in, he smoothed the concrete with the power trowel, his arms floating back and forth gracefully.

"Ryan said it was okay to watch," Drew told them, "if I stand back just this far."

"Well, he doesn't know," Eric said, pulling Drew away by his jacket hood. "He's just a kid. He doesn't know what's safe."

As if he had heard, Ryan glanced up at the Knoxes but only grinned.

Looking down, Katie wondered how deep they would go, digging that pit. How deep Teddy and Eric would make them go.

Ryan seemed down so far that he might disappear.

*   *   *

After that, while Eric took Devon to practice, enduring her stony silences, Katie chaperoned Drew at BelStars to view the progress: the installation of the rebar grid, the curing and coating of the walls, the padding on the edges glued and screwed down. And the best part, the filling of the pit with the vivid-colored foam cubes, cobalt and gold, tumbling down into it like alphabet blocks.

"You sure are a nice mom," Ryan once shouted up at her. "Bringing your boy every day."

Katie smiled, her face warm.

The grand opening of the pit took place on the final day of the Olympics.

As benefactor, Gwen led the christening, tossing in the final foam block, spray-painted gold by the Level 3s. Then her nine-year-old daughter, Lacey, leaped toward the runway, ready to perform the inaugural vault. But Gwen quickly put both hands on Lacey's tiny shoulders, patting her white-blond braids and pulling her aside as all paths cleared for Devon.

Of course Devon would be first. And more than one hundred gym members, relatives, and supporters watched as she took the floor, shaking her fingers, breathing deeply. She hadn't vaulted since the Disappointment. Since qualifiers. Would she now?

Lacey's alarming white eyebrows slanted like antennae, and she said something under her breath. Katie could hear Gwen's sharp response.

"Well, life isn't fair, Lacey. Do you think I asked for these ankles? But you have to be strong and push through. We all endure a lot of things. I slept with your father's chain-saw snores every night for six years. I have him to thank for my tinnitus. You can sit through this. Watch how it's done. Watch Devon."

Standing before the pit, padded on all sides and filled to the brink with foam blocks, each one a jewel facet, Devon couldn't even speak. Her hand finding Eric's arm, she set her right foot on one of its soft foam edges, and then she looked up at her dad as if unsure.

But he nodded, and she nodded. Across the floor, Katie found herself envying them the moment, it felt so potent.

As everyone watched, Devon walked over to the foot of the vault runway, eyes on the springboard, the vault table. Rotating her wrists, shaking them. Then, at last, charging down that runway with no hesitation at all, her body soaring into a double-twist Yurchenko that made the whole gym gasp and *aah* before nearly disappearing into the gaudy pit.

Everyone cried. Katie couldn't stop.

Later that night, Katie found Drew at the kitchen table, viewing the Olympics closing ceremonies on her laptop.

"Devon didn't want to watch," he said, shrugging at the hallway leading into the den.

Walking by, she saw Eric and Devon absorbed in old footage of Devon's first meet, a bowl of popcorn between them. She almost felt like she was intruding.

There was such a look of calm on Devon's face, for the first time since Elite Qualifiers, that Katie found herself retreating, not wanting to disturb. So she sat at the table with Drew, the sound turned low so Devon couldn't hear the fireworks, the jammy-voiced children's choir, the big horns.

After Drew went to bed, she could still hear Eric and Devon through the wall.

"The new vault table, it's the greatest ever, Dad," she said. "And my landings are sticking. I'm going to do better."

"Devon, you don't——"

"It won't ever be like that again. Like at qualifiers. I'm going to make up for everything."

"Hey, Devon," Eric said, and Katie could hear him shushing her, soothing her, telling her she was perfect as she was and that all he and her mom wanted was for her to be happy.

Katie listened, closing the hot laptop to muffle it.

The Olympics over, the foam pit and new equipment in place, along with a sense of renewed purpose, it felt like a spell had been broken.

To celebrate, Teddy engineered a (booster-sponsored) overnight trip to attend something called Gymnastics on Ice at the state capital. It would have been a forgettable experience had Hailey and Ryan not been invited and had Ryan not arrived two hours late, long after the postshow dinner during which Hailey texted helplessly at the table, certain he had perished on some remote roadside. *What would I do, Mrs. Knox?*

An hour later, all the BelStars and booster chaperones looked on from their balconies at the Ramada as Hailey and Ryan, resplendent as a pair of movie stars, bucked and brawled down by the pool, or Hailey did. You couldn't help but watch, Hailey crying and casting the sunflowers he'd given her into the searing chlorine, and Ryan still as a statue, gently pleading, or so it looked.

"Teddy must've taken a whole bottle of Nyquil to sleep through this," Eric said, coming up behind Devon. "Should I go down?"

Katie shook her head, watching from the sliding glass door.

"Why does he just stand there?" Devon asked, but she looked captivated, moving closer to the balcony edge, her toes curling there. Her face open in ways Katie rarely saw.

"Give them some privacy," Eric said, summoning her back into the room.

"That'll be Devon someday," Katie whispered to Eric. He gave her a queasy look in return that made her laugh.

Everyone inside, Katie stayed a moment longer. Soon enough, as the sunflowers, dark and sodden, drifted across the acid-blue surface of the pool, Hailey had pressed herself against Ryan's chest and all was forgiven.

The next morning, Katie saw them in the lobby sundries shop, their arms around each other sloppily, their faces glazed with sex.

Ducking behind a rack of energy bars, she tried to sidle past them unseen. She could hear Hailey whispering, over and over, in his ear, "You make me crazy, baby. You make me crazy."

Turning sharply, Katie hurried into the lobby, thick with exultant eight-year-old gymmies, high on mochas, nose-high with whipped cream.

But Ryan had spotted her.

"Mrs. Knox," he said, running after her as Hailey paid for something at the register. (What had she bought? All Katie could think was *condoms,* the word whirring in her head.)

"I'm sorry," he added, shoving his hands in his pockets. "About last night. I saw you guys on your balcony. What a couple of jerks we were."

"Young love," she blurted, trying not to look at Hailey's ballet-pink lipstick on his jaw.

"Young idiots," he said, shaking his head.

His hair still wet from the shower, the wrinkled shirt—boys that age, everything was so easy, and that ease was the centerpiece of their charm, wasn't it?

"You should enjoy it. It's a great time," she said, without even thinking. "You...you feel things so deeply."

"But then you stop?" he said, smiling. "Feeling deeply?"

She was startled to hear her own laugh, sharp and fast, almost a bark.

Then, in an instant, Hailey was behind him, smiling at Katie, giggling. "This creep!"

Her arms wrapped tight across his chest, like a shield.

When they returned from the trip, Coach T. convened a strategy meeting at his home, Mama T.'s famous sun tea and biscuits, Eric and Katie in those stiff-backed dining-room chairs.

Pulling out his flow chart again, he directed their pensive faces back to the Track, dog-eared, coffee-rippled.

"It's not over," he said, his voice firm, eyes intent. "Not for our girl."

"You think she can try again? For Junior Elite next year?" Katie asked. They'd talked and talked about it, she and Eric, endlessly.

"She could," Teddy said. "But I think she feels like she's going backward. And she's aging out soon, and if she—she won't—but if she fails again, the crush to her confidence, the impact on her ranking..."

"So what are you saying?" Eric asked. "Tell us."

"I didn't want to raise the possibility before, but that pit, it's a game changer," he said, slapping one hand on the damask tablecloth. "Listen to me, you two: There's a loophole. A shortcut."

With the thickest marker he had, he drew a line that went from Level 10, through the doomed Junior Elite, and straight to the next arrowed box.

Stopping there, he circled *Senior Elite,* drew a looping star around it.

"You can do that?" Eric asked. "You can skip?"

"No one does that," Katie said. "Do they?"

Teddy looked at them, the pouches under his eyes quivering with intensity.

"Very few. But there are exceptions." He drew another line, even thicker this time. "And we all know Devon is deeply exceptional."

Eric nodded, Teddy nodded, their eyes locked on each other's. After countless nights spent talking about Devon, raising money for the gym, watching footage of Devon's routines, standing below her as her feet fastened on the practice beam, the two of them didn't even need to speak.

"And she's stopped the clock," Coach T. added. "You know?"

At first Katie didn't. Then she did.

"Devon's going to get breasts, Teddy," Katie blurted. "And hips. And everything else. She's going to be a woman."

"No one's disputing that," Teddy said, smiling tightly. "After all, only Peter Pan gets to keep his baby teeth!"

Katie turned to Eric, but his gaze was fixed on the chart, on the thick black arrow leading off the page.

"But what if she doesn't want to?" Katie asked Eric that night, brushing their teeth side by side. "Is it even good for her, all this pressure? It's been so hard since qualifiers."

"Well, we'll ask her," Eric said. "She's the one who has to decide."

So they did. And her eyes shuttled between Katie and Eric, watching them, doing that one-sided lip-biting thing that meant she was thinking.

Then she said, "Okay."

*   *   *

The plan was in place. The new one.

For the next twenty months, Devon would compete as much as she could, increase her ranking and improve her prospects and get better and better and better. It would mean out-of-town trips, out-of-state trips, invitationals, classics, all the state and regional and national competitions—which meant arrangements had to be made with Devon's school, Eric pleading Devon's case, pointing out this unique opportunity, her strong GPA, her immense promise. He would handle everything, get tutors, pay for private lessons. Whatever it took.

Then, in July of her sixteenth year, Devon would try for Senior Elite. The first qualifier of her sixteenth year.

Just knowing they were back on the Track, even if it was a new one, made everything better. Brought order back into their lives.

So Katie had forgotten about it, or tried to. The possibility that the foot injury could have been to blame for what happened at qualifiers, and everything that might mean. Until months later.

She hadn't meant to do anything but deliver the laundry, the teetering basket of leotards and warm-up sweats, and change Devon's sheets. Tugging the mattress pad, that awkward crawl to the corner that pressed too close to the built-in bookshelf, her hand hit something soft. The felt fabric of a fat diary—I HEART EVERYTHING across its crimson cover.

The idea that Devon kept a diary, and hid it between mattress and wall, felt so charmingly old-fashioned, or out of time entirely. Devon wasn't ordinary or typical in any way, after all.

Katie, her hand on the cover, hesitated.

These are the things you just don't do.

But your child's privacy, what did it even mean after you'd spent so many years with your daughter's body at the center of your life? So much energy focused on whatever hurt most—the once-sprained arm, the soft-backed left knee, the chest bruised after Devon drove her own knees into it. All the talk, the open talk, about bras and panties, which ones might show during meets and lead to deductions, and when it was time for bikini waxes. And all those nights: hard strokes on her calf muscles, ice on her bar-bruised pelvic bones, on the inside of her beam-bitten thighs, and, not in years, but still, rubbing Vaseline where the seams of her leotard rubbed and bristled.

Katie opened its pages.

Today: straddle jump ½, ¾ & full on the beam...Working on: Giant ½ + front giant ½, giant full, toe-shoot, double layout dismount.

Entry after entry about gymnastics, chronicling the minutiae, and photos of her favorite gymnasts glued onto pages, silver-Sharpied arrows and circles over their poses, stance, muscles.

It wasn't a diary at all. It was more like a training log.

6 a.m. workout before school. Stretch, run for 15 min. Half-hour of conditioning, 25 min stretching or ballet, then squat jumps and pull-ups, then start with beam. I had trouble with my front pike half, but the rest went ok. Coach says I am achieving. He pumped his fist at me three times.

Reading it, standing the whole time, leaning against the window for light, Katie was struck by how different it was from her own private ramblings at fourteen, all boys and song lyrics and fake IDs and where to hide the purloined pint of Jack Daniel's for Friday night.

But then, closing the diary, her eye caught a photo pasted inside the back cover.

A snapshot taken in that very room, her bedspread visible. The boomerang of Devon's mutilated right foot, close up.

Under the light, her desk lamp, it looked like it was glowing.

It was horrifying, and beautiful.

Why was it the picture felt more intimate, far more intimate, than a secret disappointment, a boy-crush confession?

And why did looking at it feel even more like a violation?

Beneath it, Devon had written:

I had the dream again last night. The one where I look down and my right foot is ten times its size with skin like scales. So I take a knife from the kitchen drawer, the one Mom has to use with both hands, and I chop it off. The blood is like a fountain.

But Dad sees me and runs up the basement stairs. He ties his belt around my ankle and pulls it tight. The buckle is shining.

You need this, he says, grabbing my foot, twisting and molding it like art-class clay. It's your superpower.

And I know he's right.

What is this? Katie thought, covering her mouth. It was like turning over a heavy rock and finding something alive there, wriggling. Prying something open and pulling at its hot wires.

That can't be Devon, she thought.

Who was this girl?

Katie put the diary back into its tight wedge and vowed never to look at it again.

"Mom," Devon said that night, calling out as Katie walked past her doorway, "were you in here?"

"What? No. Just cleaning. Why?"

"Nothing. I just thought maybe you were."

Katie didn't want Devon to see her face. She was worried her face would reveal something.

All she could think of was the photo, and Devon's dream. The strangeness of the foot, the belt. But dreams were that way, weren't they? And they were private, maybe Devon's only private things.

Never again, she told herself. *I won't be that mom. She needs someplace to be herself. To be messy and sad and human. Real.*

To be whatever she was becoming.

II

Necessity is what you do in life when there is only one path, choice, or desire.

—Nadia Comaneci, *Letters to a Young Gymnast*

Chapter Four

Eighteen Months Later

"Today, some of the most anticipated moments will be when Devon Knox takes the floor," the play-by-play announcer said, voice hushed as if this were the Olympics. "Just shy of sixteen, Devon has proven the most formidable talent in the region who has not yet gone Elite. That may all change in six weeks, when she'll take her chances at the Senior Elite Qualifiers."

High in the stands, Katie and Eric watched. The purr-purr of Devon's feet during her floor routine, the zinging violin strokes of "Assassin's Tango" skittering through the air—she was excelling.

Katie had seen the routine a hundred times or more, but it looked different today. She couldn't say why.

"She's more confident," Eric said, as if reading her mind. "That's what it is."

Katie wasn't sure, but her daughter's body—slithering on the mat, then rising—seemed alive in ways she had never seen before, her scarlet leotard like a flame, leaping and flickering and flaring hot.

"Now at the vault," the announcer said, punctuating with dramatic pauses, "Miss . . . Devon . . . Knox."

Grabbing for each other's hands, Katie and Eric watched Devon wait patiently for her cue.

Standing at the foot of the runway, the massive FLIP INTO SPRING INVITATIONAL banner behind her, all the playfulness of her floor routine gone, Devon wore the face of a stone Artemis.

It was remarkable, when Katie thought about it. How her daughter, so strong already, her body an air-to-air missile, had metamorphosed into this force. Shoulders now like a ship mast, rope-knot biceps, legs corded, arms sinewed, a straight, hard line from trunk to neck, her hipless torso resting on thighs like oak beams. Sometimes Katie couldn't believe it was the same girl.

"She's up," Eric said, pointing to the judges.

"Stick it this time, Knox!" someone called out behind them, and Eric's head swiveled around, red charging up his face.

Katie pressed her hand on his arm until he turned back to the floor.

A moment later, she snuck a glance behind her, but instead of the heckler, her eyes snagged on Ryan Beck, his delicate face in repose. Like a sculpture, *Handsome Youth.*

"Here she goes," Eric said, face still flushed. "Here goes Devon."

On the floor, Devon bounded down the runway, her knees churning like pistons, face impenetrable.

Leaping from the springboard, legs tight together, toes like arrows, she flew. Front handspring, double tuck, twist.

And landing, a hard slap on the mat. Because of course

Devon stuck it, her legs like steel pikes, her arms flung elegantly above her head, wrists bent, a ballerina pose.

"Stellar performance," the play-by-play man intoned, "which definitely bodes well for Miss Knox at qualifiers six weeks from today."

And after, walking off the mat, she waved up at the crowd, at Katie and Eric.

Puffs appeared, like magician's smoke, fairy dust. The chalk that never left her hands.

"You nailed it, champ," Eric said as they walked through the parking lot, Devon moving slowly, punch-drunk. "When I saw that Yurchenko, my heart almost stopped."

"I got it. I finally got it," Devon said. Then she looked up at him with an expression Katie had never seen, almost obscene in its pleasure. "That's what it's supposed to feel like."

It almost made Katie blush, and Eric dropped his keys, flinching at the sound.

The triumph was short-lived. When they returned home, all the things postponed until after the meet—laundry, groceries, printer out of toner, wrapping paper for Lacey Weaver's birthday present, rock salt for Drew's fourth-grade science project—toppled back into their laps.

The evening blurred by and before Katie knew it, she was crawling into bed.

But a few hours later, a distant car radio, a radiator rattle, something, woke her at two a.m., bringing with it that unexpected, that tantalizing thing: rousing to Eric's hands on her, one in her hair. The surprising way he came at her, like the world might break to pieces if he didn't have her. Her face pressing into the pillow. The way he shivered against her after, clutched at her before sliding away. The other side of the bed seemed so far. She loved him so much.

The next day, back at the gym for a four-hour Sunday practice. But no one could find Coach T. And nothing began without the Mighty T.

Katie could not remember ever walking into the gym and not immediately seeing his retired colonel's brush cut, the expanse of his pink neck, the swath of his red polo shirt stretched across his former footballer's body, the lumbering gait of a longshoreman. And not hearing his bark: "Dev-*on!* Ice Eyes, girl. Come *on!*"

Except today there was no Teddy.

Six weeks before qualifiers and he wasn't there.

Nor was Hailey, whose honeycomb locks, long past her shoulders, could always be seen, even from high in the stands.

It shouldn't have felt significant, Teddy's absence, but it did. Not just to Katie but to the whole buzzing parent brigade.

"Where *is* he?" Gwen said, her phone, as ever, in her hand, like a weapon, a discus she might hurl.

"I don't get it," Molly Chu said. "I don't understand."

The girls, in their scarlet leotards, dotted the floor, the older ones doing split stretches, handstands, but the youngest ones ambled anxiously, hopping on their tiny red feet.

Finally, the skills coaches began leading drills, but the feeling was haphazard without the organizing thunder of Coach T.'s voice, the polestar, the heart.

"You listen to Amelise, Lacey Weaver," came the familiar, flinty shout of Gwen Weaver, who was calling to her daughter even as she ascended the stands. "You are wasting everyone's time."

From the beam, Amelise's grip on Lacey's tined legs, Lacey

nodded, hair as white-blond as a Hitler Youth's.

Hands still cupped around her mouth, Gwen turned to Katie, two rows down.

"Six weeks," she said, dropping her hands. "Lacey's first shot at Junior Elite, and I just cannot get her to self-discipline."

Katie nodded. "It'll come." But not soon enough, she knew.

"I need to motivate her. Like you did with Devon."

"We didn't do anything," Katie said. "Devon always motivated herself."

"Lacey'll be twelve next month," Gwen said, not seeming to hear. "You have to eat the apple when it's ripe."

Fifteen minutes passed before Bobby V., the gym's administrator, walked in, an odd slump to his shoulders, his shoes squeaking on the waxed floor.

"I have very bad news," he said, hands shaking slightly. "There's been a car accident."

There were gasps, and Katie raised her head from Drew's science book. Scanning the gym quickly, she spotted Devon in perfect straight-is-great pose, rib cage lifted, tummy in, toes forward.

"Our Hailey, she..." Bobby started, voice rising high and stopping.

A whimper came from somewhere and a swooping gasp, breaths held.

Not Hailey! Oh God! came the scattered murmurs.

"No, no," Bobby blurted, running a hand through his brush cut, just like Teddy's—all the men in the gym like 1950s astronauts. "I'm sorry. Hailey wasn't in the accident. It's Ryan, though. Well, he's dead."

Katie felt a jag in her chest.

Ryan. Hailey's sweet Ryan. He'd been in the stands just the night before, cheering the squad on. He'd been in the background for so much of their gym life, which was their life, for the past two years. He was the one who once opened Katie's car door with a coat hanger to retrieve her keys. Who'd rescued Devon's retainer from the bottom of the tumbling pit. Who danced with all the moms at that booster tiki party a few months ago—remember that? He'd even danced with Katie; the chip in one of his front teeth when he smiled. When he dipped her, everyone whooped, Katie's hair grazing the confettied floor.

Several parents began eyeing the bleacher steps anxiously but not moving, not yet. Forbidden from the floor during practice, they were helpless, like spectators behind glass.

Katie's eyes fixed on Devon, on the tight braided knot at the back of her head. Her rigid neck.

Two rows behind, the booster parents drew closer.

"Terrible," said Molly Chu, hands pressed to her cheeks. "Just terrible."

"I wonder if someone was drinking. Or texting," whispered Becca Plonski, the social chair. "Or drinking *and* texting."

"God," Katie said, "his parents. I don't even know where his family is." She vaguely remembered Hailey saying his mother lived on the other side of the state somewhere.

"Gwen, did you know already?" Molly asked. For the past year or more, Ryan had been working as a line cook at one of her Weaver's Wagon restaurants. You could see him through the kitchen window, under the bank of heat lamps.

"No," Gwen said, shaking her head, tapping her manicure on her phone case, watching Bobby as he tried to comfort Amelise, the other skills coaches. "No, I did not."

"We don't know much," Bobby said, clearing his throat over and over. "He was by himself when it happened. And he died over at St. Joe's. Teddy's there with Hailey now."

Down on the floor, the girls began clumping together, their leotarded backs hunching forward, shuddering like red birds.

Fourteen-year-old Jordan Siefert's palms were pressed against her eyes, her sparrow's body trembling.

Off the beam now, Lacey Weaver had sunk to the mat, was sitting on her hands and staring up, searching for her mother.

"Mom," a voice said, and it was Drew, beside Katie, fingers on her arm.

But at that moment Devon's seal-slick head finally turned and Katie could see her profile, a faint quiver of her chin.

"Mom," Drew said again, tugging on her sleeve, "shouldn't we call Dad?"

Katie looked down at her son, that grave face, his long-lashed eyes.

Nine years old going on ninety.

He was only a few blocks away, catching up on work e-mails at a diner.

"Eric," she whispered into her phone, "can you come here now?"

"I've still got another couple hours to go on this job—"

So she told him.

"Oh God," he said, after a long pause, a long breath. "Ryan. That poor kid."

*   *   *

Moments went by without anyone knowing what to do, Coach T.'s absence creating a formless confusion, Bobby V. fiddling with his clipboard, checking his phone, avoiding the parents' glare.

"Bobby," Gwen shouted down to the floor, "are you going to keep us in the Mama Cage forever?"

Bobby looked up, scratching his neck anxiously.

"I guess you all can come down here, comfort your girls," he said.

Spry Gwen was down on the floor in seconds, and the stands started unfilling with worried parents.

Taking two steps at a time, Katie hurried down, but Devon was nowhere to be found amid the satiny nuzzle of leotarded girls and all those identical ponytails.

"I never would've gotten to Level Seven without Hailey," little four-foot-seven Cheyenne Chu was saying softly, a hand dragging along the suede-topped trainer block. "She was the best tumbling coach I ever had."

Her mother, Molly, palms still planted on the sides of her face, seemed unable to speak, staring plaintively at Katie.

"Honey, nothing happened to Hailey," Katie said, touching Cheyenne's jutting shoulder. "She'll be okay."

But it was hard not to worry for Hailey, Coach T.'s heart's darling. Soft lilt and side-tilting head, she'd become more than a tumbling coach. She pitched in at the fund-raising car washes, sometimes bringing soy lattes for the parents who'd driven far. Laughed with the girls, gossiped with parents, even told the occasional salty joke. And, after every meet, could be seen dangling one of those long tan swimmer arms around her uncle's neck and kissing his leathered cheek.

"There she is," Drew said, startling Katie, who'd almost forgotten he was beside her. "There's Devon."

He pointed to the far side of the gym, Devon lingering by the chalk bowl, face red from the dust.

Just as she was about to push through the scrum, Katie felt a hand on her arm.

"I think he was going to propose." It was Becca Plonski, standing behind Katie, so close her fleece collar tickled Katie's neck. "I think he bought a ring."

"No," Katie said. "I don't think so." She wasn't sure why she said it. Or why she thought she might know better.

"I don't think so either," Gwen said, walking up to them. "After all, I sign his paycheck."

But Becca insisted she'd spotted Ryan at Ahee Jewelers the week before, his hands curled atop the glass cases, rocking anxiously on his feet, the ribbed neck of his windbreaker zipped up over his chin.

"No way," Gwen said, shaking her head. "A boy who wants to get married doesn't duck his girlfriend's calls."

Before Katie could ask what she meant, Eric rushed up, face flushed, his phone nearly slipping from his hand.

"I'm here, I'm here," he said breathlessly, his other hand damp in hers. "How's Dev?"

Arms wrapped around Drew, Katie watched from outside Coach T.'s windowed office as Eric spoke with pouch-eyed Bobby, who kept shaking his head.

When he returned, he pulled Katie aside.

"A hit-and-run," he whispered.

"Was Hailey with him?"

"No," he said. "The police are over at St. Joe's now, talking to the Belfours. But let's keep that quiet, okay?"

Katie nodded. *The police.* And she didn't know how anything like that could be kept quiet. Not among these parents.

"Sounds like it was instant," Eric said, his face pinched. "Snapped his neck."

A picture came to her: Ryan Beck laughing at something someone said, rubbing his nape, sun-brown always. "Oh, Eric," Katie said, covering her mouth.

From several yards away, Devon turned and looked at them both. She couldn't have heard them, not with all the chattering parents and the yelps of the younger girls, but she seemed to.

They walked over to her.

"What happens now?" she asked, looking up at her dad.

"We go home," he said, gently tugging her ponytail. "And think good thoughts for the Belfours."

"And no practice?" she said, looking down at her chalked feet. "Qualifiers are in six weeks—"

"Devon," Katie said quickly. Feeling eyes on them. Parents', other gymnasts'. Seeing Gwen and Becca turn and look at them. Eyes were always on Devon. "Everyone needs to go home now."

Devon looked up at both of them, her palms pressed together in front of her, and nodded.

The four of them made their way across the thronged gym floor, the families slow to disperse, the gymnasts seeming to find comfort in remaining there, with one another.

The lower-level girls, tender and pink-faced, hived together in their BelStars leotards, their feet so light, dipping their heads in the quietest of sobs.

Not so with the older ones, the Level 10s, who remained poker-faced, as they did after a big loss, an accident on the floor. With their matching solemn expressions, arms crossed, ponytails tight, and posture erect, the 10s ranged from ten to seventeen but all looked the same age. Under five feet, each was one of two types. The ballerinas, graceful, spritely, and pixie-ish; and the powerhouses, the corkers—barrel-thighed, thick-necked fire-plugs who succeeded by strength and will and shoulders like a man's fists.

All of them, Katie knew, had, long ago, learned to shake off, hide tears. Even, it seemed sometimes, to sort of reabsorb them, draw them back inside so no one else could see.

They had learned it from watching Devon, though she had never needed to learn it herself.

As Eric talked briefly with Gwen, with fretful Molly Chu, as Katie helped Drew pack up his things, Devon slowly drifted from them, walking farther and farther toward the empty center of the massive gym.

Chapter Five

"I just can't believe it," Katie said. "Who does something like that and just drives away?"

Next to her in the car, Eric was making calls, talking on the phone with one booster after the next.

"Well, I know...yes, but we can't get into those questions yet, and you know it, Jim."

In the rearview mirror, Katie could see Devon's face, her eyes glassy.

"Do we send flowers?" Drew said. "When Mr. Watts's wife died, you sent flowers."

"Yes," Katie said, relieved to have someone talking to her. "We'll do it right away."

"And I'll call Teddy tomorrow," Eric said, setting down his phone, rubbing his face wearily, "after they've had some time."

Then the car went quiet, just the *pfft-pfft* of the tires on the highway, and Katie flitted back into her thoughts. No one that young, with eyes so bright and the loping walk of a boy who would live forever, be a boy forever, could die.

Abruptly, Devon spoke.

"Poor Hailey," she said, her voice high and grasping. "She loved Ryan so much."

"I know, honey," Katie said.

In the mirror, Katie saw Drew looking at his big sister, puzzled and maybe unnerved. As if he'd never seen her so openly upset, but probably he hadn't.

"I'm sorry," he said to Devon in that lisping voice of his.

Devon looked at him, startled, like she'd forgotten he was sitting next to her.

"It's so, so sad," she said, more quietly now, to no one in particular. "Nothing like this has ever happened before."

Staring helplessly into kitchen cabinets, wondering about dinner, Katie could hear through the laundry chute. The whir of the treadmill from the basement.

First canceled practice since February's snowstorm, and qualifiers six weeks away, Devon wasn't going to let her body go soft.

"I wish she'd just take it easy," Katie said.

"She needs to work off some of these feelings," Eric said, reaching out to knead her shoulder.

Neither of them was saying the thing they were both thinking: the rotten, rotten timing. Right before qualifiers.

"Becca said Ryan just bought Hailey a ring," Katie said, remembering. "He was going to propose."

Eric looked at her.

"Oh Jesus," he said. Then, after a pause: "He was so young."

Katie drew a bath for Devon, even lit her favorite Island Nectar candles.

"It's okay to feel bad," Katie said. "We all liked Ryan."

"Thanks, Mom," she said, but she wouldn't meet Katie's eyes, just like after a bad meet, when she'd hide in the concessions-area restroom, as if she'd been caught doing something shameful. As if everyone had seen her with her clothes off, or read her diary.

The bathroom door closed behind Katie.

They were never home this early, and for a few minutes, Katie didn't know what to do with herself.

"Mom," Drew said from across the kitchen. "You said you'd take me to Petorium for more shrimp eggs."

"More? What happened to all the ones we did last night?"

"The container spilled in the garage." He pointed to the re-cycling bin, a squashed two-liter bottle, its sides veined with crusting salt. "I have to do it all again."

"Tonight?" she said.

But he looked so anxious, she couldn't say no.

On the drive, Drew seemed unmoored by everything, asking a hundred questions about Ryan (*But how do you know he died right away? How does breaking your neck mean you die?*).

But once they returned home, the science project focused him.

He looked so serious, measuring the rock salt, studying the dried shrimp eggs under the light, and taking notes, pencil tight in his careful fingers.

And he never said anything about what happened, seemed to have forgotten it deep in the marrow of his effort. Of the win-ning project he was creating.

He was like Devon that way.

Nearly midnight, Eric clapped his laptop shut, lifting his hand-some head and watching as she turned off all the downstairs lights, one by one.

She couldn't remember the last night they'd gone to bed at the same time. Eric working fifty hours a week, Katie working twenty-five from home, creating commercial logos, designing annual reports on her overloaded computer between carpooling, car repairs, more errands. They had such a meticulously coordinated schedule, calendars synced, pop-up reminders, both of them always needed somewhere and then always coming home to the rest of it. All their duties hung like heavy raiment over them all the time, only the sight of Devon spearing into the air lifting them up.

So it was nice to walk up the stairs together, the only balm on a gloomy day.

"I sent out a mass e-mail," he said, "to try to settle everyone down."

Walking past him earlier, she'd seen his in-box filled with breast-beating messages from parents, the gym's Facebook wall cluttered with concern and prayers. *What shocking news! Has anyone talked to Hailey? God bless him and keep him. He was loved by all.*

"The Connors told me they already saw a wreath on Ash Road," he said. "They said it's that spot with that dangerous turn. The hairpin."

Lying in bed with the cruel clarity that can come in late-night thinking, Katie foresaw how hard this would be for the gym, a tear in the seam of everything.

Ryan had been such a welcome and constant presence since that very first day he'd arrived at BelStars to help build the landing pit. That dark ruff of hair and easy smile, he was always around, waiting for Hailey in the parking lot, at competitions. Who could forget him selling raffle tickets out of the Weaver's Wagon or wielding the power hose at the booster car wash, his

T-shirt soaked through? The younger girls had squealed, whispering behind hands. The older ones, Devon's age, twitched and fidgeted helplessly, their faces red.

For the BelStars girls, he was that perfect crush age, the older-than-high-school-boy-but-not-yet-dad guy. So many of them homeschooled or marginally schooled, he was the only young man in their lives. Part of it was an infatuation with Hailey too, unerotic (probably) enchantments with Hailey's sunbleached hair and swimmer's shoulders and womanly body, so different from their own straight lines (whenever anyone asked her why she hadn't been a serious gymnast herself, she'd laugh and say, "Not with these," finger guns aimed at her apple-round breasts).

The girls marveled over Ryan's gallantry, the way he carried her gym bag, opened doors for her, bought her perfume and chocolate-covered raspberries on Valentine's Day. The flush of their love, his devotion. Even their lovers' quarrels, like the epic one at the Ramada Inn almost two years ago, were part of their allure. Their fights were exciting, and always ended with a flashy clinch.

And now he was gone. For all of them.

Being a girl is so hard, Katie thought. *And it only gets harder.*

The next day, Monday, they arrived to find no Coach T. again, his absence like a new scar.

"I don't understand," Molly Chu said, "why he can't at least be in communication with us." She looked at Katie. "Have you heard anything? There's a rumor that the police are very involved."

"I don't know," Katie said carefully. "Aren't the police always involved with a hit-and-run?"

The other parents in the stands nodded, all eyes returning to the floor. Bobby V. and the skills coaches were straining to simulate a normal day, but without Teddy, that great oak in the center, it felt awkward, stilted.

There was a peculiar tension among the girls, all of whom wore the blank expressions and big eyes of figures in Keane paintings. No one would listen to the substitute tumbling coach pitching in for Hailey or to the halfhearted drilling by Amelise.

Girls kept falling. Dominique Plonski rolled her ankle in the landing pit and limped off to her mother's arms.

At the vault, Devon struggled with her Yurchenko, the first twist so painfully slow she couldn't make the second. Foot hopping on the dismount, her face dazed and puzzled.

Then, from the corner of her eye, Katie spotted Gwen Weaver's approach, that shimmering bob and sleek purple jacket, the one Molly Chu called a Glamorak.

"I went to Coach T.'s house, to pay my respects," she said. "Hailey was there, but he wouldn't let me see her. The doctor sedated her because they couldn't calm her down."

"How horrible," Katie said, shaking her head.

"It is," Gwen said, almost impatiently. "And, you know, Hailey's nerves run high under the best of circumstances. But I thought you might know more."

"Me?" Katie said. "Why would I know?"

Gwen shook her head, her eyes veering to her daughter, Lacey, charging down the runway. The number-one vaulter in her age group, Lacey still couldn't approach Devon's talents at her age, much less Devon's now, legs fused, all air and drive. When Devon's palms hit the table, everyone gasped. Up she went, a torpedo. What was gravity, then?

"Jump big, like you dream!" Gwen shouted, one of her favorite motivational phrases. They both watched Lacey spring onto the vault table, lock into a handstand—mouth open, that slightly panicked look in her eyes always, like a wee bird that couldn't believe it was flying—then somersault off.

"Well, I'm sure Eric'll hear more. Teddy confides in him," Gwen said, leaning on the riser, rocking on her knees. "Did you know Hailey had to identify the body?"

"No," Katie said, wincing. She wondered how Gwen knew so much. But she always did—which gym let girls skip levels, which one sandbagged, the parent-lobby drama at the one on Route 7, and the gym over in Hartswood where a coach had a cozy live-in-guardian situation with a sixteen-year-old gymnast.

"His skull was crushed," Gwen said, and Katie felt her body tighten. "When I was little, my mom ran over our border collie, Hanro. I saw the whole thing from my bedroom window." She paused. "Obviously, this is much worse."

Neck snapped, skull crushed. Katie couldn't say anything, and she wanted Gwen to stop talking.

"That's why I never let Lacey have a pet," Gwen concluded, unzipping her jacket with a jerk and leaning back.

She thought of Ryan, that graceful boyish body, how he moved so easily, his arm like a slip of silk sliding across Hailey's shoulders, head dipping. At Weaver's Wagon she'd always see him coming from the kitchen in his line-cook apron, that bright ribbon of teeth, waving to the booster club, to Eric, to her.

"I have to go," Katie found herself saying, rising abruptly, gathering her bag, book, headphones. "I'm taking Drew to the museum after swim class. I'll be back."

"Right," Gwen said. "Well, I'll talk to Eric later. About everything. A plan."

"A plan?" Katie felt her ponytail unfurling slowly from its

band but didn't want to stop to fix it. She hadn't intended to leave or take Drew to a museum, but now it seemed like the perfect thing.

"I wouldn't say it to everyone," Gwen said, lowering her voice and moving closer, "but we do have to think ahead. I don't need to tell you Elite Qualifiers are forty days away. I know Devon's had that clock ticking inside her for two years."

"You're right," Katie said. "You don't need to tell me."

"Teddy says he'll be back by tomorrow," Gwen continued, "but who knows if he'll be in any condition to address gym issues. I'm going to send out some feelers."

"Gwen, this isn't the time. It was just two days ago."

Conversations with Gwen often felt like assaults and Katie never knew when to duck. *Best to duck the whole time,* Eric always said. He suffered the most, from the constant e-mails, the way she tried to dominate at meetings, the courting of other club members for key votes ("Gwen took me to Haven for a spa day and we talked a long time about the new floors. And I think the extra money is worth it. It's a safety issue, really").

She's passionate, Eric once said, with a shrug.

She's passionate when you agree with her, Katie replied.

She was nearly to the final set of steps, nearly free, when Gwen called out after her.

"Oh, and Katie," she said, swooping down the steps like a falcon. "I meant to tell you, it was so nice of Devon to come to Lacey's party Saturday night. The girls look up to her so much. I always tell Lacey: do as Devon does."

"She wouldn't have missed it," Katie said. She couldn't summon much memory of Saturday as separate from any other night. Laundry. *Lawrence Welk* bleating from Mrs. Martz's house next door. Going to the dollar store, late, for rock salt for Drew.

Had she gone to bed early? When had Eric taken Devon to the party? Had Devon had any fun at all?

The only thing she could recall vividly was that two a.m. surprise. Feeling Eric reach across, sleepily grazing the small of her back, the tenderness turning so quickly into something else, his hands between her thighs. Something different about it that she couldn't put her finger on, but it made her face warm now just thinking about it.

By then, she realized with a jolt, Ryan Beck was probably already dead. The thought was so odd and ugly, she shivered.

"So how is Devon dealing with all this," Gwen asked, looking closely at Katie, "with Ryan?" As if she could read her mind.

"It's hard for all of us."

"You know how dramatic girls can be at that age. With their crushes."

"Crushes?" Turning too quickly, Katie nearly lost her footing on the bottom step.

Gwen paused, looking at Katie, blinking three times.

"Well, who didn't have a crush on that sexy young man?"

"Everyone liked him," Katie said, dropping her foot to the floor.

"Didn't you?" Gwen added, head tilting like a debutante.

"I wasn't the one who bid a hundred bucks for a dance with him at the spring booster auction," Katie said, returning the head tilt.

Gwen's eyebrows lifted. "The things I do for BelStars," she said, laughing throatily. "Though he couldn't samba to save his life."

Katie flinched, but Gwen seemed not to notice. "As for Lacey," she continued, relentless, "she appears to be constructing a kind of pagan memorial altar."

"Well," Katie said, "that's not really Devon's way."

"No," Gwen agreed. "That girl's all head. Ice, ice, baby."

Katie started to nod, and then stopped.

Radio crackling, antenna thwacking in the wind, Katie turned the key over and over again, knowing she was flooding the engine, but anything to shake Gwen Weaver's voice from her head. Every conversation, she dropped in a half dozen tiny bombs. You only realized after, when the ticking grew louder.

Neck snapped. Skull crushed.

Crushed.

And *crushes*. Had there ever been a more perfect word for a feeling? The way the girls looked at Ryan—sometimes it had made Katie's heart hurt. She wished she could spare all of them the pain of those infatuations. The ones doomed from the start.

They were all, including Devon, young for their age in many ways. And so inexperienced in the countless ways boys could break your heart.

Her phone rang, the violin strokes of "Assassin's Tango."

"Eric," she said, fitting on her headset, "I've been calling you all day."

"I'm sorry," he said, sounding tired. "Was I supposed to get Drew? The car's been giving me trouble. That goddamn alternator. It's going to cost us another two hundred when that goes. And it's been so busy."

When Eric first started as an audio engineer at SoundMasters, back when Katie got pregnant and they decided to get married, it was going to be temporary. But everything happened so quickly, Katie's growing belly and the city hall nuptials and a mortgage. Except it turned out he was good at it, very good, with his way with people and his "sensitive ear," and eventually he'd taken over the business.

Sometimes Katie convinced herself there were parts of the job he liked, in the dark studio, that cocooning, the way he could curl into himself, ears trained, and eyes sometimes shut.

Occasionally, he seemed lost in it, in sound, and it was hard to shake him out.

Devon's concentration, her single-mindedness, it came from him, from Eric.

"Frank from WKBR called," he said. "You know how last-minute he is. And they use these cheap mixers, so I had to go back to the studio and get one of our own."

"For tonight's news?"

"Yeah." A pause so long she thought she'd lost him. "They sent me over to Ash Road."

"Oh," Katie said. *Neck snapped, skull crushed.*

"They were shooting that redheaded reporter. A standup in front of that crooked tree, her talking about the accident."

Katie knew the tree, an elm that always seemed to erupt from the ground just as you made the turn, springing up like a giant's claw.

At night, though, you could barely see it.

"There were some wreaths and flowers leaning against the trunk." His voice was slightly breathless. "You never think you'll know the person."

"He hit that old elm?" Katie asked. A picture came to her, blood on the asphalt, like those driver's ed movies. Ryan's long golden arm hanging from an open car door. "It can jump out at you after the turn if you're—"

"He wasn't driving," Eric said. He sounded very far away, like he was talking through wind or his hand was over his mouth. "He was walking."

"Walking? On Ash Road?" This revelation seemed worse still

to Katie in ways that would prod and tear at her in the hours to come. "Was he . . . do they know if he was drinking or something?"

She'd never seen Ryan drink. Once she saw him at a boosters' barbecue with a nonalcoholic beer snug between two fingers. Sometimes, when glasses were passed around, it seemed like Teddy studied him closely, as if watching for something.

"It's not really the safest place to walk," Eric said. "There's almost no shoulder." A pause, the sound of a car horn, of Eric taking a breath. "At that age, you don't think anything will ever happen to you."

Nothing ever felt so true. But the way Eric said it, voice creaking slightly, made her wonder why it felt true for him.

"Eric," she started.

But there was a siren coming from somewhere, and he had to go.

Hair wet from the pool, slicked back like a miniature financier, Drew stood in front of the Y, head bent over his phone.

"Business?" Katie asked, stepping out of the car. "Or personal?"

Just looking at him, Katie felt better about everything. Her sweet, serious boy.

"Look," he said, pointing to a silverfish squashed on the sidewalk.

She smiled. "You're going to be one of those photographers who takes pictures of taxidermy and headstones."

"It's a night insect," he said. "It doesn't have wings, but it runs really fast."

He handed her his phone. There were dozens of snapshots, extreme close-ups of metallic scales glimmering, antennae like points on a star. And other photos, beetles and cicadas. An explosion of jewels, a glamorous bracelet fallen, sprawling its gems everywhere.

"You, kid, are something else," she said. "Wanna go to the museum?"

"We can watch the rest of Devon," he said, shrugging. "I have stuff I can do."

He always made it all so easy, never seemed to mind any of it, or at least he never complained. His entire life had been sitting in bleachers. And ten o'clock dinners, weekend trips to far corners of the state, strapped in the backseat for most of his early years, all the hours high up in the stands, the noises of the gym, of all the squeaking girls and mat pounding. Katie tried to make it as fun as she could, bleacher picnics with a steaming thermos of hot chocolate, fat cream cheese sandwiches stained with grape jelly, greasy-papered blondies from Zerillo's bakery. It was always the two of them, with a stack of coloring books and puzzles and crazy eights. It was the kind of mother-son time they'd never have had otherwise, up there in the echoey stands, their elbows and forearms striped from the aluminum ridges.

These days, he'd mostly read by himself, books about magic and electricity and volcanoes. Earbuds in, he never seemed to mind.

He'd never known any other way.

"It's damn late, Katie-did. I'm sorry."

It was nearly nine o'clock, and there was Coach T. at their screen door, a six-pack of beer sweating in his big red hands.

"Is Eric around?" he asked.

From the kitchen window, Katie watched them at the picnic table, crouched over cans of Schlitz. It was a beer Katie didn't even know existed anymore but that reminded her of her granddad, of long, crowded Sundays with crunched beer cans and football and the front door always swinging open. Every other night of the week, she and her mother had their Lean Cuisines, hands burning on the puckering pouch, but Sundays were filled with leisure and the encroaching smell of pot roast, carrots broiled to tinder sticks. Her grandparents, both long dead, always had real Sundays like no one had anymore—comics in the paper and football on TV and *God is great, God is good, we thank you for this food, amen.*

BelStars, of course, didn't leave room for Sundays like that.

Silver hair glinting under the moon, Teddy leaned over his knees, shaking the near-empty can, saying things softly to Eric, too softly for Katie to hear.

They'd been talking a long time, Eric nursing the same can and Teddy peeling off two more from the plastic curlicue.

Finally, as the neighborhood quieted, the dishwasher cycle shushed, and the beer gave ballast to Teddy's voice, she could hear them.

"She'd had a few drinks at dinner, you know? So Ryan drove her back to her apartment in her car and left it there for her. She says she hates herself for letting him walk home at that hour. Just thinking of it makes her want to die. What do you say to that? To your little girl saying she wants to die?"

"She doesn't mean it, Teddy."

"I only had sons, all off to college and beyond. Not a flipper in the bunch. So Hailey's special to me. She's like my own."

Teddy peered into the beer can as if looking for something.

Katie waited, hoping Eric would offer a soothing phrase. It took a long ten, twenty seconds. For a crazy moment, she was afraid he was going to ask Teddy when he was coming back to the gym.

"Hailey's strong, Teddy," Eric said, at last. "She'll get through this."

"Sure," he said, with a hint of his usual buoyancy and vigor. "Sure she will."

Eric glanced over at the house as if looking for her.

"It's hard not to think of doing things different, though," Teddy said, pulling on his ball cap. "I had my worries about him."

"What do you mean?"

Katie moved over to the screen door, so close her earlobe pressed against its mesh.

"Drugs. He was just a kid. An arrest for possession, no charges filed. Petty stuff." Listening, Katie felt her eyebrows lift in surprise. "But it makes you wonder. I always had one eye on him. For Hailey."

"You have to be that way," Eric said, shifting in his chair. "You have to protect them."

Teddy nodded, pointing a finger at Eric, like *That's right, that's right.*

"We do. And like my own granddad used to say, if you get down to the nub of it, people don't change."

That's not true, Katie thought. *Not at all.* Everyone changed, all the time. That was what was so hard.

As if sensing her at the screen door, Eric waved her outside eagerly.

She walked over and when Teddy looked up at her, she could see the measure and breadth of his face under the bug-eyed security light, a look of such weariness, hollowed-out dismay.

With both hands, she grabbed for one of his massive shoulders, rubbed it. She'd never seen Coach T.—or any of the strong, durable, steadfast men she'd known—like this.

"Oh, Katie, thank you, honey," he said, smiling up at her. "I'm sorry to be taking up your night. Sorry to be..."

His voice drifted helplessly into nothingness, and Katie felt her eyes filling, though it was too dark for anyone to see.

It was after ten, Eric and Teddy still talking outside, when Katie peeked behind her daughter's half-open door. At her desk, Devon was leaning over her book, *Physics Principles and Problems*, brow wrinkled, face close enough to touch the pages.

"It's all so strange, Mom," she said, not lifting her head, her earbuds dangling. Katie hadn't even realized she'd seen her at the door.

"Which part?" Katie said, stepping inside quickly.

"Everyone at the gym was saying things today." Devon looked up, her earbuds sliding off. "I hope Coach hasn't heard what they're saying."

"What do you mean? About Ryan?"

"I don't know," she said. "Is it true the police are interviewing people?"

"What?" Katie said. This was new. "That's their job, honey. Who told you that?"

"I don't know. Lacey Weaver, I think. I was trying not to listen." She flexed her thumbs, staring down at them. "I've completely lost my double Yurchenko. My turnaround is pathetic. There was just so much noise."

"People are going to gossip. Don't listen. Just keep your focus. Like you always do."

"That's what Dad said."

"You already talked to him about this?" Feeling a twinge.

"Yeah." She tapped her highlighter on the edge of her desk for a second. "He said he saw the spot it happened. On Ash Road."

Katie looked at her. "He told you that?"

"He seemed freaked out by it. Is he okay, Mom?"

Katie felt herself taken aback. "Your dad? Sure he is, honey."

They looked at each other for a moment, then Devon's eyes darted away. Katie tried to hold on to a thought she had, something about how Eric sounded on the phone earlier, but couldn't.

Then, realizing: "Devon, are you okay?"

"Everything feels different."

Katie reached out to touch her shoulder. It was the most Devon had talked to her about anything other than gymnastics in so long and it made her want to throw her arm around her daughter, do something. With Drew it was so easy, Drew who would still rest his pelted head against her when he was tired, asking her questions until her head ached from them.

She wanted the moment to last, to deepen.

"Honey, did you . . . did you like Ryan a little?"

There was a brief silence, the only sound a pop in Devon's jaw, gum between her teeth. The highlighter rat-a-tatting on the pages of the book.

Then—"What? No. That's not what I'm talking about. I'm worried because qualifiers are—who said that?"

"No one. I . . ."

"Boys don't look at me," she said, uncapping her highlighter pen briskly. Straightening her back.

"Honey, that's not true," Katie insisted. "What—"

"Did someone say something to you, Mom? At the gym? Because the girls there are all . . . you know how they are."

And she did. They talked about Devon all the time, speculating and watching and wondering. Whenever she appeared in the local paper, they pored over the article for clues. Whenever

Coach T. pulled her aside, they tried to eavesdrop, to hear what he whispered in her ear and what she whispered back.

Still, Katie felt like she'd struck a nerve, the mortification of having someone stumble upon a secret feeling.

"But, honey, if you *did*, it's nothing to feel bad about," she said gently. "I'm sure half the girls at the gym did. He was so good-looking and nice to all of you. It's only natural—"

"I know," Devon said, cringing back in her chair. "But I'm not like that. Not like the girls at school, talking about boys and their abs and muscles. And their phones. All they do, Mom, is take pictures of themselves all day and send them to each other."

"Well, that's what girls do," Katie said. "Some girls. And it's okay if you look at boys. Because, Devon, they're definitely looking at you."

Devon pressed her highlighter hard onto the page, a blot spreading.

"Everything's always ending," she said.

Katie had no idea what she meant. What was ending? Childhood? She started to ask, reaching out, but Devon pulled her book up, gathered it closer to her face, as if starting to read.

Like any teenage girl might.

The hard thud of adolescence still hadn't fully arrived for Devon, or for any of the other girls at the gym. Like any parent, Katie'd braced herself for it, and then at some point stopped waiting. Ages thirteen, fourteen, fifteen, sixteen, even seventeen came and went for the BelStars, and their bodies remained flat and smooth as scythes except their perky muscled behinds.

Once, when she was seven or eight, Devon announced that she didn't need to worry about growing, as if she could control it through sheer force of will. "I'll grow a few inches when this is all over," she said, her eyes grave, as if the words *all over* bespoke an unimaginable horror.

We need to get her before she changes. That's what Teddy had said, all those years ago.

But Devon's body didn't seem to change. It only got harder.

It wasn't until a few months ago, February, that she'd had any reminder at all that Devon was a teenager, nearly a woman.

Arms pushed in the laundry basket, Katie saw it. Glaring at her from the knot of leotards, white, blue, red. The glossy red-brown stain, smaller than a dime, at the center of one crotch.

At last, she thought, and smiled to herself.

But it was fleeting, then the next thought: *Oh no.*

The Mom Moment anticipated and dreaded was, in Devon's case, magnified a hundred times. So many years past the expected age, the anticipation had stretched thin, the dread deepening as Devon would talk about other girls who'd "turned," their hips and breasts slowing them down, heavy and monstrous.

Can you believe what happened to Michele McAlpine, Mom? She was so good, but look at her now. I feel so sorry for her, all that new flesh dragging her down.

Whenever Katie asked Dr. Kemper, the BelStars' favored pediatrician, about it, about what he called "delayed-onset puberty," he'd assured her everything was fine and it would come.

"You'll be sorry then," he said. "They all are."

But it had happened, and Devon held the tampon Katie handed her as if it were a loaded gun.

"Do you need me to show you how to put it in?"

Devon looked at her like she might die.

Together, mother and daughter curled on Katie's bed. Heating pad, half a muscle relaxant, Devon's hands between her legs, Katie stroking her hair. It was what her own mom had done, one of the few motherly things she'd managed, her life so full of the tripwires of bad men and paycheck-to-paycheck living and now the slippery signs of early dementia at only fifty-eight, the result of a brain softened by margaritas and two bad marriages.

"Oh, honey," she said, her hand on Devon's back, workout T-shirt stiff with sweat. "It's okay. Everything will be fine."

"No, Mom," she said, running her hand over her stomach queasily. "You know it won't."

Katie did know. No matter what, it was a sharp slash into the center of your life. It changed things and you couldn't pretend it didn't.

"Don't tell Dad," Devon said. "Mom, don't tell Dad."

"Why not?" Katie said without thinking. Then adding, "I mean, of course. It's private."

She knew it wasn't possible that Devon might fear her dad's disappointment, that he might see it only as the loss of that aerodynamic missile of a body, low, tight, no drag. An efficient machine. Devon knew her dad better than that.

("Oh," Eric said when she finally told him. "Okay. Well. You sure? She's so small." Almost as if he didn't believe her.)

"I don't want anyone to know," Devon said. "Not anyone."

And moments went by, Devon descending at last into some kind of sleep, the telltale shift of her body weight.

"No one ever tells you there'll be so much blood," she whispered, ebbing away.

"How much blood?" Katie asked. "There shouldn't be—"

"No one ever tells you any of it," Devon mumbled. "No one warns you."

"Baby, it's nature. Your body."

"I made it happen," Devon murmured, and she had to be talking in her sleep. "And now it's forever."

Which was true, in a way.

The next day, Katie had been unable to stop herself. So she repeated her most shameful act as a mother. Stretching across Devon's bed, she dug for it, breathlessly. And there it was, though wedged much, much deeper: the I HEART EVERYTHING diary, Victorian-novel-thick, its velvety cover rubbed worn in spots.

When she opened it, she saw it was no longer the training log it had been a year and a half ago but seemed filled with thoughts, feelings, phrases jumping out at Katie—*so nervous! And next year, trig and there's more homework than ever*—but she unfocused her eyes, vowed not to read anything but the most recent entry.

And there it was, dated the day before and written with silver Sharpie:

It finally happened. I'm a woman. Everything was beautiful and nothing hurt.

The pressure of the pen leaving marks on three pages to follow.

And that was it.

A complicated but palpable relief spread through her.

To know that, deep down, Devon was just a teenage girl in the throes of her first period. A regular girl, with feelings, big feelings she couldn't explain.

It was late, and Teddy had finally left, but Katie could still hear Eric outside, returning phone calls, his voice echoing up to the bedroom where Katie sorted laundry.

She waited for him until she couldn't wait any longer, her eyes dry-socketed, her body giving way.

Sometime later, she woke to his hand resting on her stomach, his body collapsing beside her on top of the comforter, the bedside lamp still on.

They both climbed under the sheets wordlessly and she burrowed up against him, sighing in his ear.

She was glad she had him to herself at last. His familiar smell, cotton and shampoo and the faint secondhand tang of the Kools his technician Jimmy smoked at SoundMasters all day.

And later, the lights off and the house quiet, he threw his heavy arms around her, which was her favorite thing.

Just sunk back into sleep, the light off and socks tugged free, she heard his voice, and it was almost like a dream voice.

"I saw one of his shoes."

"What?"

"I saw it. One of Ryan's shoes. On Ash Road."

"What do you mean?" she whispered, pushing against him, claiming the cool space on the sheets between them.

"He got hit so hard he was knocked out of them. One rolled down into the ravine. They missed it the night before. But there it was."

"That's not true," she found herself saying. It just seemed too awful to be true.

"I'm sorry," he said. "Forget it."

He was still whispering in her ear for a while, saying things that Katie couldn't hear, his mouth on the back of her neck.

She wasn't sure why, but they were breathing so hard, like there wasn't enough air for them both.

Chapter Six

"Kirsten, tell them what you told me. About Saturday night."

All of them were straining toward each other, phones in hand.

Gwen, Molly Chu, Becca Plonski, all the regulars, their tinted water bottles tumbled at their feet.

Katie had stationed herself far from everyone, her laptop propped on her knees. With Drew off in the rec area, absorbed in the timeworn Puzzle Bobble video game, she could put her earbuds in, focus on the screen, and get some work done. And not have to talk about things.

But they were unusually loud today, a level of animation typically reserved for an injury, a bad call at a meet, the time Missy Morgan's mom was ejected for spitting on a judge.

" . . . at Randello's. They were in the corner booth. Everyone knows that's the engagement booth. It must have been just a few hours before the accident."

It was Kirsten Siefert. Standing above them, holding court. She almost never came to practice and had asked on her first visit where the pommel horse and rings were (*At the nearest boys' gym, ten miles over*, Gwen had snapped). Today, however, she brought an invaluable tale from Saturday night.

"He looked as adorable as ever, but Hailey did not look her best. Sweats and no makeup. A girl with those shoulders needs to wear makeup. Greg and I decided he must've sprung it on her. Maybe she suspected something, because she couldn't sit still, practically jumping out of her seat the whole meal, didn't touch her primavera. Boy, did that sweet boy make her wait!"

The story felt more than a little gilded, but it was sad to hear, just the same.

Hell, let's do this thing had been Eric's proposal all those years ago. The circumstances so different, a beer-can pull tab as an engagement ring, cutting her finger so badly it bled for hours, and they didn't care. *I never thought I'd get married*, Eric kept saying, dazed and smiling. *I never thought I would.*

They'd known each other five months.

"So how did he do it?" Molly asked, huddling closer to Kirsten.

"I didn't see the actual proposal part," Kirsten admitted, puncturing the moment for everybody. Then, trying to recover through sheer conjuring, she added, "We were waiting for an engagement ring in a tiramisu. Then champagne. What a romantic guy, right? And a gentleman. You know, Ryan always opened the door for me."

"Me too," Becca said, rubbing her wrists together. "He always did. Every time."

"Once he gave me a jump in the parking lot," Molly added, face pinkening.

"Champagne? On his salary?" Gwen said, stroking one groomed eyebrow. "If that happened, I better have Carlos check the bar supply."

No one said anything for a minute, or looked at Gwen.

Kirsten took a seat next to Molly. Something still seemed to be fluttering behind her eyes, in her mouth.

"But it was odd too," Kirsten said, slowly. "Greg saw her on his way to the men's room. He said her face was dirty."

"What?"

"Sweaty. He said she looked sweaty and worked up."

Katie glanced at Kirsten, who didn't appear to like the turn her own story had taken.

"Then we looked up at one point and they were gone," she said, more quietly now. "And the dessert just sat there, melting."

"Well, that's just sad," Becca said. "Gosh."

There was a pause, then Molly said, "But why did he walk home? Who would walk on Ash Road at night? Jim nearly got sideswiped running there years ago, I won't let him near it."

"Maybe they had a fight," Gwen said. "She was a moody girl."

"Hailey?" Kirsten said. "Come on. My girls are in love with her. Tansy wants to marry her."

Gwen's mouth twisted. "She wasn't just sunshine and vanilla cupcakes."

"What does that mean?" Katie interrupted, jerking her ear-buds out. "And why are you talking about her in the past tense?"

Everyone looked at Katie, then back at Gwen, who shook her head ruefully.

"I've seen things you haven't. That girl has eyes on the back of her head. She'd surprise Ryan at the restaurant. Wanted all the waitresses to know he had a girlfriend. Young women can be that way. Especially when they lack self-worth. It's not a criticism. It's just the kind of person she was. Sorry, *is*."

"Well, she loved him," Becca said, punctuating with a head nod. "Loves him. Loved him."

"Hailey was a runaway, you know," Gwen continued. There was no stopping her now, that mouth of hers, its lilac lines whirring, like a clatter toy.

"Her mom kicked her out of her house when she was just thirteen," Katie said. "That's not a runaway."

Gwen shook her head. "Teddy likes to tell it that way. Auntie Tina told me the truth once. Auntie Tina likes her gin and tonics."

And Gwen proceeded to share how Hailey had snuck out of her bedroom window with her mom's credit card to chase after some boy.

"Poor little rich girl. Once her mom canceled the card, she ended up sleeping in strangers' cars, in lounge chairs at apartment pools," Gwen said. "Finally, the police found her in Tampa, sitting on a bench, smoking a cigarette. Torn shirt, scratch marks up her whole face. She claimed a girl she'd been hitching with had jumped her and beaten her with a sandal."

"A sandal?" Becca said, as if that were the worst part of the story.

"And she said to the cop, 'What took you so long?'"

Katie rolled her eyes, nearly laughed. "That is definitely made up," she said. "Besides, she was a kid. We all did crazy things when we were that age."

The other parents always tried to do this. To drag her into their little circle, their gym drama, their coven, rubbing their hands over their water bottles, fire burn and cauldron bubble.

She had stories she could share too, but she never would. Once she found Hailey in the parents' lounge, hand stuffed wrist-deep in a bag of ice. She said Ryan had fallen asleep after his shift, missing their date.

I got so mad I punched my own wall, she said, and then started laughing, a jangling, sad laugh, her face pink and crimped like a carnation. *I love him so much. I just want to be with him all the time.*

And Katie had taken her hand and held the ice there and said some things, about young men, men at that age, and how he'd come around. And that Hailey just needed to be patient, she just needed to hang on a little less tight. It was hard, Katie knew, loving that much.

Sliding her earbuds back in, she turned her eyes to her laptop. But before long, her gaze wandered to the gym floor, to Devon swinging hypnotically on the bars, hands gloved with chalk, the arrow of her body, her feet melded into one sharp point.

This is why I'm here, she thought to herself. Not for the boosters, not for BelStars. Devon needed her at practice, always had.

The rumbling din, the hum, the freighted silences, the smell of damp leotards and pit foam, the tarry Bag Balm—they were all linked intricately to Devon. Sometimes it felt like the gym was Devon, was her body, its rhythms and pulses and tremors.

At night, the gym left its trace. Its thumps and thwacks still echoing in Katie's head, swirling chalk dust and raw puberty still in her nostrils, under her skin. In her sleep, she could hear the panting of the girls, their fire and desperation.

"Is it him? Really?"

"I saw him, I did!"

"Quiet!"

A slam and the sharp twang of a springboard and groan of bars ceased.

On the floor, there was a flurry of leotards assembling, Bobby V. shouting, *Tut-tut.*

Smiling to herself, Katie watched Devon stride elegantly to her spot. *Coach T., he's back!*

The parents rose to their feet. Thirty or more of them in pockets throughout the stands.

Then Coach Teddy swept in, his familiar red polo and bright blue track pants swapped for a graying dress shirt and sagging tie.

He stood at the bottom of the bleachers, one foot on the stands like a ship captain with his foot on the prow, an even bigger presence than when Katie first met him all those years ago.

He wiped his face three times before lifting his head and trying for a kind of smile, the one he wore when they lost badly but forgivably.

"I want to thank you all so kindly," he started, voice catching slightly. "We are all touched by the outpouring of support. Tina says we have more flowers at home than a French cathouse."

Everyone tried to laugh a little, straining to hear Teddy in the cavernous gym, all the girls lined up like soldiers, shoulders back but heads down.

"We picked up Ryan's mother from the airport yesterday. She asked me to tell you that you are all welcome to attend the services tomorrow. And I know I speak for her as well when I thank all of you for your notes, your thoughtful remembrances of Ryan. And of course Hailey thanks you." He bit his lip, stared down at his white sneakers.

Having seen Teddy the night before, the beers and self-reflection, Katie found it hard to watch him now, attempting to play the part.

"As Pastor Matthews reminded me this morning," Teddy said, chin up, jaw tight, "blessed are they that mourn, for they shall be comforted."

Katie had never heard Teddy talk this way. It felt mysterious and moving, his head bowed and a few parents crossing themselves or *Amen*-ing.

Scanning the girls, their respectful attention, she found Devon, who stood stock-still, arms folded across her chest.

Her face, what Katie could see of it, looked formal, composed.

Like Devon always looked when Coach was speaking, or when she was waiting for her score.

The practice that followed was clumsy and tense, with yet another substitute tumbling coach and Teddy distracted, his phone ringing all the time and the mistaken delivery of a laurel serenity wreath to the gym rather than his home.

At first, Devon struggled too, standing on the beam, doing her counts over and over, postponing the one-armed back handspring, not engaging with the encouraging Amelise ("Come on, girl, I know you got it!"), not even looking at her.

As soon as Amelise turned her attention to other girls, though, everything changed. Taking a breath, Devon threw herself into a beauteous back handspring and double full dismount, her feet landing on the mat with a tight smack.

Then back up on the beam to do the full routine, her lovely switch leap and aerials and cat-leap half turn, that one-armed back handspring, as if she were weightless, a gossamer strand. The eight- and nine-year-olds kept sneaking glances, like they always did, craning heads, ponytails twitching. Trying to figure out what they needed to do to get to *that,* to Devon.

To be capable of shutting the world out, even death itself, and surrendering to the body, trusting in its powers, its secrets. No feeling but this. No feeling.

The striated bands of old flesh tight around that foot.

It just doesn't feel as much.

* * *

After practice, they picked up Eric at the studio, his car in the shop again, a hundred and ten thousand miles on that barge, the side door unlocking only with a butter knife and both of them wondering what they would do when Devon moved past lurching practice turns with Eric in the church parking lot and got her license.

He was waiting outside, looking sweaty and adrift.

Katie wondered if he was getting sick. Though, like Devon, he never, ever got sick.

"Let's go to the Wooden Nickel," he said. "We could all use a break, right?"

Dinner out with just the four of them, which almost never happened. It was like old times, before BelStars, even. As if, walking under the thickly varnished rafters to the corner booth, its puckering vinyl and doily-edged place mats, they all decided to forget everything else.

Patty melts on big china plates, waffle chips with three kinds of relish, Drew's favorite "Italian spaghetti," thick as rope, its sauce sweet as candy.

And there was Devon, even eating a breadstick, or part of one. Chewing the soft dough languorously, stretching it between her fingers like taffy.

"I bet you're glad Teddy's back," Katie said.

"Yeah," Devon said. "But it'll be better when he can lead practice again."

"Is Hailey coming back?" Drew asked. "What'll she do now, without a boyfriend?"

"She'll be okay," Eric said. "Ready for the science fair, kiddo?"

"Yeah," Drew said, then spoke excitedly and with conviction

for several minutes about his experiment with the brine shrimp ("Some kids call them sea monkeys, but they're not like monkeys at all so that's wrong") and motor oil.

"Well, that sounds terrific," Eric said, fingers tapping the edge of his phone absentmindedly.

"The first batch spilled in the garage," Drew said, looking at his dad's phone too now, "so I had to start over."

"I'm sorry about that, buddy," Eric said, ceasing the tapping and looking at Drew at last.

Devon stared down at her butter-glazed hands. "I'm going to the restroom."

"How did they spill?" Katie asked Eric, who shrugged.

"It's okay," Drew said, reaching out for the clouded decanter of salad oil on the table. "Mom helped me do it over."

"Mom's the best," Eric said, stacking all the plates for the lurking bus boy, placing the utensils in the center on top, ever the former waiter.

"I think the oil will make the shrimp die faster," Drew said, holding the decanter between his pink fingers, peering at his dad through the filmy oil.

"Makes sense," Eric said.

Katie could see something dimming on Drew's face, following his dad's drifting gaze as he watched Devon return from the ladies' room.

"That sounds like a good hypothesis," Katie jumped in. "Look what cars are doing to the environment."

Drew paused a minute as Devon slid into the booth soundlessly.

"But Dad"—Drew tried again—"they're at the bottom of the food chain."

"What are?" Devon asked.

"The shrimp. So if the oil kills them," Drew said, bringing the salad oil closer to his face for a better look, "everything else goes away too."

"Everything?" Devon asked.

Drew nodded solemnly. "Everything."

"Well, maybe not everything," Eric said, a slight rasp to his voice. "But it sounds great, kiddo. You'll tear the lid off that science fair."

Eric's phone flashed. *Coach T.*

"Maybe I'll win," Drew said.

"You always win, buddy," Eric replied, rising and picking up his phone. "Be right back."

"But even if you don't win," Katie added, throwing her arm around him, "I say you win."

"I hope I get first place," Drew said, tilting the decanter so precariously Katie reached out to upright it. "But I know the shrimp will die."

Back at the house, Katie had just begun to confront the kitchen, the counter stained by gritty creep of that morning's coffee, a scattering of Cheerios mysteriously caught in the stovetop burners, when she heard Drew calling her name from the den.

"It's on TV," he said, remote in his hand.

"What is, honey?" Katie asked, Eric and Devon behind her.

"Ryan," he said, pointing. "Being dead."

On the screen a stern-faced reporter stood on Ash Road in front of the grappling elm. Despite the harsh lights illuminating him, everything looked so dark.

. . . The third accident in a year at this location. The latest victim

is twenty-five-year-old Ryan Beck, who was struck and killed Saturday night in an apparent hit-and-run.

A photo of Ryan appeared. Chin lowered, mouth slightly open, eyes vacant, like he was staring down a hole. He looked no more than sixteen.

"Why are those lines behind him?" Drew asked.

"Christ," Eric said. "Did they have to use a mug shot?"

"I guess that's all they had," Katie said. "I didn't realize..."

"Is that Ryan?" Devon said quietly, her gym bag slipping from her arm. "Is it him?"

No one spoke for a second, all eyes on the TV. Ryan's glower.

Behind her, Katie heard a soft thud and realized Devon had left the room. She couldn't blame her.

... Speculated Beck's fall down the shoulder and into a ditch is the likely cause of the fatal head and neck injuries. A formal autopsy will confirm...

"What's a mug shot?" Drew asked.

"I'll explain later," Eric said, hand on Drew's shoulder, turning him. "Time for bed."

Police are urging possible eyewitnesses to come forward.

Ryan's image remained on the screen for a second. He looked both baby-faced and sullen, a spray of acne up one cheek like a scar.

A memorial service for Beck will be held tomorrow at noon.

"Are we going to go?" said Drew, looking at Katie. "To remember Ryan?"

"You both have school," Katie said, fumbling. "So."

She looked at Eric, who was still watching the TV.

There were no skid marks on the road, the reporter continued, gesturing down to the inky asphalt. *Whoever the driver was, he never even set his foot on the brake.*

"We'll figure it out," Eric said, not moving, not blinking. "Don't worry. Everything's okay."

Chapter Seven

Car still up on the lift. I'll get there as soon as I can. Eric's text arrived as Katie drove to the funeral, alone. I'm so sorry, K.

It hurt her eyes, everything so garishly beautiful, the entire cemetery blushing with late-spring flowers, petals scattering everywhere, gathering at everyone's feet.

Everyone came, all the parents. A half dozen brought their daughters, the younger ones who trained under Hailey, taking them out of school, thrusting their hard little gymnast bodies into stiff dresses, shoulders straining eyelet.

Teddy and his wife, Tina, both pewter-haired, tanned, long-limbed, soared over everyone else, their eyes downcast. Grand and conspicuous, they moved like mourning royalty.

But then there was Hailey.

At first Katie didn't even recognize her, her hair thick and uncombed, her athletic body seemingly wedged into someone else's black dress. Her face looked raw, her freckles more conspicuous against her fading tan. Among the others—with their dark shades, the older women's hats, all their funeral masks—she looked naked.

Through the service that followed, she didn't cry at all, despite the large lace handkerchief that she held awkwardly, as if someone had forced it into her hand.

The small-boned woman next to her had to be Ryan's mother, a likeness in the soft dreaminess of her features. Weeping openly, her fingers over her nose and mouth, her delicate body shook and swayed. The more she cried, the more Hailey tensed beside her, even leaning away, averting her eyes.

Katie kept hoping someone would comfort the woman. If Eric were here, he would have. If he hadn't been so sure the car would be ready, which it wasn't (was it ever?). He was always there for important events, dispensing appropriate words, accepting shared-sympathy hugs, letting Becca Plonski wrap those bony arms of hers around his waist, snuggling up to him like Katie had seen her do after her daughter's coccyx injury.

Can't you get your car after? Katie texted, her thumbs pressing so hard the letters kept repeating. Everyone's expecting you.

I'll try. I'm sorry. I'll try to get there. I'm sorry.

Lost in thoughts during the sermon, Katie kept pondering that mug shot, the things Teddy had said, *If you get down to the nub of it, people don't change.* But Ryan surely had.

And hadn't Hailey? And, of course, Eric. And Katie herself, no longer that wayward girl who couldn't sit still, who once painted her phone number on her midriff at the beach. The midnight-blue nail polish took days to crack off, fade.

By the time Pastor Matthews finished speaking, Ryan's

mother was sobbing so throatily it almost sounded like singing. Katie moved forward, touching her shoulder lightly.

But then Teddy was there, reaching out to let her take his arm as they strode up the knoll.

Turning, Katie caught sight of Hailey, wind-whipped, hair caught in her mouth and her eyes narrow. It looked like she wanted something, nearly lunging toward Katie, her heel catching on a random footstone.

"Hailey, I'm so sor—" Katie started, but in the crowds, she lost her, couldn't get to her in time.

The Belfour house—butter yellow, rambling, sun-filled, with a massive new cedar deck that stretched through half the yard— was packed as tightly as it was for a booster event, a preseason kickoff.

As Katie moved through the rooms, everything reminded her of everything: the first welcoming party, held just for Devon, with Teddy singing a karaoke "Welcome to the Jungle"; all the season kickoffs and strategy sessions, Tina's snipping terriers underfoot. That vast trestle dining-room table, where Teddy had, six years before, unfurled the flow chart, Devon's pathway to the gold.

Now, Katie watched as the table vanished under large platters of food arriving aloft in the arms of boosters, the same macaroni salad, meatballs, and cucumber salad, Molly's dream bars, Gwen's no-carb lasagna brought to every other event at the house. Katie's fruit basket, which had seemed right at the time, sat untouched in the corner, its jaunty bow and pink cellophane spattered with food.

"I knew he had a record when I hired him," Gwen was saying to Molly as Katie sidestepped her sight line. "But I believe in second chances. It's the American way."

With picture windows and sliding glass doors or mirrored walls in every room, there was nowhere to hide in the Belfour house. Before anyone could see her, Katie ducked into the hallway, where she found Ryan's mother, wandering with a soggy, tilting paper plate.

"Mrs. Beck, I'm Katie Knox. Can I do anything for you?"

"No," she said doubtfully, brushing her hair from her face with her free hand. "I packed in a hurry. My dress isn't right."

"It's great," Katie said, even though the dress was very short, and something you bought quickly at the mall, its threads puckering the first time you wore it.

"I don't even believe this is happening," Mrs. Beck said. "He's my little boy."

"I know," Katie said, but she didn't want to imagine what it felt like. It was what all the parents did. Nearly every time Devon threw herself into the air, Katie had to fight off logic. But sometimes, still, she'd stop breathing. Like she had all those years ago, the whir and screech of the lawn mower. "I'm so sorry, Mrs. Beck."

"Call me Helen," she said. "You knew my Ryan?"

"Not that well," Katie replied, a twitch above her brow, "but I liked him."

"I could tell by your face during the sermon."

"What?" Katie felt her face warm. "I . . ."

"I only visited Ryan once since he moved here."

"Airfare is so expen—"

"I don't know anyone here," Helen said, swiveling a little, looking around helplessly for a place to set down the plate. "This house is so big, and I don't know anyone. And it's not very . . . friendly."

"What do you mean?" Katie asked.

Helen leaned closer, only the paper plate between them.

"I'm not sure they want me here," she said, lowering her voice. "I—"

"Katie!" It was Molly Chu, charging toward her, Cheyenne's little brother tangled between her legs. "I thought I saw you."

Suddenly, Katie was surrounded by boosters—Jim Chu, balancing a plate of food, hovered after his wife. Kirsten Siefert, Bluetooth forever hooked to her ear. Becca Plonski, gesturing with the same celery-stalk wrists that plagued her daughter, Dominique, clinging to her side.

Turning back, Katie saw Ryan's mother was gone, only the scent of hotel soap and ChapStick remaining.

"Katie! Where's Eric?"

"I sent him two e-mails about the practice situation. Do you know if he got them?"

"We're running on one car," Katie said. "He wants to be here."

The surprise and confusion on their faces struck her, confirmed that it was surprising, and confusing. Eric never missed anything.

"He's going to try to make it," Katie said, all eyes still on her. "You know Eric."

There was nodding, and Jim returned to the smeary chicken leg on his plate.

"I'm going to pay my respects to Teddy," Katie said, turning. *The investigation.*

The front door swung open, the sunlight tearing their eyes.

"Have you seen Teddy's new deck?" Gwen said, sunglasses dangling from her hand. "I mean, have you seen it?"

Following the sound of Teddy's voice, Katie made her way to the back of the house.

That Foghorn Leghorn voice, lungs filling, each word a hard push from an organ bellows.

But whenever he yelled at the girls (*Stick it, lick it, no weak stuff!*), which was a lot, though never at Devon, not in years, you always felt it came from love. He reminded Katie of the uncle on that TV show her mother always adored, the bachelor saddled with three kids, always rubbing his face like a weary, loving giant.

She found him in the den, in front of the gold-veined mirror tiles flanking the fireplace, his shoulders sunk, face wrung like a graying dish towel behind the perennial tan.

He was looking out the picture window, talking into his phone, his jaw clenched.

"Well, you upset her...I'm telling you, we'll get her there. But we've just had the goddamned funeral."

Discreetly, she moved away, nearly stumbling over Tina Belfour, paper towels in hand, scooping Jell-O salad off the lemon-colored rug.

"I'm sorry, Mama T.," heron-necked gymnast Shailee Robins said, shaking her head. "Everything's terrible now, forever."

"Hey," Eric said, his voice tinny on her phone, "should I still try to come?"

"No." Sliding open the glass door, Katie stepped onto the old back porch, empty and forlorn now. "I don't want to wait. I knew you wouldn't come."

"What? Katie, I promise I didn't know it would take so long."

"Forget it. It's just...sad here. And strange," she said. "I'm leaving soon. The Hargroves are driving Devon from practice. I'll see you at home."

After she hung up, she stood for a moment, the babble and hum of the reception muffled behind the patio doors, looking out onto the swimming pool, its magnificent opal surface. No one knew how Teddy could afford such an opulent addition to his already opulent home. It was probably a tax write-off for BelStars. He'd always understood the importance of show. *Smile, smile, smile at those judges. Devon, you do know how to smile, don't you?*

Besides, the pool was how Hailey had met Ryan. He'd been working for Deep End Pool Service, the prelude to digging the BelStars pit and, finally, the job with Gwen.

Diving to the bottom, he'd rescued Hailey's infinity-knot necklace from the drain.

Thinking of the gesture reminded her again of that time Ryan reached up from the depths of the foam pit and handed Devon her lost retainer. How shy Devon had been, her legs shaking.

Just then, it began. Katie felt it under her feet first, the redwood planks of the porch.

The low rumble came from inside the house.

Turning, she caught a glare off the sliding glass door.

On the other side stood Hailey, her arms tugging at the handle, the door shaking.

Mouth open wide as a trumpet bell, lips moving, she seemed to be trying to get her attention, frantically.

Katie reached for the door handle, struggled to drag the door, stuck on its track, open.

"Mrs. Knox," Hailey said, voice smothered by the glass, both of them yanking now, on opposite sides, "I thought you were my friend. Are you my friend?"

At that moment, Teddy appeared behind Hailey.

"Mrs. Knox!" she was shouting, her arms bulging as she pulled on the door, her face gray behind the tinted glass. "Mrs. Knox, I know what's happening—"

"What?" Katie shouted, wrenching the handle.

Behind the glass, Teddy took Hailey by the shoulders, flipping her around the way he had dozens of crying gymnasts, their bodies wilting toward him, his thick, strong Coach T. arms.

Katie watched as he buried her against his chest, her face seeming almost to slip away into the dark of his blazer. Her arms pinned to her sides, her body started shaking wildly.

"Hailey," Katie said, the door finally popping open, a surge of warm, cloying air, "what is it?"

But Hailey didn't hear and Teddy didn't seem to see, instead spiriting his niece away as a squall of guests entered, the kitchen swelling with mourners ready for cake.

"She got hysterical when the detective called," Teddy explained, standing with Katie in the kitchen, his hand on his meaty brow. "She just lost it."

"Detective?" Katie asked. "Do they have some kind of lead?"

She couldn't guess why they kept needing to talk to Hailey.

"They just want to ask more questions. Routine, I guess. I don't know." He turned before she could meet his eyes.

Upstairs, they could hear Hailey, a sob throbbing through the floor for a few moments, then ceasing, replaced by Tina's calming voice.

"I should go up and see her," Katie said. "She wanted to talk to me."

"About what?" Teddy's tufted brows lifted.

"I don't know."

He paused for a second.

"She was just confused. Mama T.'ll calm her down before we head over to the station."

A flinty voice sounded out, "Maybe you should take Ron."

It was Gwen, standing in the kitchen doorway, her abalone earrings glinting under the incandescents.

"No, no," Teddy said, shaking his head. "That's not necessary."

"Lawyer Ron?" Katie asked. "To sue somebody?"

"Teddy," Gwen said, fiddling with her earring, rubbing the shell, "he's the gym's attorney and he's in the living room right now eating your chili, drinking your beer. Why not take him?"

Gwen insisted on attorneys for everything—booster tax issues, liability protection, contractor squabbles, labor disputes, for her attenuated divorce, five years of litigation and a million-dollar settlement.

Teddy kept shaking his head. "Hailey has enough to handle now. She doesn't need Ron Wrigley peering over her shoulder too."

"She may need someone to protect her."

There was a pause, Teddy staring down at the kitchen floor.

"Protect her from what?" Katie said. "That's ridiculous. Why—"

"Hailey has her family," Teddy interrupted, looking up at Gwen, her mouth just beginning to open. "She doesn't need any more protection than that."

Walking to her car, trying to unravel everything, Katie heard footsteps behind her, the *skim-skim* of espadrilles.

It was Tina Belfour, sailing toward her, serving apron still on, the bright white of her perennial crisp oxford shirt like a flag.

"Katie," she said, moving very close, in the way she liked to talk, a woman's woman, a Southern expat, crinkle-eyed, always a flicker of a smile no matter what words came from her mouth, "did Hailey say something to you?"

"She was trying to. She seemed very upset." Katie paused. "She seemed angry."

"Don't pay her any mind," Tina said, walking alongside Katie, even increasing their pace. "The doctor gave her some pills and she's not herself."

"I understand," Katie said as they arrived at her car. "Give her my love, okay?"

Tina smiled, those white teeth, perfect and even, like the former beauty queen she was.

"You got it, hon."

Driving home, radio loud, muffler scraping the pavement, Katie tried to shake it off, but there was no shaking it off. Everything had been so exaggerated, stretched like in a carnival mirror—that jagged mouth, those slit eyes, the heave of those swimmer's shoulders smeared against the smoked glass, Hailey's muscled arms jerking, head knocking back as she tried to pull the door.

It reminded Katie of the time her stepdad raged on the front lawn after her mother locked him out. Howling and shouting for hours, chucking pebbles and gravel at all their windows, snagging the screens. Running around looking for something—anything—larger to throw.

And there was something else she'd never seen on Hailey's face before.

A kind of intensity that reminded her, in some small way, of Devon.

"But Dad," Devon was saying, her voice high, "look at it."

Katie found them in the garage. Eric was standing outside his car, apparently back from the shop, leaning over Devon as she sat in the front seat, legs shaking.

"You picked her up from practice?" Katie said to Eric. "I told you she was getting a ride with the Hargrove girls."

They both turned and faced her in the same moment, their matching gray eyes.

"It's my hand again, Mom," Devon said, rising, holding her wrist. "That same spot."

"Okay," Katie said, head aching from garage smells—solvent, or aerosol, the epoxy they used on the floors. The musky shrimp smell from Drew's science project. "Let's go inside."

Under the harsh glare of the kitchen light, the wrist looked pink and puffy, a doll's.

"Can you feel that?" Katie rested her fingers gently on Devon's skin, hot to the touch.

"It's not broken," Devon said. "I know the difference."

"Did you have your Tiger Paws on?"

"I told you they make my wrists weaker."

"But for the vault—"

"Mom, no," she said, pulling her wrist away, holding it against her flat, hard chest. Looking at it made Katie feel extravagantly bosomy, fleshful. Obscene. "I just need to ice it."

"Dad thinks you've been overdoing it too," Katie said, in case that might matter more. "We both agreed."

"What kind of box did they put him in?" Drew asked. "Ryan."

"A nice one," Katie said, taking a breath. "Help me set the table."

Drew was the only one who'd asked about the funeral, wanting to know how deep they had to dig. And if it would be quiet down there, and if Ryan would like it, even though he was dead.

"He likes it, sweetie. I'm sure of it."

She grabbed the forks, pricking the heel of her hand. She was still wearing her black dress. It felt wet inside.

"Like how beetles are," Drew decided. "They make a hole in the wood and stay there."

From upstairs, she could hear Eric moving. From the basement, Devon.

"Sometimes it's for years. All by themselves," Drew said. "Do you think they get lonely?"

Katie looked at him, half hidden behind the stack of dinner plates he carried.

A rush of heat pushed under her eyes.

The thing you try never to think about when you go to a funeral is the thing that's really happening. The body in the box going into the ground.

But now, with Drew there, his chin resting on the plates, looking at her gravely, talking more about beetles, all she could think of was Ryan Beck, in a box in the ground, all alone.

Everyone picked at the defrosted ziti except Devon, who held her wrist and sipped a green smoothie through a straw. Practice had been confused and unproductive again, she said. Everyone kept wondering about the funeral, talking about the mug shot of Ryan on the news.

"And saying things about Hailey. All kinds of things."

"What things?" Katie asked. "Was it about the police?"

"The police?" Eric asked. "What did you hear?"

Devon shrugged. "I tried not to listen."

"You shouldn't listen," Eric said, leaning back. "Those girls, they can't help it, but they'll also distract you if they can."

"The flexion, I could feel it," Devon said, staring at her wrist. "There's no time to rest it before qualifiers."

"I like Hailey," Drew said. "I feel bad for her."

"We all do," Katie said, rubbing his hand. But all she could think about was Hailey's face behind the glass, Ryan's body in that box. Her head ached.

"I wonder when it'll get back to normal," Devon said, chin resting on the rim of the glass.

"Soon," Eric said. "Try to put it all out of your head."

"It's only been four days," Katie said, looking at Eric. "The Belfours are in mourning."

But they were talking over her, talking about Devon's heel drive and the new vaulting table. It all seemed impossible, the way they were just charging forward.

"The vault's pitched too low," Eric said. "I saw it right when I walked in. I'll talk to Bobby."

"No, it was my fault," Devon said. "There was just so much noise in the gym. Everyone talking, no one working. Dad, I can't get that double twist back on my Yurchenko."

Eric nodded, a stitch of worry over his brow. "Slow and low, I know."

"The funeral was just today," Katie tried again, louder.

But only Drew seemed to be listening to her.

"Mom," he said, staring at her between the tines of his fork, "how come they didn't burn him? Ryan, I mean. Like when Mrs. Wheeler from school died."

Something in Katie's chest contracted painfully, her fork dropping from her hand and clattering onto the table.

"Hey, everybody!" Katie said. "The funeral was very sad for everyone. For Ryan's mother, for Hailey. It was all very sad. That boy died just four days ago."

They all turned and looked at her, and at her fork in the center of the table.

Drew reached over and retrieved her fork, handed it to her.

"Katie," Eric said, but before he could say more, Devon stood up, fingers ringed around her swollen wrist.

The wrist looked bigger than ever; it looked alive, the pulsing throb of a fat heart.

"It *is* really sad, Mom," Devon said, backing away. Her face pale and strained. "No one ever said it wasn't really sad."

"I'll talk to her," Eric said, crawling beside Katie in bed. "Practice is how she works through feelings."

"And how do you work through feelings?" Katie asked, pulling their bedspread back with a snap.

He looked at her. "I'm sorry I wasn't there today." Then adding, "And I'm sorry it was hard for you."

"For me?" she said. "Funerals are pretty hard for everyone. And, you know, people were surprised you weren't there."

He reached for her arm. "I should have been there."

And there was a pause, and she was so tired.

"Okay," she replied, because in the end it was so easy to just surrender to it. To his handsomeness, his dedicated dad–ness, the depth of his feelings, which he seemed to wear all over that car-tanned face, in all the smile lines around his eyes.

"Oh," she added, her own voice sounding so small, girl-like. "Except Hailey. I need to tell you about Hailey."

"What about her?" His fingers drifting down her sternum, his other hand on her hip.

"She was upset. Very upset."

"Of course she was. God."

"But...no, I mean, she...she was angry. And she really, really wanted to talk to me."

"Why would she want to talk to you?" he said, his fingers pressing on her pelvis.

"I never found out," she said, looking down at his hand.

The weight of the day began sinking into her. Sinking her. She wanted to hold on, to talk about it, but it seemed too involved, too heavy and strange.

"It's a hard time for everybody," he said, and he seemed suddenly so far away on the bed, the warmth of his body gone, his voice so distant she could barely hear him.

Sometime in the night, she opened her eyes.

It was Drew standing in the doorway in his shark pj's, the teeth that glowed.

"Mom, Devon won't stop yelling."

"What?" she asked, pulling the bedspread up over her bare legs, Eric deep in post-beer stupor. "You're dreaming."

All Drew's dreams of Devon, Devon flying, jumping off the roof, riding his bike, sneaking into the garage and driving away in their cars like Batman. She'd meant to ask the doctor, or someone, about them. But then, drifting down the hallway, Drew leading the way, she heard it too.

From the closed door, Devon's voice, a snarl of sounds, stutters, rasps.

"She's just talking in her sleep," Katie whispered. "Go back to bed."

Tapping lightly on Devon's door, she watched Drew slip back into his room, eyes still on her.

There was no answer, so she opened the door.

There was Devon, her comforter kicked off the bed, standing

in the middle of the room, her head in her hands, red wrist blazing.

"Devon." Katie rushed toward her. "Devon, wake up!"

Pulling her hands from her face, she stared at Katie, eyes burning.

"He was standing there," she said, pointing to where Katie stood. "Mom, it was Ryan."

"No," Katie said, touching her arms, trying to soothe her. "You were dreaming."

"He was right there, where you are," she said, a soft moan. "He looked so sad, Mom."

The skin on Katie's shoulders quilled.

"You were having a dream," she said, trying to hug her, but Devon's elbows kept jabbing, her body twisting. "Usually it's your brother with the crazy dreams."

It took several minutes for Katie to calm her, to guide her back to the bed.

"Are you sure he wasn't here?" Devon asked finally, voice softening, head sinking back into the center of her pillow.

"I'm sure, honey. Ryan's gone. He's not coming back."

"I know. Is Dad sleeping?" she said, her hair tangled over her face, hiding her.

"What? Yes," Katie said.

"Remember that song?"

"What?"

"At the tiki party last winter. The one you danced to."

"I danced to it?"

She sang in a soft, lisping purl, like when she was very small – a line about a blister in the palm of a hand.

But no, Katie couldn't remember it.

Still, she brushed her hand through Devon's hair and Devon let out the smallest sigh, like an *aah* after seeing things had turned out okay after all.

"Mom," she said dreamily. "Don't be mad at Dad. I think he's sad."

"What?" Katie said.

"We're all sad," Devon said. "Aren't we?"

Her hand pressed on Eric's back, she tried to settle herself. He'd never woken up, and the only sound now was his breathing, hoarse and ragged. For a second she thought she saw his lashes lift, the white of one eye looking at her, but she was wrong.

Chapter Eight

"Mrs. Knox, it's Nurse Patty."

"Who?"

"Nurse Patty. From Carver Elementary."

"What?"

Everything was moving slowly in her head, a night of bad dreams, of beetles boring through smoked glass, of swimming pools coated with beetle shells.

Devon, that nightmare. The way she was standing in the middle of her room, seeing ghosts.

Then the day had hurdled past. Eric had gone to work before dawn, leaving Katie with the school drop-off, a conference call with the printer, a design deadline at noon, four parents trying to reach Eric. Then, just before two o'clock, came the call from Nurse Patty saying Drew had a sore throat and needed to be picked up immediately.

Looking at him now in the rearview mirror, his lips waxy and head lolling, Katie decided to drive straight to Dr. Kemper, who jabbed a swab down there and confirmed what she already knew: strep.

"Mom," Drew said in the car after, "I think Devon made me sick. I dreamed she put rocks in my mouth."

The line at the pharmacy was long, a shouting man with a fistful of prescription bottles at the front and behind him a woman scrambling on the floor to recover her phone's battery cover.

A jumble of feet, a woolly roll of dust floating from under a towering vitamin display, the woman dropped to her hands and knees as the cover spun away. Finally, she collapsed in cross-legged defeat on the floor.

That was when Katie noticed the gentle tilt of her jaw, the sleepy eyes, just like her son's.

"Mrs. Beck—Helen," Katie said, "are you okay?"

She looked up at Katie, nodded.

Katie helped her to her feet.

"Thank you," she said, crinkling her prescription bag between nervous fingers. "I'm having a bad day."

"Here," Drew said, stepping forward, her sooty battery cover in his infected hands.

"Thank you, honey." She smiled, her eyes filling. "A little gent."

First, Helen couldn't find her rental car, then she wasn't sure which way her hotel was.

"I thought you were staying with the Belfours."

"I'm at the Days Inn now. I needed to get out of that house. It felt bad. All these whispered conversations. The police calling all the time."

"The police?"

"And I haven't been sleeping," Helen said, shaking her head. "I came to pick up my meds before I head over to the station again. Your daughter's Debbie, right?"

"Devon," Katie said, looking toward the car, Drew now belted into the backseat, his face chalk white. She was eager to get him home, but Helen hooked her hand around Katie's wrist. "The police station?"

"Yeah. You know, things finally seemed to be coming up roses for him," she said, her face crumpling slightly in a way that made Katie ache. "Well, carnations at least."

"I'm so sorry, Helen. I guess I already said that."

"He would always find the lonely person in every room and go talk to them. Make them feel special." She looked at Katie, smiling faintly. "I'm sure he did that for you."

"Everybody liked Ryan," Katie said.

Finally, Helen found her car but not her keys, so Katie offered to drive her to the station a few blocks away.

As Drew waited in the car, Katie walked Helen to the entrance, the precinct building so old that green-tinted lanterns still stood sentinel on either side.

For a second, Helen just stood at the door. Then she took a deep breath.

"Thank you again, Katie." Waving her phone, she added, "And thank your sweet boy for me."

Behind her, a whey-faced man nearly stumbled to hold the door open for Helen.

"Ma'am," he said, tipping his baseball cap as she walked past him. "At your service."

"Did you see his hat?" Drew asked squeakily when she returned to the car.

He was watching the man stroll across the lot.

"No," Katie said, taking a breath and then turning the ignition. "Don't hurt your throat."

"The orange cap he was wearing. It had two eyes on it. And one was droopy. It made his face look droopy."

"That's not very nice," Katie said.

"Sorry, Mom."

But she looked in the rearview mirror, watched the man amble toward a panel van. Something in the way he'd stood there holding the door—the way he'd rocked from foot to foot as Helen passed through—felt familiar. Like her uncle Don, who also rocked like that, back ruined by years of lifting drywall. He used to carry around sandwich bags filled with blue pills. One day he came to the house streaked with gray sweat and tore the TV out of the wall and stole the new rims off her mom's car.

That was all a long time ago. Sometimes it was like none of it ever happened.

"I'm sorry he's sick," Devon said, dragging the spare air mattress into the basement. "But I can't be around it, Mom. You know I can't. Qualifiers are thirty-six days away."

"He's on antibiotics," Katie assured her. "By tomorrow he won't be contagious."

But Devon refused to share a bathroom or even a hallway with her brother (*Sometimes he licks his hands when he's nervous, Mom*).

Instead, she disappeared into the basement, the treadmill vibrating through the ceiling, and no one seemed interested in dinner, Eric on the phone with booster after booster, Drew tunneling into a narcotized sleep, his mouth open, his comforter and pillows massed on top of him in that cavelike way he liked, the humidifier purring beside him.

"Mom," he said as he drifted off, "the shrimp are dying. Or they're dead already. The science fair..."

"That's days away, honey."

*   *   *

Spray bottle in hand, Katie started by wiping down all the chair rails, the doorknobs and jambs. Her head humming with thoughts, so many none could take shape.

At Devon's empty bedroom, she stood in the doorway, bleach stinging her fingers.

It was always so quiet, so clean and pin-neat, so contained.

Occasionally, Katie would see the bedrooms of the other girls. Pink-zebra-striped, sparkly G-Y-M-N-A-S-T-I-C-S! lettering across purple padded memo boards, mounds of leotards swirled onto mamasan chairs.

But Devon was different, once again.

It isn't how I pictured it, Kirsten Siefert said once when Katie found her sneaking a peek during a booster meeting downstairs. *I thought you must've covered the walls with gymnastics posters, inspirational quotes, seven-point creeds.* She looked at Katie. *I don't know what I thought.*

Parents always wanted to know what they'd fed Devon as a child, if they'd ever tried homeschooling, if she'd ever been given hormones and was she vaccinated. They always thought there was a code they could crack.

They never understood that it was all Devon, just like the room. Spare, almost puritanical.

All her awards were in the family room, the special shelf Eric built for all the trophies, wooden dowel pegs beneath to hang all the medals and ribbons. In here, everything was simple.

A small corkboard with a meticulously pinned printout, ELITE COMPULSORY PROGRAM RULES, REV. A desk wiped clean with a feather duster every night. File boxes with labels. Everything labeled: ALGEBRA. HISTORY I. ROUTINE MUSIC. FAMILY PHOTOS.

The quote taped to the side of her computer monitor: *The only way to escape fear is to trample it beneath your feet.*

Her first grips looped in a ribbon and hanging on the wall.

The only odd piece: that gaudy LeRoy Neiman tiger poster from their old gym. The day they left Tumbleangels for BelStars, Eric had torn it from the wall and given it to her. Devon had always loved it, its million colors teeming and frothing from its whiskers, shooting from its slanted eyes.

Spraying from door frame to baseboard, the air in the room misted with bleach, Katie heard a chirp.

There, on the floor, was Devon's phone in its tidy plaid case.

Leaning down, she picked it up.

She didn't mean to look, precisely. But she didn't see any reason why she shouldn't.

Swiping her thumb across the screen, she saw the flare of the Missed Calls icon, the harsh red arrows.

And then the same number, over and over again. Every ten or fifteen minutes for hours.

Hailey Belfour.

Hailey Belfour, Hailey Belfour, Hailey Belfour.

She found Eric in the kitchen, halfway through the screen door to the backyard, deep in a phone conversation.

She could tell from the way he spoke—earnest, enunciating, patient—that Gwen was on the other end.

"First, competition fees. That's eighty dollars per gymnast and forty dollars per level, per team. Then coaching fees at one hundred dollars per session, sixty-four cents per mile for travel times four coaches, plus thirty dollars for coach meals times four coaches—no, the bylaws require us to pay for meals, even for the skill coaches...Well, that's what we voted on."

She waited a minute, Devon's phone like a hot iron in her hand, but it was taking too long.

Hurrying down the nubby carpeted steps into the basement— the chalky smell of the mats, the gust from the laundry room, the churn of the treadmill—she could feel Devon even before she saw her. The energy she held so tightly until she let it thunder forth: a soaring vault, an epic tumbling pass, a delirious aerial on the beam.

At the foot of the stairs, Katie stopped, watching her daughter run, her face bone-white under the gooseneck light looped around one of the posts.

"Mom." She looked up, surprised, hands reaching for her headphones. "What is it? Did something happen?"

"Has Hailey been trying to call you?"

"Hailey?" she said, eyes scanning the room quickly, the floor beneath her, her book bag.

Looking for her phone, of course. A classic teenager move, but not one Katie was used to from Devon, who barely seemed to notice her phone other than to look at TumbleTally after meets. Who'd never been like the other girls Katie saw at Devon's school, with their glittered fingernails clawed over their phones, trapped in a constant storm of entanglements and betrayals.

"Yes, Hailey," she said, waving Devon's phone. "Several times."

"What? No." Slowly, Devon untangled her headphones from her ears, the cords caught, her fingers gently pulling them apart. "You have my phone?"

"It was on your bed, flashing." The lie came easily.

"Oh. And you started looking through it?"

"No," Katie said, noticing something in Devon's expression, a sense of the breach. It was unfair, to feel like an invader. She, who sewed cotton gussets into the crotch of Devon's competition leotards if they were cut too high for underwear. She, who, like every gymnast mom, was so acutely attuned to her daughter's body, hands on her thighs, massaging a groin pull, that sometimes she felt it was her own.

"I just saw the missed calls. That's not the point, Devon. Why is she calling you?"

"I don't know. I didn't answer."

"You have no idea?" Katie wasn't sure why, but she didn't believe her.

"I guess she's sad and calling a bunch of people. Everyone said she was acting funny at the funeral. I didn't answer. I don't want to say the wrong thing."

"I'm sure she'd appreciate whatever you had to say," Katie said. It made sense, her daughter's life so blessedly untouched by the loss of a grandparent, or even a pet. By the time Katie was Devon's age, her uncle had died in a fall, her mom had burned through two marriages, she'd moved six times. "But you and she—you aren't close. Why you?"

"I don't know. She probably won't call again. There's lots of people who know her better than me. Like you."

"What? I'm not close—Devon, if she calls again, you tell me," Katie said, but Devon had already slid her headphones back on and started running again.

Katie sat at the kitchen table, waiting for that morning's tarry coffee to heat. Gwen had finally released Eric, but now he was upstairs checking on Drew.

The vinyl place mat bore the imprint of Eric's jottings, the ballpoint pressed so hard. Rows and rows of numbers, mysterious hieroglyphics (Eric's perpetual vault-table doodle), and something that had been crossed out vigorously, over and over again.

She held it up to the light without knowing why. All she could see was a doodle, a pair of slanty eyes, a *V* between them, like a cartoon owl.

"Poor kid, his throat looked like a slab of raw beef." Eric's voice startled her, her hand dropping the place mat quickly, face flushing. "What're you doing?"

What had she been doing?

Before she could answer, Eric's phone lit up once more.

They both looked down and saw the name: Gwen.

Exchanged looks.

"Not a chance," Eric said, hands in the air.

The phone stopped, but seconds later, Katie's leaped to life. Gwen.

"It might be important," Eric said gently.

"Things are happening here. Did you know Hailey's been calling our daughter over and over?"

"What?" he said, his face very still.

They both watched as the phone finally stopped.

Then the text message came:

There's a witness.

"Gwen, it's really late," Eric said into the phone.

"Put her on speaker," Katie whispered.

He set the phone down, and Gwen's voice filled the kitchen.

"Somebody saw the car. A trucker. Apparently he called the day after the accident, but he'd been on the road. He finally showed up at the station yesterday to make a statement. He didn't see it happen, but he saw a car speeding past. Up by the highway, just before the turnoff to Ash Road."

"So have they found the driver?" Eric asked, standing up and walking to the sink.

"No. But the guy said it was a woman. He didn't get a good look at her, but she was driving very fast. Like she had someplace she needed to be."

"Gwen, how do you know all this?" Katie asked.

"You don't own six restaurants and ten parking lots in a town as small as this without having friends at the district attorney's office."

"Well," Katie said, "for the Belfours' sake, I hope this leads to something."

"But here's the kicker," Gwen said, the speaker crackling as her voice rose. "He said the car was purple."

Katie looked at Eric, who turned around slowly, eyes on the phone.

Hailey? he mouthed.

"No way," Katie said, looking at him and then looking at the phone. "No, Gwen."

"I'm sure there's other purple cars," Gwen said, her voice breathier now, like she was right there in the room with them. Her excitement palpable. "We shouldn't jump to any conclusions."

They couldn't find anything on the Internet except the news article from the day before.

"It doesn't make any sense," Katie said. "Five days later he suddenly remembers this?"

"Gwen said he called the next day," Eric reminded her. His eyes were on the screen, the photo of a spotlit Ash Road, the crimped guardrail, the dark earth massy below.

"The police called Hailey in for more questions," Katie said. "And Helen. I dropped her off at the police station. She's not staying with the Belfours anymore."

"Well," he said, "I guess we know why."

"You don't believe this, do you?" Katie said. "Because some guy says he saw a purple car near Ash Road that night, it has to be Hailey? And so she must have run over her own boyfriend?"

The words themselves seemed to startle them both.

He looked at her. "No," he said softly. "I don't believe it."

She told him about the missed calls on Devon's phone and tried again to explain about Hailey after the funeral. Hailey through the sliding glass door.

She tried to tell him, but it all felt cryptic, the whisper of a story rather than a story.

"She kept pounding on the door," Katie said. "She told me she knew what was happening."

"Knew *what* was happening?" Eric asked, leaning forward.

"I don't know."

"Katie, I think we need to keep out of all this," Eric said. "This is something Teddy has to deal with. It's not our business. Our business is Devon."

Our business is Devon. She knew what he meant, but it reminded her of something one of Devon's teachers once said to her: *You may be in the Devon Knox business, but I'm in the education business.*

"She's under so much pressure right now," he said, his face strained and weary.

She thought, as she had many times, of how it must feel for Devon, everyone's hopes pinned to her, the gym's reputation waiting for her burnishing. The *Gazette* calling her the town's "brightest star." How heavy it must feel, all the time.

But there was something in Eric's eyes, a jittery urgency. "Molly told me she was struggling with her Yurchenko again. A few months ago, she was nearing the Amânar, now she can't even get her second twist. Amelise said she looked disoriented in the air. Devon told her she just got lost up there."

The words scissored through her. *That's how necks get broken,* Teddy always said. She couldn't help but think of Devon's first accident, the thump of the mower.

"Maybe she shouldn't be practicing at all," Katie said. "Not until things settle down."

"She needs practice. It's what grounds her," he said. "It's just that gym. Right now, it's not the safe place it used to be."

"Okay, but if the gym isn't a good place, maybe we should just—"

"We need to keep her out of all this," Eric interrupted, so loud Katie flinched.

"Yes," she said, tightly. "That's what I'm trying to do."

He looked at her. "I know you are."

Arm darting, he reached for her hand, but she pulled it back without knowing why.

"I'm sorry," she said, returning her hand to his. "You surprised me."

Chapter Nine

"Mom."

The nicotine-graded voice of a fifty-year-old, pack-a-day woman.

"Mom. Mom!"

Two forty-five, the clock read.

Stumbling down the hall, her feet catching on a humidifier cord, a stray tennis shoe.

Drew's room was unbearably hot, his glass of water untouched, film around its rim.

"Honey," she said, "what is it? What do you need?"

"Devon jumped off the roof."

"What? What?"

Sitting straight up in bed, he looked at her, face red as a candy fireball.

"She had wings. White wings, like a gypsy moth."

"Oh, honey, you're dreaming again."

She looked inside his throat, scarlet and pulsing, webbed white. It did look like beef, she thought, with thick striations.

"She jumped off the roof and into the car. Then she drove away."

"Oh, honey."

"And you," he said, pupils widening, boring right through her. "You had scales over your eyes, like a snake."

"Lie back down," she said, "try to rest. You and Devon, your crazy dreams."

His hands on hers, sticky and hot.

"Mom," he said, "you can't go anywhere."

"I'm not going anywhere," she said, hand to his face.

"You'll miss everything," he said. "Mom, you'll miss what's happening."

Just after five, she felt Eric's body lift from the mattress. For a second, she forgot about everything that had happened in recent days and just watched him in the blue morning light.

Watched that familiar span of shoulders, the way his hair curled up his neck, his hand there, that early-morning piano-key dance he did with his fingers, prodding at kinks from days spent leaning over the soundboard or toward the glaring computer screens.

Watched him walk across the room, rolling his shoulders, yawning.

Watched him emerge from the bathroom, the shower's fog, the smell of soap and shaving cream shuddering from him as he moved.

Watched as he took his phone from the dresser. The steady thrum of texts, e-mails rippling from it, his head curled down, reading them, all of them under his fingertips.

There were furtive thoughts she tried never to linger over. Like maybe Eric never would have married her if she hadn't gotten pregnant (the night it happened, drunk on a softball victory, the company team, and three jubilant hours at Rizzo's Tavern with everyone toasting his grand slam, Eric had been the one sweet-talking her into the back of the SoundMasters van. The one who promised her it would be okay, promised her everything). Or the other thought: that he never would have stayed married to her if it weren't for Devon.

It's just, he'd said once, that shaky first year, Devon swaddled to Katie's chest, *I don't need you the same way.*

But, thank God, everything was different later, and had been ever since.

Before he left, that kiss on her cheek, his breath tanged with mouthwash—she loved him so much.

Then the last week sharp-kneed its way back into her brain.

The shower still warm, she stood under the water a long time.

Everything was beautiful and nothing hurt.

The sentence came to her, dizzy from the steam. What was that thing Teddy always said during practice? *Don't let me see it hurt. Everything's beautiful, nothing hurts.*

Dreams and waking mingling all night, purple cars and whey-faced strangers, and poor Ryan slipping into her half-conscious state, she felt like she hadn't slept at all.

He would always find the lonely person in every room . . .

That's when the memory came. A few months ago, Ryan in the gym's lobby—he'd caught her as she tried to change the bottle in the watercooler, the cold, wet thing slipping perilously from her arms, like a wriggling child.

That's bigger than you are, Ryan had said, reaching out for her, saving her.

Rubbing her wrists, she watched him, forearms clamping the bottle, the cuts, scars, and puckered burns of a line cook.

As he leaned over, turning the water bottle, she spotted a worn paperback gaping from his back pocket.

It tumbled to the floor, resting on Katie's shoe.

Picking it up, she touched the book's fading red cover, soft as felt.

I missed a lot in high school, he said, screwing the glistening bottle into the stand. *I'm taking classes at JCC. Making up for lost time.*

She didn't know the book.

You shouldn't be lifting things like that, he said, shaking his head. The bottle left his shirtfront damp.

Maybe not, she said, her face warm and her hands still slippery.

Now, your daughter's another story, Ryan said. *Small as a peanut, strong as a tiger.*

Oh, Katie said. Her shoulders slumped a little. *Yes. Yes, she is.*

He smiled, filling a cup of water for her, and it felt—

Of all the moms, he said, winking, *you're the nicest.*

Stepping from the shower, she heard the trill of her ringtone.

The opening thumps of "Assassin's Tango."

A number she didn't know.

"Hello?"

"Mrs. Knox." The voice was brittle and low and she didn't recognize it. She wasn't even sure if it was male or female. "Why won't your daughter talk to me?"

"Who is this?"

"You can tell her for me that I know everything."

"Hailey," Katie said, just realizing it. "Hailey, what are you—"

"You can tell her I'm watching her. I know all about her. She can't hide from me."

"Hey, calm down," Katie said, trying to keep in mind what Tina had said about her niece, all the medication.

"I won't calm down," she said, that surly tone, clenched jaw. "People have been telling me my whole life to calm down."

"Hailey, you're going through a lot right now."

"I am, Mrs. Knox. I'm going through *a lot*, and thanks to that stunted freak daughter of yours, that little monkey—"

A lurch in her chest, her voice rising. "Don't you dare talk about—"

"I thought you were my friend." Her voice hard, hammering. "I thought you were a decent person. Maybe you are. But I'm telling you this: you have no clue about that thing under your roof."

"Jesus, Hailey, what do you—"

"Your daughter's a fucking animal."

There was a click, and silence.

Seated on the edge of the bed, Katie stared at her feet on the bedroom carpet, trying to catch her breath, trying to control herself, fists clenched.

There were all kinds of troubling ways grief could work on people. Probing with hard fingers, scraping underneath old scars. Maybe Hailey needed a focus, she told herself. A gathering point. Though why she had landed on Devon, Katie couldn't guess.

Except she could. There were many things she'd had to get used to as Devon's mother, a competing gymnast calling her daughter Boulder Shoulders, Bitchface, Ice Dyke, or when that science teacher accused her of cheating: "No one who misses that much school could score this high on a test."

But those remarks were easy to dismiss, the anger fleeting, a hot wave that came over her and settled, Eric calming her, reminding her that some people would always be jealous of Devon, the way they were jealous of all beautiful and brilliant things.

From Hailey, though, it was different. Those words, the sharp thwack of them—they were words she'd never heard Hailey use. It was like a Disney princess hurling foul epithets, oozing dirty talk. And the words made no sense. They seemed to spin from some far-off place and now latched hard in the center of her.

"Mom?"

Jolted, Katie looked up to see Devon in the doorway, showered, ponytail wet and sleek.

"Why were you yelling?"

"Was I?" she said.

"Who was that on the phone? I thought I heard you say 'Hailey.'"

"No. Yes."

"Why were you yelling at her?" Devon asked, her fingers running slow down her ponytail and landing at the bottom. "What did she want?"

"I don't know," Katie said. "She wasn't making any sense."

Everything felt backward. Katie was seated, still in her bathrobe, dripping all over the bedspread, as Devon loomed in the doorway, T-shirt straining over her muscled arms. Questioning her. And Katie was lying.

"Mom," Devon said, eyes downcast, "what about the purple car that guy saw?"

Katie looked at her, not sure what to say. "Who told you about the car?"

Devon didn't say anything.

"Did your dad tell you?"

Devon paused, then shook her head. "Everyone knows. Everyone's texting about it."

"Honey," she said, "all we know for sure is that Hailey's not herself right now."

"Kind of like Grandma?" The last few visits with Katie's

mom had spooked Devon. Once, she forgot Devon's name and called her Marie, and then another time, which alarmed them all, she thought a leaf on the sidewalk was shrieking at her. Accusing her of things. *It says I steal!*

"If she calls you again," Katie said, "tell me right away."

"She can't," Devon said. "I blocked her."

"Good, Devon."

"Dad told me to."

This sensible, sensible girl. A girl who knew how to protect herself. Never a daredevil, never stunting without a safety mat, without spotters. A girl for whom instability was the ultimate enemy. Who'd never known divorce or slamming doors or slamming fists. A girl whose home was a peaceful sanctum, even the basement padded. A life that had to be made safe because of the risks she put her body through. She was the most dangerous thing in her own life. Her body, the only dangerous thing.

Katie looked at her. *Of course he did.* "When?"

"This morning, before he left. He said to block her."

"Teddy, I'm calling about Hailey." She didn't even know what she was going to say, but she couldn't stop herself. The minute she dropped Devon off at school, she pressed the number.

"Katie, dear," answered Teddy, his voice gruff and creaky, wind whining in the background. "Don't listen to what you might hear, okay? Or read."

"Teddy, this isn't about that eyewitness. It's Hailey."

"I can't talk now," he said. "I'm waiting for Ron."

"Ron Wrigley? The gym attorney?"

"I think that's him pulling up now."

There was a rustle and then he hung up.

*   *   *

All day the picture kept returning, the picture of Hailey as Katie had always known her. That thick mane of yellow hair pushed back as she grasped those tumbling seven-year-olds by the waist, guiding all their landings. That sunny, capable smile of hers.

Each time the picture returned it became stranger.

To imagine a darkness at the center of that bright-lit, summer-skinned, effortless girl was very hard. But she'd seen it, the contorted face on the other side of the patio door. And now she'd heard it too.

Of all the girls she'd guess to have a secret self inside, Hailey would have been the last, or close.

"That's what you get for owning a purple car," Gwen said when she called Katie, just before noon. Katie could almost hear the tapping of her nails through the phone.

Not even Gwen seemed to know much. She knew Teddy had retained Ron Wrigley, that Hailey was still cooperating with police, and that no other eyewitnesses had come forward.

There was an article in the *Gazette* about dozens of reports of damaged purple cars and suspicious paint and repair jobs coming in from across the county. An unidentified man with a plum Toyota had been questioned but released after it was determined that his torn bumper came from running over a dog. Another man claimed the new paint job on his magenta Sentra was due to a rancid egging by a deranged ex. "She called in the tip," he told the *Gazette*. "She thinks I stole her stereo and poisoned her cat. She wants to destroy me."

It was upsetting, like the seam of something had been torn, ever so slightly.

But the boosters were all focused on Hailey.

"The more you think about it, the weirder Hailey's story is." Calling during her lunch hour, Molly spoke breathily between what sounded like long tugs on a straw. "Ryan drives her home and leaves her car there? Why not drive himself home? And let me ask you this: Who walks two miles at eleven o'clock at night? On that road? I hope they're testing for drugs."

"Maybe Ryan had dealings that came back to haunt him," Kirsten Siefert whispered, calling Katie from the ladies' room at BelStars, her voice echoing high. "You saw that mug shot. Who knows what kind of life he led?"

And there were questions no one could get the answer to: What really happened between Hailey and Ryan at that dinner? Were they engaged? (No ring had been spotted on Hailey's hand at the funeral.)

They were questions you couldn't ask anyone but Hailey, and now, with Ron Wrigley on retainer, word was she wasn't talking to anyone.

Except Katie didn't really believe she would stay silent. The girl she'd heard on the phone that morning seemed unready for muzzling. She seemed to have so much to tell that her throat might burst.

In the laundry room, the dryer knocking sneakers violently beside her, Katie loaded the washer with everything Drew had touched in the past three days. She almost didn't hear the phone.

It was Eric, saying something had come up, he wouldn't be home for dinner, he'd explain later. And Devon was getting a ride home with the Chus, and he'd explain about that later too.

"Eric, I've been trying to call you all day. Hailey called me."

"What?"

She told him about Hailey's call, a version of it. She couldn't quite bring herself to use Hailey's exact words. They were a blur anyway.

"God," Eric said, after a pause, "she sounds completely unstable."

"She wasn't herself. She was so...angry. The things she called Devon..." As she spoke, a thought fluttered in the back of her brain, something Hailey said: *You can tell her for me that I know everything.*

"Well, look at her history," Eric said, impatience edging into his voice. "Her own mother couldn't handle her."

"That was ten years ago," Katie said. "She was a teenager. Didn't you do things when you were young that seem impossible now?"

"Maybe it's still in her," he said, not answering her question. "Maybe that's why she was dating someone with a rap sheet."

"Eric," she said, surprised. "You know Ryan was a good kid. He was—"

"You're just like him."

That's what she thought she heard him say, the line crackling. "What? What did you say?"

"You just liked him," he said. Which was not the same, even remotely. "We all did. We all liked both of them. But we don't know what this is, do we? All we know is we don't want her bothering Devon again."

Katie didn't say anything for a moment.

And she couldn't account for how upset she felt, her face hotly throbbing with it.

"I tried to talk to Teddy."

"Don't talk to Teddy," he said. "I'm going to talk to him. I don't want her calling us again."

"Okay," Katie said.

"And Katie, whatever you do," he said, "don't tell Devon that Hailey called."

"Why not?"

"She has enough pressure. She doesn't need to know this."

The pause that followed felt very important. It was one of those moments in a marriage when you have to make a critical decision with alarming speed and the consequences could last a long time, even forever.

The words almost came out: *I already told her.*

But they didn't.

"Right," she said. "Whatever you say."

The house felt small and sweaty and polluted.

Devon came home, rubbing her hands with antibacterial cleanser. Hovering at her brother's door, she looked at Drew, asleep again, only his shuttered eyes visible above the swoop of the comforter.

A cup of melting ice chips in her hand, Katie asked her how practice had gone.

"He's so red," she said. "Look at him."

He was, a little flame curling from beneath the covers.

"He's not contagious anymore."

And Devon, backing away, nearly covering her face with her hand, hiding it. "Everyone's counting on me."

Chapter Ten

Their tracksuits were shining in the night as they marched up the driveway.

"Didn't you tell them about the strep?" Katie asked, peeking through the curtain.

Eric nodded wearily. "They promised they wouldn't come inside."

It was after ten, and the boosters had arrived.

Maybe it was all those arched backs, those manicured nails gripping water bottles, their glossy manes, the high, whinnying sounds they made, their beady eyes. It reminded her of the hyenas in Drew's favorite animal book. *They have excellent nighttime vision and hearing.* True. *They have powerful jaws and sharp teeth that they use to break open bones so they can feed.* Also possibly true.

"It's time to take matters into our own hands," Gwen was saying. "Every day they don't practice, our girls descend into mediocrity. Our responsibility is to our kids and their performance at qualifiers. Not this tabloid drama."

Katie watched them from the upstairs window. Drew long

asleep, Devon was holed up in her bedroom, studying for an exam. Katie hoped she couldn't hear them.

They were all arrayed on the patio. Gwen, Kirsten, Molly, with husband, Jim, in tow, gnawing on an energy bar as if he were straight off a run. The former college track star. And in the center now, Eric. Always.

She'd never really gotten used to it. To sharing him with all those antic mothers, their clicking heels and clucking heads and private confidences about their own homemade sorrows: absent husband, nefarious sisters-in-law. Molly's breathless hugs, breasts seeming to draw circles on Eric's chest. Kirsten's late-night calls whenever she opened the Drambuie in the minibar on one of her business trips and wanted to settle in for a "chat about the gym's future and Jordan's place in it." Becca Plonski's birthday gifts, which last year included a pair of boxer shorts that read *Boost This!* And Gwen, always Gwen, who sometimes unclamped her talons at the booster parties, donning her skyscraping snakeskin heels and singing "Delta Dawn" on karaoke after tequila shooters with Eric and Jim Chu. (What Katie remembered: how she said, that night, pounding on a tabletop, *Mark my goddamn words, Eric Knox, we will ride your daughter all the way to Olympic bronze, silver, and gold!*)

"Can I get anyone anything?" Katie asked, finally stepping outside. "Coffee? Vitamin C?"

All their heads lifted, their bodies straining from their perches on the rusty lawn chairs, the same squeaky ones she'd meant to replace last summer. Gwen's had a center of fraying slats, tendrils ready to snap. Behind her sat her daughter, Lacey, hoodie-hunched in a ball, her short, sinewy legs thick as banister knobs, and that face. The face of a cartoon dog, soulful eyes and slight jowls and the general aura of sorrow.

But no one was listening to Katie, all eyes returning to Gwen's laptop, laid forth on the patio table like a holy book. A competition video played, the floor-music score chirping, katy-didding in the night air.

"Lacey," Katie said, touching the girl's shoulder, sharp as an arrowhead, "would you like some juice?"

"Orange juice has twenty-four grams of sugar," Lacey replied, looking up. As if it had been a test, and she was passing it.

"John's done terrific work with those girls," Gwen interrupted, "but, *entre nous*, he is not happy. He's talked about opening a new gym right over in Indian Springs."

"Who's John?" Katie asked, feeling Eric's eyes on her.

"John Ehlers," Molly said. "At EmPower."

EmPower. An Olympic training gym two hours away in Hartswood, a woody, lush community near the water. The kind of place Katie and Eric had always dreamed of vacationing—canoes, paddleboats, cracked crab on the water—before the second mortgage and the most recent round of competition fees. And it was the place that, in the past five years, had propelled a half dozen girls to the national level, girls who, rumor had it, still had their baby teeth at twelve.

"Why are you talking about EmPower?" Katie asked, moving closer. "That's where they do daily weigh-ins. Girls work out with broken toes. At regionals, we saw an EmPower girl compete with a leg brace."

And the thing Katie didn't say: that EmPower parents paid eighteen thousand dollars a year, which might be manageable for the banker, the married attorneys, the dominating business owner seated around her. But not for the Knoxes, with their debt and their sagging roof and their creosote-lined chimney and the spidery foundation cracks their neighbor Mr. Watts kept pointing out, poking with a screwdriver and shaking his head.

Gwen paused the video. Behind her, Lacey rocked nervously, her bare legs goose-prickled in the night air.

"Katie, we need to be prepared," Jim said. "All we have now are Teddy's skill coaches—minus the one possibly under suspicion by the police—and none of them are competition material."

"Teddy's always hired from the heart, not the head." Molly sighed.

"Teddy hires from the wallet," Gwen said. "Why pay for a good tumbling coach when you can get your unstable, possibly criminal niece to do it for pin money?"

"Jesus," Katie said, "you guys don't waste much time, do you?" Looking over at Eric, waiting for him to join her.

"Teddy is focused on his family," Gwen said, "and it's up to us to focus on ours."

"Without a high-level coach in place now, we don't achieve," Jim said, punching the words with military rigor. "Each day we lose before next month's qualifiers we risk full collapse."

"Thirty-five days," Molly said, nodding vigorously. "We have three girls going for Junior Elite, and I'm not just saying that because Cheyenne is one of them. But she is. And Devon, of course, for Senior Elite."

Everyone looked at Katie and Eric, both of whom crossed their arms.

"Forget Cheyenne, forget our daughters," Gwen added more quietly, reaching down and smoothing Lacey's braids. She looked at Katie, eyes fixed. "We know who this matters most for. Devon. She is our star. And we all know this may be her last chance."

Katie counted to ten in her head.

Several seconds of awkward quiet, Lacey digging energetically at the callus on her palm.

"Devon's ready," Eric said coolly. "She will be ready, she will be flawless and she will dominate."

Katie looked at him, surprised. They never talked that way outside of the family. Or even inside it. There'd never been any need to assert anything before the foot bobble two years ago, but all this reminded her of some of the chatter that had followed: That Coach had skimped on equipment, failing to invest in good skill coaches. That he counted on the boosters to pick up the slack while he expanded his swimming pool, added the cedar deck. And the part that was only whispered: that Teddy might be squandering Devon's remarkable talent, and on her talent the gym's prospects rode. *The rising tide lifts all boats,* Gwen once told Eric, *and I just hope Teddy's not a sinker.*

No one ever said anything directly to Katie, only to Eric. Occasionally, she'd wonder if Eric had doubts too. But she always reminded herself that he loved Teddy and, most of all, Devon did. *Mom,* she'd once said to her. *Thank you for finding him for me.*

She'd thought, but didn't say, *Honey, he'd have found you anywhere.*

"I have no doubt about Devon," Gwen was saying. "My doubts are with Teddy's attentions right now. They need to be on BelStars, not on his hysterical niece and her doomed romances."

"Hey," Katie said, looking around at them, "we all owe Teddy a lot. You want someone like John Ehlers? Who says gymnasts are like scorpions in a jar, the one who crawls out is the winner? You think he's going to care about your girls like Teddy does?"

There were a few halfhearted nods, though Gwen's eyes wandered back to the laptop screen. Lacey squeezed her sneaker toes anxiously.

"Katie, I know you love Teddy," Kirsten said, removing her Bluetooth and leaning forward in the squeaking chair, "because he has done nothing but shower your daughter with attention since the moment she landed on his doorstep. But your darling Coach T. was at the police station with Hailey for four hours today. And we need to get real."

Katie looked at Eric as he watched it all. *Say something*, she thought.

"You want a gym exodus? That may be fine for you," Katie said, "but I don't feel ready to make any big decisions for Devon."

"That's because you don't have to," Kirsten said icily. "Because your daughter's a star."

There was a long beat, Kirsten glaring, her Bluetooth crackling in her palm.

"Hey, everyone," Katie said, rising. Someone needed to say something, and Eric stood there silently, almost as if he were one of them.

Katie cleared her throat. "Let's step back a second and remember a few things. Molly, how about the time he missed his own fiftieth-birthday party to visit Cheyenne at St. Joe's after she dislocated her knee playing soccer? Or when he drove seventy miles on black ice to get Nikki Hargrove home from regionals before her PSATs?"

She turned to each of them, softening her eyes as Eric always did.

"And Kirsten, before State last year, when Jordan couldn't find her good-luck grips, Teddy spent two hours looking before he found them at the bottom of the pit, under that mouse nest."

"Thigh-deep in the pit," Molly said, with a small grin, "holding up those stinky grips, saying, *Nothing I won't do for my girls, our girls!*"

Katie could feel Eric watching her so closely. So intently it almost hurt. It felt like a heat on her.

"And Gwen," Katie said, taking a few steps toward her, the screen saver on her laptop spattering *blood sweat & chalk*, "Lacey's last coach, the one at that fancy gym we lured you from—he told you Lacey would never make it to Level Eight with her confidence issues. Teddy saw her potential."

Katie looked over at Lacey, who was staring fixedly at the bug zapper above.

"He did," Gwen said. "But that's not helping any of us now. And no offense, Katie, but you're not even a booster officer."

There was an anxious silence, and Katie looked over at Eric, filling her face with urgency.

"For God's sake, Kirsten, your daughter isn't even a Level Ten yet, she—" Katie began, but Eric stepped forward, grabbing for Katie's wrist, pulling her toward him and then behind him.

"Can I say something?" he said, leaning against the edge of the tilting patio table. "Katie's right. We need to slow down. Teddy's concentrating on his family right now, which is what any of us would do. And a big disruption so close to qualifiers—the upheaval of changing gyms and coaches—is that good for our girls? Is that what they need?"

All their eyes had turned to him, their faces filling with expectation. It was such a power, one she could never match. Even more good-looking as the years skipped by, his features settling on himself, the hot gaze of booster moms and dads transforming him, he was always able to convey the feeling that he believed firmly in all the right things. And, in ways magical and obscure, the way he looked seemed to confirm it.

"So instead of talking exodus," he continued, hooking his fingers around Katie's wrist, "I think if we all pause here on this moment, we'll remember we owe him more than poaching plans and knee-jerk second-guessing. We should be doing for him what's he's done for us: hold steady through the storm, steer with confidence, and be there for him. Because we're lucky to have him."

There was a brief pause and then Molly and Jim nodded firmly, rising, and Jim shook Eric's hand, *Hear, hear, my friend*. Kirsten sighed and tucked her Bluetooth back in her ear, its light pulsing jauntily. Gwen slid her tablet back into her purse.

"Eric," Molly said, voice shaking, moving closer to him, "really so much of that is you. We are so lucky to have *you*."

Katie watched as Molly walked over and pressed her soft bones and, as ever, her quivering breasts against Eric's chest. As she nestled against him, Eric turned slightly, and that was when Katie saw the look on his face. A look only she would understand. It was the same one he always wore right before Devon attempted a terrifying stunt for the very first time. A look of acute trepidation, even a hauntedness. As if he held a private knowledge that this wasn't going to end quickly, or cleanly. That all the foam pits and pizza parties and booster brawn and stalwart can-do spirit in the world weren't going to count alongside the dark matter of Ash Road.

And maybe that's what the tightness in his voice earlier had been about, when he spoke about Hailey. Maybe that's what everything with him these last few days had been about. The desperation to try, to try against all the epic forces at work in the world, to hold everything together.

For Devon.

That night, Katie couldn't remember him coming to bed at all.

At one point, she thought she saw him, felt him, but it was just a shadow, a passing car, a trick of the light.

Chapter Eleven

"How does it work?" Drew whispered as Katie shook the Chloraseptic and sprayed it down his meaty throat.

"I don't know, honey. It just numbs you."

"Where's Dad?"

"He had to work."

"It's Saturday."

"It is."

Eric rarely missed Devon's weekend practices, but he'd fallen behind, with everything. That's what his text said:

Need to catch up at studio after dropping off D.

"I hope I'm okay soon," Drew said, his voice thick and funny from the spray. "Can I go check the shrimp?"

"What?" Katie said.

Her eyes drifted to her laptop. The BelStars Facebook page. Someone had posted an old photo there. Ryan, his face breaking into a grin, alongside Hailey in cutoffs and a BelStars T-shirt in front of that purple car of hers, Maiden Pond shimmering in the background.

She wondered if it had been posted in memory of Ryan, or to remind everyone of Hailey's purple car. The car in question.

In the photo, it didn't look nearly as vibrant, as grape-crush delicious.

Instead, it looked muddy, mysterious.

And Hailey—her freckles blurry, her hair wind-stirred, her side smile—looked mysterious too. Obscurely primitive. The way she was holding on to Ryan so tightly, her neck cords visible, her painted fingers like purpled claws.

You make me crazy, baby. You make me crazy.

That's what Katie had overheard her saying to Ryan that time at the Ramada sundries shop. Moments before she'd lunged up behind Ryan as he talked to Katie, her arms bolting around him: *He's mine.*

Or maybe it was Hailey's phone call still hammering in Katie's head. But the picture. It looked like evidence for something.

Two hours before practice normally ended, the text came.

Mom, no Coach T. again. Short practice. Dad not txting back. Can u get me?

"You sure you're up to the drive, sweetie?" Katie asked as they walked into the garage.

"Yeah," Drew said, peering down at his two-liter bottle, thick with scum. The science project, of course. "It smells funny in here."

"You mean like old shrimp?"

"No."

* * *

150

A jackknifed truck held her hostage on Route 11 for an extra twenty minutes and by the time she pulled into the BelStars parking lot, gymnasts were already streaming out of the building in their matching warm-up suits, matching hollow-chested postures, matching stoic expressions, their mouths all straight lines. But no Devon.

Looking in the rearview mirror at Drew's wan face, mouth open and lips coated white, she didn't want to leave the car. But Devon wasn't answering her phone and Katie had the sneaking sense she was still at the vault, making use of every spare minute, feeling her progress whittled away by circumstance and tumult.

I just get lost up there. That's what she'd told Amelise.

"Drew, I'll be right back," she said, leaning into the rear seat, resting the back of her hand on his forehead for the hundredth time.

Jogging inside the BelStars lobby, the familiar bite of Steri-Fab and Tinactin, she kept her head down, avoiding eye contact with the stray parent or staff member.

As she pushed through the heavy doors into the gym, she saw only a few assistant coaches, a handful of girls in leotards over at the Resi-Pit, one girl still practicing handstand pops on the tumbling track, Bobby catching her legs.

"Where's Devon?"

"Katie. She was looking for you," Bobby said, the girl's ankles caught in his hands, her upturned face blooming with blood. "But that was a while ago."

"I saw her in the locker room," Missy Morgan said, zipping her gym bag. "But I think she's gone now."

Wending her way past the practice beams and uneven bars, Katie started to pick up her pace. Some feeling in her chest.

Approaching the locker room, eyes fixed on the long line of red cubbies veining through the door's cutout window, she heard the scream, like a tear in the throat.

"Stop it! *Stop it!*"

Heart pommeling against her chest, Katie charged through the double doors.

At first, she couldn't see anything, just heard a tight shriek, a hard clang.

"Devon?" Katie cried out.

Running past the locker stalls, her chest lurching, everything was a red blur until she saw them:

Two girls interlocked on the floor, almost like an embrace. Katie could see only the tall one on top, golden hair sprayed across the back of a red BelStars hoodie, and beneath her a pair of tanned legs scrambling, sneakers squeaking on the tiles.

"Help!" came a strangled voice as Katie forked her arm under the torso of the hoodie girl and lifted with all her might, which seemed infinite.

Wrenching the girl by her hood, barring the tanned expanse of her broad shoulders, Katie hurled her aside, somehow stronger than ever in her life, and found beneath the bloodless face of her daughter.

"Devon," Katie cried. Sprawled on the floor, her daughter still grasped the girl's hoodie cord so tightly it had cut into the center of her palms, blood-whorled.

"I'll kill you," the hoodie girl screamed, and Katie's head whipped around to see who she was.

Though she already knew.

The freckled nose and bright teeth, that corn-colored hair rippling.

"Hailey," Katie panted, her arms wrapping around Devon, shielding her hunched body. "Oh God, Hailey."

"Call the police! Call the police!" someone was shouting as the doors to the locker room swung open behind them.

There was a swirl of noise and doors and shouts, Bobby and Amelise descending upon them, propelling Hailey backward, legs kicking, punching air, and the crash and rattle of locker metal and the skidding of sneakers and the savage howl of a girl who barely sounded human.

Her face, Katie thought, *her face—who is that?* Teeth bared, veins rising everywhere, a face swollen with blood.

In an instant, turning her body, Devon lifted her muscled leg and pounded, with a force like the force she marshaled to punch the springboard, her foot landing on something with a deafening crunch.

The stray bits of a lavender cell phone scattered across the floor like confetti.

Hailey let out one last howl.

"I called 911!" came a shout from the hallway.

Huddling over Devon, Katie looked up at Hailey, who stood panting wildly, a thick strand of her own hair caught in her mouth, her neck scored with nail marks.

Held back by Bobby's trunk arms, Hailey breathed in, bent her head, and let loose a warm spray of pink saliva that scattered across Devon's chest, onto Katie's calf and ankle.

"Bitch, I know you," Hailey muttered, Bobby pinning her arms back fiercely, "I know you."

Devon, eyes sheeted black, her expression as stony, as pitiless as Katie had ever seen, looked up at her and said nothing.

* * *

Katie's hands clutched the wheel tightly even though the car was not running.

Bobby had tried to get her to wait in Teddy's office until the police arrived.

"If we don't handle this right," he'd warned, "there could be trouble. People trust their children with us."

But she'd needed to get Devon out of there, and Drew was alone in the car.

Now, all three of them sat, fogging the windows, and there were too many things to do all at once, and Eric's phone went straight to voice mail.

"What happened?" Drew asked. "Did Devon fall?"

Her head felt like it was whirring, her hands shaking.

Devon was leaning forward in the front seat, hand pressed on the dashboard as if she might fall.

"Devon, look at me," she said.

But Devon wouldn't, and wouldn't, until Katie finally reached across and pulled her sharp shoulder back.

She supposed she'd imagined it would be worse. But other than Devon's chin, scored with red half-moons, her daughter looked remarkably intact.

Except: Was that a strand of Hailey's hair caught in the corner of Devon's mouth, like corn silk?

"We may need to go to the hospital," Katie said, reaching out for Devon's chin.

Flinching, Devon pulled back, covering her chin with her hand.

A police car turned into the lot.

"Stay here," Katie said. *"Do not move."*

* * *

"You can meet us at the station," said the officer with the shaved head and soft lower lip. "We'll get some other statements here first."

His nameplate said Officer Crandall and his severe affect was oddly comforting. Shaking his head as he took notes, he wouldn't let her back in the locker room. The sounds coming from there, piercing girl squeals echoing, reminded Katie of the time they'd found the dead raccoon trapped in the gym air shaft.

Back in the car, Devon was still pitched forward, her eyes shut.

On the tan dashboard, there was a red palm print like a kindergarten art project. The palm that had been wrapped around Hailey's hoodie cord.

"Mom," Drew said when she opened the door, "Devon didn't cry once."

It's what he always said when his sister got injured, and it was very dear. Katie tried to smile for him but caught a glimpse of herself in the rearview mirror, her face and neck smeared pink with adrenaline, sweat-smudged hair, mascara striped across the bridge of her nose.

"I think Dad called," Devon said, eyes still closed.

Katie looked down at her phone, blinking rapidly.

When she called him back, he said he was already on his way to the police station. Bobby had phoned, he said. Bobby had told him.

"How is she?" he asked, breath ragged. "How's her wrist?"

"Her wrist? She's okay. She—"

"Goddamn it. I told you we needed to keep her away from Hailey."

"What?" she said. "This is my fault?"

"I shouldn't have left her there. That gym isn't safe. Can you put her on the phone?"

The back doors of the gym opened.

"We have to go," Katie snapped, turning the phone off and tossing it onto the console with a hard crack. She'd never hung up on Eric in her life.

The three of them watched silently as the officer escorted Hailey, hair sprigged like Medusa, in plastic cuffs, to the squad car.

Once, at a booster-sponsored volleyball game, Hailey had worn a bikini, and Katie could swear she had the tan poreless skin of a slick Barbie doll, not a stray blemish, not one broken blood vessel, not a single scar. A perfect, markless body.

And here she was, face ruddy, eyes lowered, angry scarlet grooves swooping up her face and neck. Officer Crandall's hand behind that honeyed head, ducking her into the backseat.

She imagined Hailey at thirteen, hitching her way down to Florida. Ripped shirt, clawed face. Fighting with another girl, beating her with a sandal. *What took you so long?*

"Mom," Drew said, "what happened to your arm?"

Katie looked down and saw the long looping fish hook of a scratch extending from her elbow to her wrist.

"And your eye."

Pulling her hair back, peering in the rearview mirror, she saw the knot of blood under her eyebrow and couldn't remember how she'd gotten it. A tigress, protecting her young.

At the police station, Katie watched as Eric's hand clenched the water bottle so tightly it cracked, leaking all over his jeans, into his pocket, blurring all the print on the speeding ticket stuffed there. The one that Officer Crandall said he'd "take care of," given everything.

She put her hand on his leg firmly.

The desk sergeant sat with Drew on the other side of the windowed room. Katie watched Drew's mouth moving, imagined him talking and talking in that funny little frog voice.

Inside, for the next half hour, Devon told Officer Crandall what had been happening with Hailey and what had happened that day.

It was hard to get her to say everything and Katie had to prompt her several times.

"Hailey called me once," Katie said, "but she's been calling Devon constantly. Tell him, Devon."

"She kept calling," she said, so quietly they all leaned forward. "I don't know."

"But you never spoke to her?" Officer Crandall asked. "Did she ever directly threaten you?"

"No," Katie said, looking at Devon, who was staring at her sore hand.

"She did," Devon said.

"What?" Katie said. "When?"

"She was sending me texts. I kept deleting them. They were creepy. Dad told me to block her."

Katie and Officer Crandall turned to Eric.

"Because of the calling," Eric said, straightening in his chair, looking at them both. "I told her to block her because of the incessant calling. I didn't know about the texts."

"Devon, why didn't you tell me about the texts?" Katie asked, her head throbbing.

Officer Crandall looked at Katie, then back at Devon, who was still staring at her right hand, the ailing wrist bandaged now, like a fat paw.

"I don't know," she said, finally.

"What did the texts say?"

Devon shrugged. "She kept calling me names. I don't know why."

The officer looked at her as if waiting for more.

"Are we going to talk about what happened today?" Eric said, squirming in his chair.

"You have no idea why she might have targeted you?" Crandall asked.

There was another brief silence.

"Sometimes," Katie jumped in, "Devon's talents make her a target. There's jealousy, you know. A lot of it."

Devon nodded, staring at her hands. "Hailey wanted to be a gymnast," she said. "But she was too big."

"That's true," Katie said, except it didn't seem precisely right. The way she'd always understood it, Hailey had abandoned serious competition back in high school for swimming, and then coaching. "Can't you get those texts from Hailey's phone?"

"We'd need a warrant," he said. "And we'd have to go through her provider since her phone was in about twenty-five pieces on the locker-room floor."

Katie remembered the sound of splintering, the skittering of plastic on linoleum. Devon's foot landing on it like a tomahawk. Hailey's banshee howl.

"Why do we keep talking about texts?" Eric said, face florid in a way Katie didn't recognize. "This woman attacked my daughter."

"Or your provider," the officer told Katie calmly. "Because deleting texts from your phone doesn't get rid of them. It just removes them from your phone."

As he spoke, the officer watched Devon, who was still fixated on her wrist, stretching the grip muscles like Teddy always told her to.

"Officer, what do we do?" Katie asked. "We have no idea what Hailey's capable of."

"We know exactly what she's capable of," Eric said. "We saw it today. And I can't be the only one wondering what this has to do with Ryan Beck."

A loud crack, and the battered water bottle in Eric's fist completely gave way this time, a sluice of water scattering across all of them.

Katie jumped back, but neither Crandall nor Devon moved. Devon's eyes blinking as if water had been caught there, her lashes sticky with it.

"Mr. Knox," Crandall said, looking down at the water spatters on the desk, "let's just keep focused on what happened to Devon. Okay?"

"Then tell me this: How do we file a restraining order?" Eric said, picking up the splintered water bottle, nearly slamming it into the trash can.

"She's locked up now, right?" Katie asked the officer, placing her hand on Eric's arm, pressing hard.

"Miss Belfour is at St. Joe's," Crandall said. "But we'll be talking to her very soon."

"She's at the hospital?" Katie asked.

"Her injuries were more substantial than your daughter's," Crandall added.

"Oh."

"A big hank of her hair got torn out," he said. "Your daughter knows how to protect herself."

Katie looked at Devon, whose eyes remained downcast.

"And her scalp opened up where she hit the floor," Crandall continued. "But mostly they need to be extra careful whenever there's bite marks. Especially under the eye." He paused a second before adding, "It was a mean fight."

They found Drew half asleep in his chair, mouth still ringed white and a fresh red rash swarming up his face.

"Come on, honey," Katie said, arms around him. "Devon's in the restroom and then we'll go."

She felt Eric's hand on her arm.

"Did you know she was violent?" he said. "Did you know any of this?"

Katie stared at him, the way his hands bulbed into fists. He was looking at her like she had done something. Like she was the one.

"You knew as much as I did," she said, trying to keep her voice calm. "You're the one who said practice is how Devon 'works through feelings.' Right?"

He looked at her, then down at Drew, the back of his hand touching Drew's bloomy face.

"We shouldn't have let Devon out of our sight after that call," he said. "That's all I meant. Sorry. Sorry."

She nodded, and stared at the ladies' room door, waiting for Devon.

That's when it came to her, the last time she'd talked to a police detective, more than a dozen years ago. They were huddled in the hectic waiting room at Good Samaritan Hospital, Eric's forearms streaked with three-year-old Devon's browning blood, the same blood that spattered across his T-shirt like scatter art, and the officer assuring them it was only routine, after any severe injury of a child.

The dropped ceiling so low, the strip fluorescents hurting her eyes, Katie had sat there, feeling like her insides had been scraped clean, like her mom once told her an abortion felt (*Which is why*, she'd added, *I put you on the pill at fifteen*).

The woman kept asking them questions.

Mr. Knox, was it common to have your daughter with you while you mowed the lawn?

Mr. Knox, were you aware of the safety mechanisms on your mower?

Eric, all of twenty-two years old, younger even than Ryan Beck, just stood there, grass blades still slashed up his calves. No belt—he'd torn it from its loops, tying it around Devon's foot. He stood there, unable to say anything but *No, no, I don't know.*

Your daughter may not even remember this later, the officer told them, walking them out. *She may not even remember her foot ever being like it was before.*

But Katie knew that was a lie. The moment her own knees slid onto the shorn lawn, slick with Devon's blood, she knew her daughter would remember this forever.

How did I do that? Eric kept asking her, his voice strange and high, like she'd never heard before and hadn't since. *How did I do that?*

The paramedics, and Mr. Watts from next door, trying to help. To distract Devon, mashed against the grass, face white as paper.

Honey, look at me. Listen to me. Mr. Watts from next door, trying to get her to look at him and not the red tangle hanging from her ankle. *Do you have a dog? Did you get an ice cream from the truck today?*

But, glassy-eyed, Devon would look only at Katie, her red-specked chin.

Mommy, where did it go?

Her foot stretched out in front of her, the bright mass below her ankle like a tissue-paper flower.

Where did it go?

She wondered if Eric was thinking about any of this now.

Looking at him, she had no idea, and would never ask.

"We'll be in touch," Officer Crandall said. Then added, turning to Eric, "And we can talk more about that restraining order."

Her bandaged hand resting on top of her other one, Devon walked toward them from the restroom. So tiny, half a foot shorter than Katie herself.

"Dee-Dee," Eric said, which he hadn't called her in a decade or more. "Dee-Dee, come with us."

Back home, after everything settled a little, after a muted dinner of freezer-scorched pizza, Drew collapsed into his bed and Devon disappeared into the basement gym again. As Eric drank whiskey from a coffee cup, Katie stood over the sink, scraping all the rice stuck to the bottom of yesterday's casserole dish, drinking beer from a can.

All she wanted was for everything to stay quiet. To be quiet.

And to keep Eric away from Devon. He still looked so on edge, a coiled thing.

"Can you go to the drugstore?" she asked him. "Some vitamin E oil for Devon's wrist?"

He said he would. She hoped to talk to Devon alone, quietly, and make sure she was really okay.

But before she could, everything started again.

"Katie," Teddy said, one foot on the doorstep.

Polo shirt untucked, neck rubbed red, eyes pouched, he stood before her, one hand tugging nervously at the fingers of the other. She was guessing he'd been up for a long time, days maybe.

Under the porch light, though, there was still that magnificent silver hair like drusy quartz. And his voice.

"Oh God, Katie."

Hurrying him inside, she shut the door to the den behind them.

"You absolutely cannot be here, Teddy. Eric's at the drugstore, but he'll be back. You know how he can be and this—"

"I can't explain what she did, Katie. I won't even try," he said. "But I need you to know, we're taking care of it."

He explained that he had checked Hailey into Gateways Behavioral Health, the only way to keep the hospital from putting her in the psych ward after she'd tried to climb out of her bathroom window.

"It's this lying, bullshit eyewitness. It unwound her. And he can't keep his story straight. First he says Altima, but cops show him pictures and he ID's a Chevy Malibu. And he's a trucker!"

"I don't care, Teddy. I don't care about this. What does it have to do with what she did to my daughter?"

Shaking his head. "All of this, it's eating her alive. It's made her do . . . shameful things. I just ask that you try to understand that that wasn't our Hailey there today."

Katie kept her eyes on the front window for Eric's return.

"Katie, when she first came to us, Hailey was headed down a crooked road—boy trouble, lots of volatility. We got her to church, got her on the swim team. Didn't give up on her," he said, voice cracking with urgency, his fist pounding his knee. "By sixteen, she was a prom queen and junior-class president."

"Teddy, I know this."

"And I thought," he said, "well, I thought: *We sealed that up. That's done.*"

Teddy covered his face with both hands and was silent for a moment. But when he lifted his head again, his eyes were dry and filled with surprise.

"I mean, I thought *this* was what I was good at. Making girls feel loved."

In spite of herself, Katie felt her throat tighten.

And there it was, Eric's weather-beaten silver Ford, lights flashing up the window.

"Teddy, you have to go. Now."

He nodded firmly, squeezed his bloodshot eyes, nodded again. But he didn't get up.

"But, Katie, I do need to tell you: At the hospital, Hailey wasn't making any sense. She was talking about how the fight started. She started saying some kinda...*raw* things about...I mean, you must be wondering too."

"You bet we're wondering, Teddy. We've known Hailey for years. We——"

"I mean about Devon. She had some things to say about Devon. About Ryan. Some stuff that kinda rocked me back on my feet."

"What?"

"Well," he said, shifting uncomfortably, "you know how young women can be."

Then the side door slammed and Katie jumped up.

"What the hell are you doing here?"

It was Eric, standing in the doorway, keys still in hand, eyes bleared.

"What did you say?" he demanded, and Teddy rose.

"Eric, he just——"

"Katie, don't you talk to him."

Katie looked at Eric. Something in his eyes she had never seen before.

"Teddy, you need to leave. You just do."

Briskly, she walked Teddy outside, afraid Eric might follow.

"Teddy, what did Hailey say?" she asked. "What did she tell you?"

"Listen, it doesn't matter," he said. "Let's just wait. Let everything calm a little."

"Then you better go." They both stood a moment on the front lawn, jungly with ground ivy.

"Katie, listen, you know Hailey," he began, voice trembling. "You know her heart. You always understood her—"

"I don't know her heart," Katie said coolly. "She came after my daughter. What would that do to you?"

Teddy nodded, kicking the curb at the foot of the drive, just like a little boy might. "I'd be the same way. I'd be like Eric. I'd be worse. You know I love your daughter."

Katie folded her arms, glancing back at the house, Eric's shadow in the front window.

"I'm tired and life is a son of a bitch," Teddy said, looking off into the distance, the neon-banded lights from the corner drive-through, cars chugging into the lot all night. Thumping bass, the drunken chirrs of girls.

"We never know," he said, "none of us, what love'll do to us." He smiled a little. "Make us buy a swimming pool, just so a niece might keep coming by."

Katie felt something inside herself open, her face red-rushed with shame over it. It felt like he had poked a hole in her.

"Or maybe we do know," he said, walking backward

down the front walkway, the deep slope of the unmowed lawn.

"What was he thinking, showing up here?" Eric kept saying, over and over and over, pacing in the living room.

"He shouldn't have come."

"After what she did to our daughter."

"I know."

"And you," he said, freshly outraged at the thought. "What she did to you."

It was the first time Eric mentioned it. Katie looked down at the spindle scratch on her arm. Felt the pulse over her brow where, she guessed, Hailey's hard knuckle—or was it Devon's, accidentally?—had pushed.

"No one ever wants to believe bad things about their own family," Katie said.

He was standing by the front doorway, and those car keys still in his hand, like he was going to leave. For a second, she wondered if he would.

"How did it happen?" he asked, as if to himself. "How did this happen?"

She wasn't even sure what he meant, but there was something in his face. She'd seen it before, years ago, during the pureed-pear-smeared chaos of new parenthood. This dangerous and endangered creature had landed like a bomb in their lives—his life—and he'd stand at the nursery door at the end of a long day and she couldn't get him to come inside, to join her at the rocker, or he'd stand over the crib rail. His face stiff and eyes distracted, he'd linger in the doorway, *I don't want to wake her.* But Devon was always awake, bantam arms swatting at Katie's chest. *Come on, Eric,* Katie would urge, *hold her, smell that sweet smell.* But it was as though he were frozen there, and he never moved at all.

But that was a long time ago, before everything.

That night, tucking Drew in, feeling his forehead, she tried to explain what had happened, that Hailey was upset and had been mean to Devon.

"Oh. I thought Devon did something wrong," Drew said, his throat clacking wetly. "I thought she was in trouble."

"No," she said, worried about the rash, his skin mottled-looking. She was going to call the doctor in the morning. "Sleep snug, okay?"

"She looked like she looked when she drove the car that time."

"Honey, you were dreaming, remember? Just like when you thought she was flying."

"But she can," he said. "She can fly, Mom."

"You poor tucker. Call me if you need more throat spray."

"It makes my mouth feel like a seashell," he said. "Like something died inside and took all the feeling away."

On the way back, she stopped at Devon's room, peeking behind the nearly closed door.

It was black inside, and loud with a warm, wet wind from the open window. Devon lay there, still and helpless, one arm dangling off the bed.

Katie stood a moment, listening to the wind, watching it rush over her daughter's body, so motionless. Her hand, palm facing out, caught the hallway light. The funny stigmata the gymnastics rips had formed in its center.

"I'm sorry" came the whisper and now she saw Devon's eyes shimmering in the heavy dark.

"Sorry for what, baby?"

"Mom, what if it's all my fault?"

"No," Katie said, stepping inside. "Nothing is your fault."

She sat down on the edge of her bed, feeling Devon's body stiffen, nearly cracking. She rested her hand on Devon's ankle, hot and heavy.

Devon looked at her closely, tilting her head like a cat.

"Was Coach T. here?"

"Yes," Katie said, not taking her eyes off her.

"What did he want?" Devon asked, more awake now, body tensing. "Did he want to talk to me?"

Katie paused. "Devon, do you know why Hailey did this to you?"

Devon said nothing. Katie waited. There was something happening. She knew it. She let the silence linger and kept her gaze fixed on Devon.

Devon held that gaze for a long minute.

"Maybe she thinks I'll tell."

"Tell what?" Katie asked, a creeping feeling on her neck, like a pin scratching.

It was like opening a diary, Devon's diary. Except Devon was doing it. Inviting her in. Katie had always thought her daughter never confided because she had nothing to confide.

It started a few weeks ago, she said. It was a Saturday practice, amid the sweat and chalk fog of the gym. Only a few parents were staggered through the stands, not even Katie, who was at swim class with Drew. Devon looked up in the stands and saw Ryan.

Usually, if he visited, which was almost never anymore, he

stayed close to Hailey's part of the gym, where she reigned over the seven-year-olds, bellybands cinched around their soft centers.

But today he was sitting on Devon's side, with a perfect view of the vault.

She focused on her routines. Round-offs to the board, drills onto stacked mats and onto the trapezoid, and especially Yurchenkos into the pit. Gaze trained on the sloping tongue of the vault table. The place she needed her hands to hit, fingers straight ahead. Telling herself: *Don't slip off the tongue.*

But at a certain point she noticed Hailey had abandoned her seven-year-olds to a round-off drill and strolled over to watch her.

After Devon's last run, Hailey approached her at the chalk stand.

Devon, Ryan thinks your vault is mind-blowing, she said, smiling but in a weird way. And the way she said *mind-blowing,* like it was a dirty word.

Later, Devon saw the two of them in the BelStars parking lot, leaning against Hailey's Altima and talking very closely.

Walking past, she thought she heard Hailey say, *Is that how you like them now,* her voice peculiar. *Like little boys.* Like that one time when Hailey couldn't get Ryan on the phone and said to Lacey Weaver, *Your mom would tell me, right, if Ryan was screwing that hostess? The one who shakes her tits at him?*

("Mom," Devon said, "that's how she talks when no adults are around. She's so . . . nasty.")

Then Ryan came to practice again. He stopped her at the vending machine. He said he was sorry if Hailey had made her uncomfortable but not to worry about it. It was Hailey's way. *She's always been jealous as a cat,* he'd said with a shrug.

But that made Devon worry about it more. And something about the way Hailey had started looking at her, watching her on the beam, even in the locker room.

Then, last Friday, she was running, shin splints aching, in Hood Park, just off Ash Road, and Ryan spotted her, gave her a ride home.

That night, she got the first text.

I know whats up.

I know u were w him last nite. I could smell yr disgusting wrist grips in the car.

And then more came, and they got nastier.

Gym bitch, nasty whore. You'll get yours.

("Mom," Devon said, "I never answered any of them. I stopped reading them. I've heard things about Hailey. How she'd beaten up girls. Crazy stuff.")

The next night, Saturday, she was at Lacey's birthday party when Hailey called.

At first, she was really nice, like the before-Hailey, the one who brought her famous funfetti cupcakes on birthdays and snuck them out for secret frozen-yogurt runs in her little purple car. She said that she was sorry about any bad feeling between them and wanted to explain in person and would Devon consider meeting up, to talk?

But the more she spoke, the stranger Hailey sounded. Her words seemed to stretch out and then speed up, and her mouth seemed too close to the phone. It gave Devon a bad feeling, and she said she couldn't see her. She didn't even have a way to get there.

Something told her not to go. It felt like a trap.

But then Hailey said, *It's because you're seeing him tonight, isn't it? He goes to you after me, doesn't he? He puts his hands on you and your little-boy body. Do you even have tits? Do you even have pubic hair? That's how he likes them. Freaks with a freak foot.*

Devon hung up.

But all night, Hailey's voice kept needling her brain.

It was like in a horror movie, when a person you are very close to, like one of your family, changes. A vampire, a zombie, voice dropping low, eyes murderous.

Like how Grandma was that time. Right after they started the dementia meds. *You're as dark as your dad,* she'd whispered as Devon leaned over to hug her powdery bones. *You're trying to murder me.*

"And then the next day, we all heard about Ryan...the accident," Devon said to Katie now, grabbing for her pillow, twisting it. "And the calls started, and more texts. So Dad said to block her."

Katie looked at her, trying to unravel it all. Her daughter snared in such big drama, a seamy love triangle with an unhinged young woman, and Katie never knew it. Freaks with a freak foot. It was too awful.

"Then, today," Devon said, sitting up to face Katie. "Mom, she must have been hiding in the locker room. She must've been waiting for me behind one of the shower stalls. If you hadn't come..."

There was a pause, Devon's chin shaking slightly.

"Oh, Mom," she finally said, turning her face away. "The way she looked. Mom, she wanted to kill me."

It was a thing you never expect to hear from your child. They had a long moment where Katie wrapped her arm tightly around Devon's hard, hewn shoulders and neither said anything.

"What happens now?"

"Your dad and I will take care of it. She will never get near you again."

"Should I have told the police?" Devon asked.

Katie looked at her, the snarl of panic over her eye. "We'll figure it out."

"I didn't want to tell," Devon said. "I mean, that's Coach T.'s niece, you know?"

"Oh, Devon," Katie said, feeling a rush of heat under her eyes. "That's very generous of you. After everything."

Sometimes, in the blur and burr of Devon's extraordinary upbringing, she worried about how Devon would ever learn people skills, social skills, empathy even. But here it was. Devon thinking foremost of her beloved coach. Always thinking of the burdens of parents and parent figures everywhere.

"But," Katie said, taking a breath, "if anything goes further, we might have to talk to the police about it. This might be evidence." *Evidence.* The word heavy on her tongue.

But Devon just bit at her thumbnail like she did before a floor routine. She'd learned long ago how to beat down her fear.

"Are you mad at me, Mom?"

"No," she said. "No, Devon. None of this is your fault."

Devon looked at her, big-eyed and immaculate, thumbnail still between her teeth, looking for all the world like Devon at age eight. Or like Devon at thirteen, still carrying that plush tiger in her travel bag, sleeping with it between her legs.

"Mom," she said, pressing her face against Katie's shoulder, "I'm really glad we talked."

It was a full embrace like Devon hadn't offered in years, not since four-year-old Drew had poured milk in her fish tank and killed all her angelfish, not since she'd left her first gym for BelStars.

"But Mom," she whispered, her head ducked down toward Katie's chest. "Don't tell Dad."

"What? Why not?"

"Because it's private," she said, voice soft, plaintive. "It's girl stuff. Stuff you share with your mom."

"Devon, I—"

"And because," Devon added, breathing in long and hard, "he'd get so mad. Sometimes, he gets so mad."

"He just wants to protect you," Katie said, feeling something churning inside.

"Yeah," Devon said, eyes black, chewing on that nail again. "I know."

In bed later, everything batting around in her brain, she decided she wouldn't tell Eric. Not yet, at least. Besides, it was something Devon had shared with her. Mothers and daughters shared things.

There is something bad here, growing. Day and night I watch it. Growing.

—Sophocles, *Electra*

Chapter Twelve

"Oh my God, baby."

Marbled red, Drew's skin felt like sandpaper under her hands.

"It doesn't hurt," he said. "But it feels weird."

Pulling off his pajama top, she found dark red lines on his underarms, his elbows, any crease in his soft little body.

Behind her, Eric was already on the phone with Dr. Kemper, his voice shaking and sleep-thick.

"He's just...it's like someone took a paintbrush to him. What the hell did you dose him with?"

"I'll take him," she said, Drew's skin bright white under the pressure of her fingertips. "You stay with Devon."

For twenty minutes she sat with Drew in the car, the parking lot nearly empty, slicked clean from all the rain the night before.

"The Knox I barely see." Dr. Kemper winked at Drew as he unlocked the front door. "You finally figured out how to get my attention."

One look at Drew's face under the exam room's fluorescent lights was all he needed.

"Don't worry," he warned Katie, "it sounds much worse than it is."

The only person she'd ever heard of getting it was Beth March in *Little Women*.

As they hurried through the waiting room, Eric called.

"Honey," she whispered into the phone. "Um."

A bleary, streaky-nosed kid and his wan parents were staring at dappled Drew, his face like raw bacon.

"It's scarlet fever," she said, covering her mouth with her hand. "It's fine, but Drew has scarlet fever."

Both parents looked up, alarmed, the mother clutching her son closer to her chest.

"Christ," Eric said. "Isn't that from the Civil War?"

"It can come with strep. The strep releases a toxin—"

"How could he get it when he's already on antibiotics? I always knew that guy was a quack. *Teddy's* doctor. All he knows are cortisone shots and horse pills."

"Who else do you know who sees patients on Sundays?" Katie said, voice low as she could make it. "He says it does happen. He increased the dosage and he says in twenty-four hours, the fever will go away and the rash will just—"

"Let me talk to him." That sharp rap again.

"He's with another patient. And Eric, you need to—"

"I mean Drew," he said, more softly now. "Can I talk to my son?"

Katie said nothing, handing the phone to Drew.

"Dad," he chirped, "it's like in *The Velveteen Rabbit*. Remember how they had to burn all the toys?"

Katie rested her hand on the top of his head, trying to breathe.

*   *   *

Devon was standing on the front lawn, gym bag in hand, when Katie pulled up the drive.

"I'm going to the Y," she said. "I'll work the weights."

"You will not," Katie said, jumping out of the car. "You're not going anywhere after what happened yesterday."

"Dad said he'd take me," she said, backing away from Drew, even from Katie. "Mom, I need to."

She wouldn't even step into the garage, or look at her brother.

"We'll just do a few hours' practice," Eric said, pulling the covers over Drew, who slumped into face-squashing sleep in seconds. "I'll be with her the whole time."

"Go, just go," Katie said, not even looking at him. "Both of you. Go."

"After, I'll take her to lunch. I'll explain."

Katie was listening, but she wasn't.

Drew's eyes fluttered like when he was a baby.

The rest of the morning, taking care of Drew, scrubbing everything with bleach until her hands cracked, she had the feeling things were happening, but no one was calling her back, no one seemed to be anywhere they should be.

Another load of laundry, the weight of the final basket branding her forearms, she fell asleep in the mamasan chair she'd dragged into Drew's room. To watch him.

She was dreaming when a sound woke her, dreaming of her hands digging into Hailey's thick hair from behind and pulling it back to see Devon hunched beneath, teeth bared and pink, her feet like little claws.

Her eyes opened to Drew sitting bolt straight in bed, mouth open, a flash of crimson that looked like a flame.

"Someone's here," he lisped. "Someone with noisy shoes."

Katie leaned over and looked out the window.

In the driveway, a familiar car gleamed like an oyster.

Reaching the bottom stair, laundry bag still in hand, she stopped in the foyer and took a breath.

There was Gwen, lodged firmly in the wing chair in the living room. It was the only fine piece of furniture they'd ever owned, a family heirloom presented, with tears and ceremony, by Eric's mother for their tenth anniversary.

Katie could remember sitting on it only once. Or she and Eric had together, the herringbone beneath her palm as she pushed hotly against his chest. A seized moment, Devon away at regionals, news of her triumph freshly arrived. The knife-pleat skirt tickling her swinging ankle, the skidding sound of its ball-and-claw feet on the floor—*claw away, claw up the floor, mark it.*

And there Gwen sat. Tangerine sheath dress just a shade too tight across her midriff, those tanned piston arms of hers bare because she was always warm. *I run a few degrees shy of Hades,* she told everyone, all the time, *always have.*

Fingers tapping on her phone.

And, now scraping along the wall-to-wall, were those noisy shoes. Pointy, soaring, python-skinned like they'd hiss.

"Look who woke up. I ran into Eric and Devon at Pancake Palace. They're upstairs."

"Thanks," Katie said, looking at her watch. They'd been gone for four hours. "What can I do for you, Gwen?"

"It's really unbelievable, isn't it? Thank God that demented girl is under lock and key."

"Yes," Katie said, trying to smooth her sleep-rumpled hair.

Trying to shove the detergent-speckled laundry bag behind her. "For now."

"You should have seen Devon at practice yesterday, Katie." Her eyes shone, python heels rasping on the carpet beneath her. "Amplitude, perfect body alignment, and the prettiest toe point I've ever seen. But, listen, Katie, that double-twist Yurchenko is not what it was two weeks ago. The stress of this is telling on her."

"Worry about your own daughter," Katie said, her eyes catching sight of Gwen's car, the top of Lacey's buttercup head inside. "Who's apparently imprisoned in your car like an over-heated collie."

Gwen sighed. "We got in some extra practice time today. She keeps saying to me, 'Mom, I love gymnastics.' But I tell her, 'Just because you love it doesn't mean you'll be good at it. There's a whole gym out there of girls who love it and are useless at it.'"

"But why is she in the car, Gwen?"

"It's hard enough to get her to practice without dosing her with scarlet fever too. And, circling back, Katie, to your question about why I'm here. I thought I'd extend the invitation to have Devon stay at my house a few nights. Until the quarantine has passed."

"There's no quarantine. He's on antibiotics. He'll be fine."

"Katie, I know I'm prone to hyperbole. Or so my ex-husband said while he was raping me in the divorce proceedings. But, really, who gets scarlet fever these days? Between whatever criminal derangement has overtaken Hailey and the pestilence under your own roof...well, it's getting pretty Greek here, isn't it?"

Katie took a long, long breath.

I wish I had your balls, she once overheard a bourbon-brewed Jim Chu say to Gwen at a booster party, shooting pool. Gwen had smiled, rolling the eight ball between her fingers.

"I appreciate your concern," Katie said, lifting the laundry bag, trying to signal an end to things, "but I'm not letting Devon out of my sight again."

"Of course," Gwen said, rising. "It's a mother's decision. Eric thought it was a good idea, but what do fathers know?"

"You two already talked about it?" Katie felt the bag slide off her narrow, toneless shoulder and catch in the cradle of her bent arm.

"He said he'd have to talk to you, but he's up there now, helping her pack."

Feet pounding up the stairs, laundry sack swinging wildly from her forearm, Katie called out both their names.

"What's going on here?" she asked, pushing open the door to Devon's room.

Both of them, backs to her, were leaning over Devon's duffel bag.

When they turned around, their faces seemed to blur before her eyes, same deep-set eyes, same hewn cheekbones. The same grave expressions.

"Mom," Devon said, hand out as if to calm her, "I need to go. Mrs. Weaver said the bacteria lives for up to eight days, maybe longer. She called a specialist."

"Not with antibiotics," Katie said, voice cresting. She knew Gwen could hear her, everyone could. "You are staying in this house with your parents and your sick brother. Have you even ducked your head in there? Have you even asked him how he is?"

"But Mom," Devon said, her hands shaking slightly, her fingers wrapping around her wrists like just before a vault run. "Dad set it all up. It's the right thing."

Katie looked at Eric, who didn't say a word.

Their bedroom door shut, Eric began talking quietly, fervently.

About how Gwen would escort Devon to and from practice with Lacey, and that not only was the Weaver house germ-free, it had a full workout room with a beam, a bar trainer, even a vault table. Devon could practice around the clock if she wanted—see? Gwen could take care of Devon, and they could take care of Drew.

"It's not just about Devon," he added, husky-voiced. "It could spread through the whole squad. All those girls who are counting on doing their best next month. And it's only for a few days."

"We need her here, Eric," she said. "You didn't see it. You didn't see her on the floor of that locker room."

"Gwen's house has a security system. It's wired for everything—fire, carbon monoxide. It can even tell if someone opens the medicine cabinet."

"I don't give a goddamn if it's land-mine-tripped from basement to roof, Eric. She belongs with her family. She belongs with her mom and dad."

Her voice sounded high and childlike. Once, in the grocery store, piling the cart with energy bars and string cheese and a tilting stack of frozen dinners, a woman came inside and said, *Whoever owns the blue Ford, you shouldn't leave your child in the car like that,* and she'd forgotten Drew, six months old and strapped in the car seat for close to a half hour and Katie crying the whole way home and so tired she snapped the wheel too hard on the final turn, hit a guardrail. *What will Eric say, what will he say?* But he'd said nothing.

And then the fear spinning inside: *What would he have said if that had been Devon?*

He would never say anything, though. He never did. But did he stow it away? Did they both have their little storage lockers of parental missteps and near catastrophes?

"Katie," he said now, with a hollow look in his eyes that rattled her, "this is the best thing. If something happened to Devon, you'd never forgive yourself."

It ended with the slamming of doors, and Katie shouting like she hadn't since she was a teenager, a hoarse and howling thing.

Eric kept shaking his head, shaking his head, his face white, eyes like two pinholes.

"What makes you think you know better?" she finally asked, voice shredded. *"You?"*

And the word itself like a charge. A long-buried indictment.

But all he said was "Katie, I'm fixing things. I have to fix this."

"You can stay in here, Mom," Drew said, his bed heavy with books. "I don't mind."

So she sat with him while he read, stopping every few minutes to tell her things, until she warned him to rest his sweet voice.

"'Boy, at sunrise it must be like diving into cotton candy!'" Drew read. "Mom, didn't you sell cotton candy when you were young?"

"I did, yes. That's how I met your dad."

At the Kiwanis fair. She'd sold him fried clams on a paper plate and a twist-tie bag of cotton candy and they spent that summer careening through back roads with sixers of Keystone. He loved to kiss the round scar on her eyebrow, the one from the time her stepdad caught her with the Wiffle bat he carried when he was drinking. Eric loved to run his hand along the *Fight Like a Grrrl* tattoo ringing her left thigh. A thousand years ago.

The door open, she could hear the zipping and unzipping of duffel bags, the shushing of Velcro grips, Eric and Devon shuttling back and forth, grabbing wristbands, liquid-bandage spray, flip-flops, a jiggling pair of ankle braces, a tower of leotards. As if she were going to a major tournament rather than to Gwen's pleasure palace a few blocks away.

Devon stealing nervous glances at her through the doorway.

From the upstairs window, she watched as Devon walked outside, bag swung over her shoulder. Gwen was leaning against the car door, saying something to Eric, as Devon slipped into the front passenger seat.

Lacey had already moved to the back.

That night felt lonely in a way she hadn't known since childhood, the endless chain of evenings with the TV tray and waxy sleeve of crackers, peanut butter jar, her mom working late.

Drew asleep in his room, she and Eric passing each other silently. For most of the evening, he sat at his computer, working with headphones on.

She couldn't tell if he felt guilty or righteous.

She missed Devon, and the energy around Devon being there, which felt elemental to everything. As if Devon's presence, quiet and focused, generated everything. In some way powered the house, the family.

She only realized it now, because everything else had stopped.

*   *   *

Nearly nine o'clock, and she was drinking vinegary wine she'd found buried in the back of the refrigerator behind a jug of bubbling kefir.

She tried to stop her mind from turning and overturning images of Gwen's house. She had seen it at parties, a half dozen over the years.

All the sconces and gilt and high ceilings of powder-blue plaster, the study's lacquered walls, the curve-backed sofas, the fresh flowers fogging your mouth as you passed through. The marble-topped kitchen island where platters of food always sat, mounds of olives, impossibly green artichokes, dewy lemons, everything wet and ready, all the time.

In the backyard, there was even a secret garden enclosed by pear trees latticed flat, candelabra-style, into a trellis, trained with the same rigor as Gwen trained Lacey's hair, planting her daughter between her legs in the stands as she flattened that white-blond hair into the tight Dutch braid, smoothing the feather wisps at her hairline hourly during meets.

Sometimes even Lacey seemed hand-manufactured, face cast in porcelain, that tiny nose that tilted up at the end as if Gwen herself had pinched it daintily, like a piecrust, right down the center.

When the phone rang and Devon's name flashed there, Katie's body shook to life.

"Mom," Devon said, "I'm staying in one of the guest rooms. It's bigger than our whole upstairs."

"Well," Katie said. "I'm glad."

"The sheets smell funny, though," she said. "Not like at home."

There was a brief silence.

"Mom, it's just a few days. I feel okay here. I do."

A pause.

"Mom, are you there? Mom, I'm sorry."

Chapter Thirteen

It's in here. It's in the bed with me. I see it.

Hair and teeth against her ankles, something gnashing, something furred and champing. The rasping of hooves and nails.

One of those night terrors she hadn't had since she was six years old, sleeping on that pullout sofa with her mom.

It's here, it's here. Help me, please, someone.

Her mother always laughing at the *someone*, saying, *How come you never ask for help from me?*

Devon used to have them too, back in kindergarten. Clutching her sherbet-striped comforter, distraught, inconsolable.

Katie had nearly forgotten what they felt like until—

I see it in the bed!

—sheets torn away, her palms white and spread on the bare mattress.

"Katie! Katie! Wake up."

It was Eric, leaning in the darkened doorway, beer bottle in hand, looking at her.

"Wake up."

*   *   *

In the violet dark of two a.m., he remade the bed for her, yank-ing the sheets back across the rumpled mattress pad.

"I can't sleep," he said. Then he went downstairs again.

You were mysterious to him and he was mysterious to you.

She could hear him walking, floors creaking, the refrigerator opening and closing.

The chime from his laptop.

The hiss of his phone.

She swore she could hear everything.

Devon had been gone less than two days, and the house felt haunted, the decaying manse of a family quarantined by fever.

Without car duty, practices, there was suddenly so much time, and Katie ended up spending far too long with Drew's sickbed meals, fashioning a banana to look like a person with raisin eyes. Cutting his sandwich into angel wings.

You really only learn your place, her mother once said, *when you're left in it.*

She had talked to Devon on the phone four times, each time a minute or less, Devon off to special air floors and ballet barres and the thirty-foot inflatable tumbling strip in Gwen's home gym.

Katie hadn't talked to Eric at all.

"Are you going to be mad at me forever?" Eric asked, com-ing up behind her as she dressed in the morning. He put his hands on her hips and ducked his head down against the top of her hair, and she felt an unexpected shiver.

"I'm sorry," he said. "I'm sorry." But then he added, leaving for work, "Katie, it's the right thing. I swear."

Something was wrong, wronger than it even seemed. She just wasn't sure what it was.

"I'm better, Mom," Drew said, seven a.m., leaning over his terrarium, peering in the resin cave the salamander liked to hide in.

"Okay," she said, her hand on his forehead, no longer the little radiator of days before. "But better isn't well."

"Remember when we watched that show about cavefish?" he asked, tapping on the resin with one red finger.

"I think so."

"They have scars where their eyes should be."

"Right. Because of evolution. It's always dark. They don't need to see."

"Mrs. Teazer said it's not true," Drew said, lifting his hand from the terrarium, a slurpy snail curled on his wrist. "They did this experiment where they mated the fish with other fish from different caves and then the baby fish could see. Their eyes were bigger and they could see everything."

"Is that so?" she said. Sometimes she wondered how she'd gotten such a smart kid. And just how smart he might be.

"Mom, it was the cave's fault. Not the fish." His voice shook slightly and she knew he must still be sick, emotional. "The cave made them that way."

"But it still doesn't matter. They don't need to see down there, baby," she said, touching his forehead again. "There's nothing to see."

"It must have been weird the first time they saw their parents," he said, peering closely at the snail on his wrist, his eyes glassed. "But their parents still couldn't see them."

"I think you still have a fever."

"Mom, what was Dad doing in the backyard?" he asked, coaxing the snail up his speckled forearm.

She looked at him.

"Dad? He just left for work."

"No, in the nighttime. Last night. Before the newspaper came."

"What was he doing?"

He shrugged. "Talking on his phone. I saw the light on his cheek. He kept spinning around, talking. Who was he talking to?"

The hydraulic drill of the landline startled her.

"Katie? This is Helen Beck. Ryan's mom."

"Oh, Helen. Yes. Are you okay?"

"I'm so sorry. I heard about what happened. Between Hailey Belfour and your daughter."

"Yes," Katie said. "Thank you. Devon's okay."

"I'm at Ryan's apartment. Taking care of things." She let out a weighty sigh. "You should see how many T-shirts he has. They all smell like him."

And then she said, "Katie, I think you should come here."

"Pardon?"

"Well, it's...I think you should come over. If you can. Do you think you can do that? It's easier in person."

There was a pause, Katie looking at Drew, who was drinking a tall glass of flat ginger ale with a leisurely grace.

"Oh, I remember this one." Helen's voice came soft. "The gray ringer. He used to wear this back in high school whenever he played baseball."

*   *   *

"That's three forty-six, Mom," Drew croaked from the backseat, Post-it in his damp hand. "Is this where Ryan lived?"

She stopped at the box-shaped low-rise buildings on the right, just past the Quik Mart. Concrete walls, two sets of balconies, a banner across the facade: AFFORDABLE RENTALS CALL TODAY!

"Yes."

She'd gotten in the car within ten minutes of Helen's call, had not stopped to think. Or even to ponder the wisdom of taking Drew outside.

Helen met them at the door, the buzzer broken.

"He was working really hard, saving up," Helen said as they walked inside, the hallway's linoleum cluttered with circulars, tented takeout menus, a waterlogged stack of aging Yellow Pages. "He would've been out of here soon."

"It looks fine," Katie said.

"Hey, devil boy," Helen said, winking down at Drew. She looked over at Katie. "Ryan used to get funny rashes like that all the time when he was little. They always told me it was my detergent, no matter which one I used. They never believed me."

They climbed the staircase, Drew's eyes jumping, his first time in an apartment building.

"This is where Ryan lived?" Drew asked. Inside, it looked like anyone's apartment, any young person living paycheck to paycheck. Small and sunstruck, everything in it beige and worn, with the same foam sofas, the microfiber shiny with age, the halogen torchiere, the set of acrylic bar stools along the kitchen counter that were in all furnished rentals, everywhere.

But there were little things that made it personal, a gently broken-in baseball cap on the glass-topped coffee table, a

Weaver's Wagon apron hooked forlornly on a molded plastic coat stand. A windbreaker, faded red, hanging over the back of the sofa. Katie had seen Ryan wear it a half dozen times. She didn't see his jean jacket. She guessed why.

"Their eyes have two thousand lenses," Drew said, pointing toward a half-eaten blondie, its plastic wrap folded back, resting on the kitchen counter. "They can see everything."

"What, devil boy?" Helen asked, winking at Katie.

They all watched as a cockroach scuttled across the counter and down the sink drain.

"We only have one lens," he said, a little wistfully.

"Oh dear," Helen said, walking over and squinting down the drain. "I saw a critter yesterday too. Well."

There was a brief pause, then Katie couldn't wait any longer.

"So, you wanted to talk?"

"In the bedroom." Helen looked over at Drew. "Maybe we can put the TV on for Big Red."

Later, many times, Katie would remember the room's particular smell, sweat and must and forest pine from the Little Tree air freshener hanging from the blinds' cord. And something else, something intimate, bodily.

She looked down at the deep blue sheets coiled on the mattress, which sat on the floor exotically, summoning up bohemian memories of youth, a youth like Katie dreamed up as a girl, beaded-curtain doorways and those Technicolor saint candles in glass jars.

There was no furniture other than that mattress and a table lamp on the floor, an open book beside it, its red cover bent back. She wondered if it was the novel he'd always kept in his back pocket. She found herself wanting to touch it.

She hadn't known him at all, really, but that made it sadder somehow.

"He'd had his trouble," Helen was saying, "but he was figuring things out. He finally had a steady job. Still couldn't afford cable or a cell phone. You try to help, but they don't want their moms' help, do they? He had his own journey."

"This must be so hard."

Helen skittered her fingers along the window blinds, peeking through the dust-laced slats. "There's a lot I'm trying to figure out now. Like that girl of his."

Katie looked over at her.

"He always had a weakness for girls like that," Helen continued. "Handfuls. I'd only met her twice, but I don't think Ryan was too serious about her."

Katie hesitated, then finally said, "They were pretty serious. I heard he'd bought her an engagement ring."

Helen's head jerked up. Then after a pause she sank down to the mattress, laughing a little, a kind of laughing.

"Isn't it a strange day," she said, "when you realize you have no idea what's going on in your kid's head? One morning, you wake up and there's this alien in your house. They look like your kid, sound a little like them, but they are *not* your kid. They're something else that you don't know. And they keep changing. They never stop changing on you."

Katie almost said something but stopped herself. She didn't want to be one of those smug parents, like Gwen, like Molly, who claimed to read their daughters' expressions with one hundred percent accuracy. But she could: the particular twist of Devon's mouth that meant frustration. The shake of her elbow that meant her wrist was throbbing. The twitch over her left eye that meant she was afraid.

"I can't imagine what you're going through," Katie said instead, touching the window blinds, warm in the sun. "Losing your—"

"You keep losing them nonstop, don't you?" Helen said. "Where'd you get that idea, anyway? About the ring?"

"Someone saw him at Ahee Jewelers the week before."

Helen shook her head. "Ah, well, Katie, I don't see him buying any ring. He couldn't pay his water bill. He didn't even have a credit card."

"Oh," Katie said, not sure what else to say, and not sure why she was here. She peeped through the bedroom door, checking on Drew, his tiny head behind the sofa back, those little ears red as Swedish fish.

Behind her, Helen was sliding open the closet door, a waft of fabric softener and old smoke. Bending down, she lifted something off the floor.

"Here," she said, handing it to Katie. "Here's why I asked you to come."

It was a vinyl gym sack Katie recognized dimly, one of those tournament giveaways a few months back. Gingerly, she slid its pull string. The room dark, the navy bag dark, she couldn't see anything except a flash of red.

Her hand inside, the familiar feel of Lycra.

A leotard. A competition one.

Red and black, with a swirl scoop neck. A spray of crystals up one shoulder. They'd paid extra for the crystals. Eric said it would be worth it. The light would pick up the sparkle.

Katie hadn't seen it since the charity invitational in Inverness six weeks ago. They'd played "Eye of the Tiger" when she came out on the floor to take her medal.

She looked inside the neck hole, and there it was: D. KNOX, the same iron-on label she used with all Devon's travel leotards.

She held it for a second, something sick in her stomach.

Helen's fingers appeared on its edges, lifting it so the light caught it.

And Katie could see the slight tear in the seam at the crotch and then, turning it, a pale, scaly stain on the back. Her stomach turned hotly, hand slapping over her mouth.

"What did he do—" Her voice thundered from her, surprising her.

"No," Helen said loudly to match Katie's sudden loudness. "That's not what this is."

"I know what I'm seeing," said Katie, trying to control herself but her voice whirling and whirring.

"You know Ryan."

"I don't. I don't know him." The words came out in sharp sputters. "Except I know that he's been arrested. He had drug problems. He had a violent girlfriend. That's what I know. And now I know he did something to my daughter."

Helen reached out and touched her arm lightly.

"Listen, listen," she said, "no one likes to imagine their daughter's been—"

"Stop it!" Katie said, or heard herself say, her face crowding with heat. "Stop it. I know my daughter."

"And I know Ryan," Helen said, grabbing the leotard from Katie's hands and turning it so Katie could see the inside.

The words written in silver Sharpie: *I ♥♥ U SO MUCH!!*

She knew the handwriting. Unmistakable. And the same silver Sharpie Devon used on her notebooks, in her diary.

"My son's had some problems in his life," Helen was saying.

"With substances. With direction. But he would never hurt a woman—"

"Devon's not a woman," Katie said, a coldness lifting up through her body. "She's a child. She's never even had a date. This is crazy."

Helen leaned against the wall, watching the leotard dangling from Katie's fingers.

"You have to decide what you want to think. What you want to know. That's on you. But I don't think Ryan would have kept that if she hadn't meant something to him." She paused. "Everything meant a lot to him."

"Have the police seen this?" Katie asked, her mind clicking, ratcheting up speed.

"I wanted to talk to you first," Helen said. "Do you think Hailey found out about the two of them?"

"No," Katie said, quickly. "No. Helen, you can't tell the police about this."

"Why not?"

She couldn't even think through all the reasons, or which ones mattered most.

"Because," Katie said, her voice breaking humiliatingly. "Think how Ryan would feel. Think about that. Everyone would find out. And everyone would know your son is a statutory rapist. Worse."

Helen lifted a hand so fast that, for a crazy second, Katie thought she might hit her.

But instead, she covered her mouth with it, shaking her head.

"I'm sorry," Katie said. "I'm just . . ." She looked down at the scant leotard, like a doll's costume in her hand. None of it was possible.

"You're worried about your girl," Helen said with a new

coldness. "People thinking things about your baby girl. Getting her caught up in this."

"I'm just asking for time. Mom to mom."

Helen nodded wearily, the back of her hand on her forehead. "No promises. But for now, okay."

"Mom," she could hear Drew say from the other room. "Hey, Mom."

"I'm coming," she said, moving past Helen, the leotard clutched to her chest. The smells of the room, the way Helen's eyes looked, she had to leave.

"None of you even cared about Ryan," Helen said. "You just let him work for you, do things for you."

"That's not true," Katie said, embarrassed to feel heat rising to her eyes.

"None of us know our kids," Helen said, reaching for the leotard in Katie's hand. "Haven't you figured that out yet? You're no different than the rest of us."

You're wrong, something inside her said. *About that, you couldn't be more wrong.*

And Katie held on to the leotard. She held on so hard her nails left ugly furrows in her own skin that would last for hours. And the look on her face must have been something, because Helen let go. She let go.

"C'mon," Katie said, seeing Drew in Ryan's kitchen, standing in front of the refrigerator. "Now."

"But look." He was pointing to a photo taped on the fridge door. A blur of greenery, stippling moss, the muddy colors of a bad computer printer.

"No time for nature, okay, kiddo?"

"Okay."

*   *   *

Standing at the dining-room table, the lulling *zip-zap* from Drew's cartoons in the other room, she punched at her phone. First, she called Eric. Then Devon. Then Eric again. No one was answering anywhere and she had no idea what words would come if someone did answer.

For a very brief moment, she tried to sit still.

Devon's room was hot, always hot. All that energy, it stayed there.

Katie hovered in the doorway a long minute, taking in all the symmetry and order. The organization so precise it felt mysterious. To Katie, her life always brim-high with chaos and distraction, Devon's order was a mystery. And, for the first time, it felt suspect.

Will it still be there? she wondered. In the same cramped spot she'd found it the first time, two years ago, and again in February, the day after Devon got her first period.

On all fours on the bed, she reached down into the wood-swollen crevice between bookshelf and mattress in the upper left corner.

Feeling for the diary, fat and weighty. Its felt fabric cover. I HEART EVERYTHING.

But her hand hit only cardboard. A box, and another. She lifted them out. Four of them. Four cardboard boxes of tampons, one for every month. Katie had bought them all for her. And now they were wedged between her mattress and the wall, un-opened except the first box, all its tampons lined up like soldiers save one empty spot for the tampon she'd handed her daughter.

Katie felt herself grow dizzy, collapsing slightly on the bed.

But what about the diary entry she'd read? She tried to re-member it; something about becoming a woman and that it hadn't hurt and—had she said it had been beautiful?

Pieces hurtling into place, it now seemed so clear: Devon hadn't been writing about her first period. She'd never even had her period. She was writing about Ryan. Her first time with Ryan, scarlet marking the spot on the leotard Katie found in the wash.

No one ever tells you there'll be so much blood, Devon had said to Katie as they lay together on Katie's bed. Her daughter deceiving her, lies upon lies.

I made it happen, she'd said. *And now it's forever.*

And, too, *Don't tell Dad. Mom, don't tell Dad.*

Katie tripped down the hall to the bathroom. Leaning over the toilet, sure she'd be sick, she waited. Then stood again.

Staring into the vanity mirror, her hand over her mouth.

Chapter Fourteen

Face fretted from sun and years and fishing and puttering in his widower's yard, he was the only neighbor still there since they first moved in. He'd been there for Devon's accident, for Devon's earliest backyard tumbling efforts (*That trampoline sure looks fun*, he'd said, watching Eric install it, *but you might want to put some shock absorbers over those springs*), for the time the *Gazette* came to take pictures of Devon swinging from the walnut tree's branch.

"Mr. Watts," she asked, glancing at her watch, "can you keep an eye on Drew for a little while?"

He straightened, looking at Drew.

"I swear, he stopped being contagious two days ago."

"Had scarlatina when I was a kid, back in the fifties," he said. "Out of school for a month. Read all the Hardy Boys stories. My favorite was *The Melted Coins*. A crazy sailor tries to tattoo Joe. That seemed much worse than hives."

What is it I plan to do? she asked herself over and over on the forty-five-minute drive.

Where do I even begin?

She wondered what Hailey knew. Had she found out about Ryan and Devon and then, with that same spike-rattling jealousy that had sent her to Devon's muscled throat, done something appalling?

An old country road, her purple bug of a car, a luscious grape, darting from the darkness and straight into her cheating lover.

A red swarm of tracksuits were gathering at the gym's double doors, a few girls peering in the windows, the rest squirming and bouncing.

Seeing them all in the brightness of the afternoon, out there in the wild, free from the carapace of glass and insulation and mats and padding and foam, Katie was struck. Everything looked vivid and strange.

They were massing, half of them as brawny as footballers, their necks and waists thickened by muscle, the other half as delicate as sylphs, girls who seemed to consume only air, chalk dust. Chestless chests and the round behinds, the few with breasts seemed to treat them as vestigial burdens, their arms folded across them, their zippers pulled high above them.

It was as if Katie were wearing glasses for the first time in her life, the world suddenly brought into sharp focus.

The eleven- and twelve-year-olds bundled at the windows. Jaws locked, veins roped across temples, corded up the neck, they reminded her of baby birds, their heads tilted back, gullets unhinged, open, cries shrill and hungry for anything.

Then there were the older ones, fifteen, sixteen, seventeen. They were looking at their phones, or their moms, these hard-

ened vets, biceps fist-thick, straight lines down to thighs powerful enough to anchor the world. None of them topping five feet
three.

See what it does to them. A comment Katie overheard once, a
parent at Devon's school, watching Devon walk across the parking lot.

Check out Popeye, Katie had heard a man say at the mall,
winking at his friend. *Too bad those are pecs not tits.*

Devon, whose toes pointed out as she slept.

Whose ankles cracked as she walked up the stairs.

Who, before she performed, would, one by one, crack all her
joints, fingers, knuckles, neck, toes, hips, and ankles. Pulling her
thumbs so far back they rested on her wrists, like tongues.

Once, she had to take Devon for an EKG and the nurse kept
telling her, *Relax all your muscles,* and Devon kept saying, *I am, I
am.* She'd looked down at Devon's pointed toes, hard as screws.
Like a ballerina, like a Chinese princess.

Now, before the bolted BelStars entrance, here was five-year-
old Ashlee Hargrove, cracking her spine into a back bend, her
tiny body like a table, shoulders pushed out over hands.

It came to Katie, that feeling. One she had known before, but
it was so much stronger now. A nagging sense of some irrevoca-
ble wrong.

What have we done to them?

What have I done?

Always there, like a flicker in the corner of her eye, she'd
learned to ignore it. But now it was, quite suddenly, right in
front of her. It was everywhere.

She shut her eyes.

*   *   *

"Katie! Katie, where's Eric? Does he know about this?" Becca Plonski said, her hands pressing down on little Dominique's shoulders. "Can you call Eric?"

Everyone was assembled around the handwritten sign on the door.

GYM CLOSED TODAY—NO PRACTICE UNTIL FURTHER NOTICE— THE MGT

"What do we do?" Cheyenne Chu asked. Her elfin fingers touched the sign as if it might give her a deeper knowledge. "What do we do?"

"He might have given us some warning," Kirsten Siefert said, chewing gum forcefully. "I cut a conference call short to get Jordan here."

"Unacceptable," whispered Becca, just under her breath. "This is completely unacceptable."

"Even if Teddy can't be here," Kirsten said, more loudly, "does that mean the gym can't run? We paid for that staff. We pay for those lights to be on."

Katie didn't say anything, scanning the crowd for Devon.

Devon, whom she hadn't seen in three days.

She felt a hand on her arm. Turning around, she saw the strained face of Molly Chu.

"I didn't think I'd see you here," she said. "So where's she getting her private lessons?"

Katie stared at her a moment. "What do you mean?"

"Come on. No one believes the scarlet fever thing and Hailey's locked up, so why else would Devon keep missing practice?" Then, moving closer to Katie, lowering her voice. "But, listen, don't be greedy. Just give me the coach's name. I don't want Cheyenne to lose the month before qualifiers either."

"Wait," Katie said, "are you saying Devon hasn't been at practice?"

Molly scratched her brow nervously, just like Cheyenne on the beam, her torso shaking. Which was why Cheyenne would never go Elite.

Molly wouldn't say another word until they were nearly to Katie's car, Cheyenne gazing after them forlornly, shivering in her nylon shorts by the gym's doorway.

"She hasn't been to practice for the last three days," Molly whispered, even though they were yards away from anyone.

"Oh."

"Neither has Lacey, by the way. People were guessing Gwen hired a private coach for her. Do you think so? What does Eric say?"

"She's been staying with Gwen," Katie said. "Devon has."

Molly's face stiffened and she paused, as if calculating something.

"I'm sure it's a misunderstanding."

"I don't think so," Katie said, quick and pointed.

"Well, it's not like Gwen kidnapped her."

"Molly, you're telling me you haven't heard anything at all? You talk to Gwen twelve times a day. All of you do."

"All of who?" Molly said, tilting her head.

"The booster klatch."

Molly looked at her, blinking. "I've told you what I know," she said, her voice newly clipped. "And aren't you part of the so-called booster klatch? Don't we all want the same thing? No practice, not even open gym, this close to qualifiers is inexcusable."

"I don't care about that right now," Katie said, her own voice sounding so insistent, grinding up her throat. "I care about my daughter. I'm trying to find out why my daughter's not here."

But something in Molly's face had changed. A veil, a mask dropped over it.

"We all know Devon's the big gold dream," she said coolly. "But there are other gymnasts here too. Other girls count too."

Katie recognized the tone. From school events—the college fair, the Mother's Day fashion show. The other parents, their under-the-breath comments, the looks they exchanged if Katie or Eric asked a question—it only demonstrated how distinct and special Devon was. Long ago, she'd learned, Eric had shown her; you had to own it.

"Well," Katie said, finally. Jaw set. Voice steady. "Only one counts to me."

The man in the GOD'S LITTLE ACRE polo shirt and cap pushed the neon-yellow machine across the lawn, punching holes in the spongy grass.

He was whistling as she walked swiftly past him, up the long curving drive studded with sacks of peat moss. *Punch-punch-punch.*

Standing at the knotty-pine door, she clapped the dragonfly knocker, which didn't seem to make any sound.

She clapped it again. *Punch-punch.*

"Don't think anyone's home," the lawn man called out, turning off the aerator.

The whirring stopped, the quiet swallowing everything.

Somewhere a cicada thrummed.

She thought she saw something move through a sliver of

blurred glass at the top of the door. A flash on the front staircase, a ghost.

From inside, she heard the beeping sound of an alarm system and the click of a bolt.

Turning the brass knob, Katie pushed the door open.

There, halfway up the spiral staircase, was little Lacey, legs matching its narrow white balusters, blending with them, as if all turned on a lathe by a master woodworker. Her hand clamped over one of the finials.

"Hi, Mrs. Knox."

One socked foot lifted and rested on the step behind her, as if she were backing away.

"Where's Devon?" Katie asked. "Sorry." She took a breath. "But where's Devon?"

Lacey's hand loosened slightly on the finial, the shape of a cannonball.

"They're gone," she said. "It's just me."

Striding past the caramel stone walls, the flagstone floors, the vaulted ceilings of the grand house, they didn't speak.

Lacey, like some sly elf from a fairy tale, silently ushered her through a doorway with the sign LACEY'S LAIR hanging over the frame.

The room smelled strongly of lavender and sweet pea.

On one wall the words *Sweet Dreams!* were painted in sprawling silver cursive, the exclamation point like a crisp command.

On the opposite wall, behind the satin headboard, hung a yard-high black silhouette of Lacey, that tilted nose and bulbous forehead.

A series of gymnast decals leaped and bounded and somersaulted over the vanity mirror. Beneath, a small banner read, in glittery ink, CONCUR YOUR FEARS. No exclamation point.

With a slightly weary wave of the hand, Lacey gestured to a button-tufted settee on which Katie was invited to sit.

"Lacey," Katie said, "you need to tell me. Where's your mom? Where's Devon?"

But Lacey just stood in front of her mirrored vanity, lustered Deco-style, like a Shirley Temple movie, and began brushing her ponytail with great care and tenderness.

Watching her in the beveled mirror, Katie was suddenly struck by what an unaccountably exquisite child Lacey was. So much time watching these girls, you looked at their bodies constantly but so rarely their faces. That white-blond hair, eyebrows that arched like a doll's painted ones, a chin that came to a sharp point, and a gap between her two front teeth that made her look vaguely amorous, even though she was only eleven and had probably never even looked at a boy.

"Honey," she tried again, "where's Devon? You need to tell me, okay?"

The girl looked at her in the mirror, slowly setting down her hairbrush, frilled with her pale strands.

"They're not here. Grandma's coming soon," she said. "Riley left early. That's why I'm by myself. But it doesn't matter to me."

"Riley's your babysitter?"

"I don't need a babysitter," she said, pulling her socks off gently. "Riley's giving me privates."

Katie looked at her.

"Beam and vault," Lacey added, eyes lifting.

Ah, Katie thought, realizing. "How long have you been getting private lessons?"

Lacey swirled her finger across the back of the hairbrush and said nothing.

"And Devon?"

Lacey's fingers danced over to the vanity's glass knobs, one hand on each side of the vanity. Twisting them.

"Lacey, did your mom and Devon go on a trip today?"

Lacey looked down at her bare, gnarled feet and lifted them, tiptoeing.

The gesture was so Devon-like that Katie felt a rush of pity.

"Lacey," she said, leaning forward on the settee. "I'm sorry they left you by yourself. It isn't very nice. Do you—"

"They left you too," Lacey said, "didn't they?"

She turned slowly to face Katie.

"They're at EmPower, which is far away. Mom takes Devon there for her privates. Mr. Ehlers thinks he can turn things around for her. It's Coach T.'s fault Devon didn't make Junior Elite. Coach T. can't even control his own family. That's what they said. I heard them."

Katie shifted, her fingernails snagging on the tufted cushion. "Heard who?"

"Mom and Devon and Mr. Knox. They were all talking on the terrace this morning." She pointed to her window. "You can hear everything people say out there. That's where my mom goes to yell on the phone."

"Mr. Knox?" The smell in the room, the lavender, the feeling of the cushion beneath her tearing. "Lacey, has he been here before? Since Devon came?"

"No," she said, lifting her brush again. "But he was here this morning. And then Mom went inside and left Devon and him alone. He was crying."

"What? What did you say?"

"I didn't hear him, but Devon kept saying, *Dad, Dad, Dad, don't cry.*"

Katie felt her fingernail gouge into the tuft and rip loose. The only time she'd ever seen Eric cry was the accident. Devon's accident.

Lacey's head lifted. She looked at Katie in the mirror.

"My dad used to cry," she said. "When he came to pick me up on weekends. My mom made him stay in his car until he pulled himself together. Do you cry?"

Katie clenched her hand, tucking her wounded finger in the center.

"Everybody cries, Lacey."

Lacey looked at her dubiously.

"I wondered if it was just dads," she said. "Mr. Knox, he kept saying he was sorry."

Katie felt something small and delicate unhook inside her.

"Sorry about what?"

Lacey shrugged, looking at Katie in the mirror.

Sorry about what, what, what—

"Blood," Lacey said, turning.

"What?"

And they both looked down at the settee, its lilac satin daubed red.

Lifting her hand, staring at her shorn nail, its red tip, Katie found herself almost laughing.

Lacey walked her to the front door, her elfin feet now in flip-flops that gently slapped the stone floors, the sound echoing into the distant rafters like wings.

"Is Hailey in a mental hospital?" she asked.

"Not exactly," Katie said. "Lacey, what if you called your mom for me?"

"Why don't you call her?"

"I have. She isn't answering. Maybe if you called..."

Lacey looked at her, her fingers dancing up to the security panel on the wall.

"I texted her," she said, "when you got here. So she already knows."

Katie wondered if, behind her aura of mute surrender, the stupor of her eyes, like a drugged pixie, Lacey knew more about her mother, and everything, than anyone guessed.

"She just leaves you alone with Riley? Does she know him well?" Katie blurted, not sure where it came from or why she was saying it.

"Riley's a girl," Lacey said. "I already have a boyfriend."

"You do?"

"We met at the county invitational. He works concessions. He has long sideburns and the keys to all the rooms at Lightning City."

Those pointy brows like butterfly antennae, and the stoned lips, numb and pink-jutted.

"Lacey, when you say *boyfriend*, what does he—"

"He has a big key ring and he said he'll take me on a tour, but not till I'm in high school."

Katie squinted, trying to be sure she was understanding.

"Don't tell my mom, okay?" Lacey was saying, her head tilted against the front door. "About my boyfriend."

A crush of questions pushed into Katie's brain, all for this candy sticklette of a girl.

But before Katie could ask them, the front door had opened, the beeps of the security system announcing Katie's departure.

"Mom says if a man ever touches me," Lacey said, "she'll definitely kill him."

The door shutting behind her, the smell of sweet pea dancing behind her, and then gone.

Katie sat in her car for a long time.

There were two missed calls from Eric—prompted by Gwen, she was sure.

"I know what you did," she said to his voice mail. "How could you? You'd better be driving home with my daughter right now. I know everything."

And she wasn't even sure what she meant by *everything*. It felt like the biggest word in the world. It felt like a black hole.

Pulling up the drive, she saw the garage door was open, gaping before her, a big ragged mouth.

Inside, Mr. Watts stood with Drew in the back corner, next to a snare of rakes and brooms, the rust-furred reel lawn mower, the only one they'd owned since Devon's accident. Long ago, Eric had taken a sledgehammer to the old one, sending sparks across the lawn, a figure eight of singed grass. Even this one—its blades looked so sharp.

"Mom, we were looking for the shovel," Drew said as she got out of the car and walked toward them. "In the book, they dig up a buried treasure."

"Hardy Boys," Mr. Watts said, gesturing toward the worn volume Drew had set on the garage floor. "*Melted Coins*. He can keep it."

"And look what we found." Drew held out his hand. "On the ground."

She looked in his outstretched palm, cherried and tender. In the center sat a trio of silver wafers, one as large as a dime, the other two almost too small to see.

Katie cupped Drew's hand in her own, eyes still on the silver, like the paint in a model-plane kit.

"He thought they were silverfish," Mr. Watts said.

"Not once I got closer," Drew insisted, looking down at the concrete floor, as if expecting to see more. "There was no antenna or anything."

"Paint chips," Mr. Watts said. "Must have come off your car."

"Dad's car," Drew said. "Mom's is blue."

She could feel Mr. Watts looking at her. Drew waiting for her.

But her brain stuttered, stalled.

"Anyway," Mr. Watts said, clearing his throat, "we had an adventure."

Her phone, like a preying animal, one eye lifted, blinked with texts from Eric: Please, I can explain.

Get home now, she typed.

It was the sole corner in the house without booster flyers and spreadsheets, without gym grips and tape and everything coated in chalk.

"I hope I get to go outside soon," Drew said, his cheek pressed against his window screen. "Not just the garage."

"You will, honey. Open the window."

"Look," he said, pointing to the black walnut tree outside.

She was grateful for any distraction.

"The catkins," she said. "You used to say they looked like demon fingers."

They'd chosen the house in part because of the dark canopy of the walnut tree. When they first came to see it nearly fifteen years ago, Katie asked the man rolling a sod cutter next door—

their future neighbor Mr. Watts—what all the long green frills drooping from the branches were. They looked like flower leis.

Happens every spring, Mr. Watts had said. *You like them now, but just you wait.*

Later, she'd realized what he meant, the way the catkins fell in soft heaps to the ground and turned brown and black. *Banana-peel clumps,* Devon called them.

It turned out there was a chemical in the tree's roots that stunted or poisoned everything around it. The petunias Katie once planted there shriveled to pale ribbons.

But Katie still loved the way they carpeted the lawn, had loved running and swinging little Devon's feet through their velvet tendrils, the pollen staining their ankles. And Drew loved them too. Every fall, he'd take pictures of the silky webworm nests that hung from the branch ends. He said they looked like his favorite teacher's hair.

Those catkins, they're wonderful, Eric used to tease her. *Wonderful tarantulas.*

And then he'd mention how they used the wood to make gunstocks, and coffins.

That's what Old Man Watts told me, he said. *Makes me wonder what happened to Mrs. Watts.*

"Mom," Drew said now, pointing out the window. "Mrs. Teazer says those are bagworms."

Rising, Katie followed his gaze to the odd, lumpy sacks dotting the branches.

"Zachary brought one into class," Drew said. "The boy worms leave the bag when they want to mate. The girls never leave at all. They don't have wings or legs or mouthparts. The girls die in there."

"Always harder on the girls, huh?"

"But just one female can make a thousand babies."

"That's some mom," she said, chin on the top of his head, peering out. "Supermom."

"They eat the whole tree."

"That's not good." She tried to smile, but the bags looked ominous, alive. Almost like something was kicking inside. "Not good at all."

Drew looked at her, nodding.

"Mom?"

"Yes, Drew." The bags were rocking, the wind kicking up. She imagined she could see the eggs inside, white as slugs.

"You have to kill her."

And Katie found herself nodding too.

You had to stop them, just like the tent caterpillars in the crab-apple tree at one of the apartment buildings she'd lived in as a kid. The landlord had burned them with kerosene.

"Mom," Drew was saying.

Rushing down the hall, she thought she heard a phone ringing somewhere. She was trying to think if they had any lighter fluid.

Then she remembered something. Grabbing for her purse in the hallway, she pulled something from it.

"Stay inside," she shouted to Drew from the bottom of the stairs.

"Mom," he said, leaning over the railing, "you look funny."

It felt good in her hands, like a sword.

She hoisted the tiki torch from the sand bucket on the patio. The heat-splintered one she'd brought home from the tiki party a few months ago.

There was a feeling inside her that was tangled and wretched, and she peered up to Drew's window while she poured the glugging fuel from the can in the garage.

Dirty sacs strung along the branches like miniature party lanterns, just inches from her son's window, her stricken son— they were everywhere and she couldn't fathom how she hadn't seen them before.

One mass, nestled in the crotch of the tree, was so large it resembled a small animal spread-eagled under gauze, limbs splayed against branches, a horror show. Others hung in the joints like Christmas balls tinseled brown.

All this time—how long?—they'd been here in her backyard, her patio, where all the boosters had perched just a few days ago.

Once she saw one, she saw a hundred, and her chest felt full and large.

Waving the torch, the smell heavy and sweet, she swooped its embered end across the woolly pouches. A husk skittered from the branch, sparking hot into her hair before she jumped away, cinders scattering.

Looking up, she could see Drew's face in his bedroom window, eyes wide as the flaming pods dropped and as one of the branches caught fire.

"Stay inside!" she shouted. "Don't you move, honey. It's not safe out here!"

The torch in her hands, saber or bayonet, she kept going until she'd vanquished them all.

It was only then, standing behind the tree so Drew couldn't possibly see, that she tossed the item looped around her arm into the fire.

That red and black leotard snatched from her purse, its spray of crystals popping like small firecrackers, the Lycra collapsing slowly into soft, black gum.

Looking up again, she caught sight of the tree itself, an enormous enflamed torch. The wind kicked up higher, and her panic was a feeling more expected than experienced. There wasn't time, the flames striping up the dark bark.

"The tree's on fire," someone said.

In the same second, she heard a squeaking sound, then the splash of cool striking her arm, skating up the tree, sizzling a moment, then trampling the flames.

Mr. Watts, turning the wheel on his garden hose.

The smell was strong, and they both held their shirts up over nose and mouth.

Looking up, Mr. Watts waved at Drew, who was still watching closely from his window, his red face abraded by the screen.

The ground littered with blackening pouches, all hissing and popping, Katie began raking the tiki torch around, encircling them.

"Next time, give a holler," he said to Katie. "We can snip 'em down first. That way you don't lose the whole tree. Don't take any houses with you either."

"No," she said, shaking her head. She was not herself, heat glazing her, making her feel invincible. "How could you ever be sure you got them all?"

He nodded, catching one last ember with a stray sluice of water left in the hose.

"When they cool down," Mr. Watts said, "I'll take them off your hands."

She looked at him quizzically.

"Fish bait," he said, winking at her. "The cycle of life."

Together, they watched all of them burn, like singed cotton candy.

Later, Katie would sneak back into the yard, knees to dirt, palms on ground, until she found the last bits of gummy Lycra, a few crystals seared into the flattened grass.

Chapter Fifteen

It was nearly ten o'clock, and she'd let Drew stay up so long, his eyes stung to tears from too much TV, and his words were beginning to break apart and float away.

He kept finding shows that seemed to come from some special planet of Drew, creepy reruns of *In Search Of* ..., a documentary about hairless, blue-eyed, and hunchbacked creatures killing livestock in Texas, another about the mysterious red rain of Sri Lanka. They all interested him and made him wonder about things, his speckled face and the softness of his boy tummy as he stretched across the cushions.

She could sit there and watch him, and not think of anything else. Not think about leotards or pixie nymphets or dark-eyed men and the lies they tell you or the silver paint in the garage, which shimmered every time she shut her eyes and which meant nothing, couldn't mean anything. Instead, listening, her entire body flooded with love for Drew, his voice creaking forth question after question, each one a balm to her.

"Mom," he said, his Hardy Boys book open on his lap, "it

says here Blackbeard used to stick matches in his beard to light up his evil eyes."

"That sounds scary," she said. "That sounds like a scary book."

Eventually, he started drifting off, curled like a glowworm in his neon-green pajamas on the sofa beside her, and she half coaxed, half carried him to bed.

Looking into those nearly lidded eyes, the gleam of his pupil trying to stay awake, to not miss *anything*, she found herself locked in something deep with him.

Like he held something she needed.

Don't fall asleep, Drew. Please.

She caught herself thinking it, maybe saying it out loud, her fingers to her own lips.

Embarrassed, she shook it off, rising from his bedside and nearly bounding to the bedroom door. Leaving him alone.

The eleven o'clock news was beginning, its familiar pulsing music.

Behind it, she heard the groan of the garage door. They almost always left it open, but she'd closed it so she would know when he returned. And so he would know she knew.

Then, the loud punch and scatter of glass breaking in the backyard.

The scrape of metal on concrete.

Hand smacking the screen door open, the thickening June air climbing into her mouth, Katie called out, "Who's there?"

He was slouched in the most ramshackle of their aluminum chairs, a half-hollowed pint of Jack Daniel's in his hand, a beer bottle broken at his feet, and the back of his neck ruddy from a day spent behind a car windshield, kidnapping her daughter and driving her across the state with another woman.

His face shimmered forth in the dark, tanner than the day before, the grand slope of eyes sorrowful. Handsome as ever, maybe more. So much so he took her breath away. And she felt sick from it.

"Eric."

"I'm gone a few hours and you set the backyard on fire?" he said, not looking at her, his feet kicking at the ashes.

"Where's Devon?" she demanded. "Where is she, Eric?"

When he turned, head bobbing slightly, she could see how drunk he was. Like she hadn't seen him in years. Like he'd sometimes been when Devon was a baby and he was still rollicking with coworkers at the end of his long days, his after-hours spent with elbows stuck to place mats at their local, a place called Huddles where the bartenders wore green vinyl aprons and drank while they poured, and Eric staying until last call, finally stumbling home at three a.m., shoes sticky and hair matted, and once, a dart caught in his finger, he'd driven home with blood soaking through the cuff of his work shirt and *sorry*s, *sorry*s, *sorry*s forever.

"Where's Devon?" she repeated, standing in front of him, the caramel smell of the whiskey thick upon her. "Where is she?"

"At Gwen's."

"Why is she still there? Goddamn it, Eric, you lied—"

"So you know," he said. "Your message. You know everything."

She looked at him, a breeze lifting the smell of the ash, the waving torch.

He looked at her, eyes white as an animal's in the woods.

They each waited, a marital standoff, the silence unbearable. But she blinked first.

"How could you go meet John Ehlers at his fancy EmPower gym with our daughter and not tell me?" Her voice bouncing around the weird dark of the yard. "You took our daughter. You and Gwen. You conspired with that monstrous woman."

There was a sudden energy in his face, and his shoulders jerked forward. "No, Katie," he said. "It wasn't like that. The boosters outvoted me. They wanted me to meet with him and I knew you wouldn't like it—"

A sound skidded up from inside her throat to stop him. "You're lying," she said. "I saw Molly. She didn't know about any of this. All you do is lie."

The weight, the bigness of the words excited her. They seldom fought, not really, so it was all here now, and she kept going, about how he had lied and lied again and *Is this about Gwen Weaver and if so what kind of man are you to let her tell you* and *What a thing to do, shanghaiing our daughter behind my back almost like a kidnapping*—and then the words had a powerful thunder to them and she said them again and again, *like a kidnapping, like a kidnapping.*

And as she was saying it, an equally powerful sinking feeling of what she couldn't say: *How could you two keep secrets from me? You and Devon.*

Thrusting that thought to the corner of her hot brain, she just kept going.

"And you lied about where you were and left your sick son and you lied about what you've been doing with our daughter and you left me here, all alone—"

"Katie, stop. Stop and listen. I needed to meet the guy. Ehlers. I needed to see Devon with him. I needed to see if it might work, if they connected. I needed to fix this. To make everything right again."

"Everything right? For fuck's sake, Eric," she said, a way of talking she barely remembered, hadn't used since she was a teenager in that teenager way of playing with words like flung rubber bands, "you're talking about qualifiers and gyms and coaches when all this is going on?"

He jumped up, the metal of the chair sparking, the bottle keeling between his sneakers, his arm diving down as it crashed. A light went on somewhere, a dog howled, a screen door banged shut.

"But this *is* what's going on, Katie. Not something that happened to a kid we barely know. This is about Devon. I can't believe I have to tell you that." He paused, and then he said it. "You never cared as much as we did. You were always ready to give up."

There it was. There it was. "How dare you," she said, her voice low and ugly. "How dare you, Eric. After everything. We've always been in this together—"

Turning from her, his chin tilted up in a way that felt strangely churchlike, a reminder of vows taken, he said, "I know. I'm sorry. I know."

And they both sat for a moment, the yard black, with the quality of witchy mystery it had had years ago, the first time a patch of browning green was all theirs, before patios, before the maze of all-weather tumbling mats, before the trampoline and the smaller trampoline before that. Before the lawn mower. When it was a place that was outside but private and wild but safe. Empty garden beds and rambling ivy and a dented air conditioner stained with black walnut husks, but it was beautiful, and theirs.

And she almost said it. She almost said, *Our daughter was sleeping with Ryan Beck.* But she couldn't make the words come.

* * *

Then they were both drinking, a half-pint of Black Velvet Eric dug out of the kitchen cupboard. He was roaming around the firefly-studded yard while she sat thinking bad thoughts, how you can be married to someone your whole life, it feels like, and not know them at all.

You never cared as much as we did.

"I did the right thing, Katie," he said. "I did what I had to because this is what matters," pointing to the yard, the house, Devon's bedroom window, lightless and lonely. "This is about our girl. Our girl. Helping her get everything she wants. Which is what we always said we'd do."

"That's not good enough, Eric," she said, rising from the squeaking lawn chair. "We're in this together. We promised way back when."

But now she was drunk, and her foot caught in the rust-pocked frame and she fell against him, and he caught her. And she held on to him so tightly, the smell of his shirt, her face pressed against it. Feeling the heave of his heart.

She was so drunk.

When he half carried her inside the house, they were both out of their minds, her foot banging against the door frame, cutting her ankle.

Her ankle was bleeding and felt warm and cold at the same time, and they nearly fell on the stairs, her back hitting the handrail and his foot slipping on the carpeted steps.

They were on the bed, barely.

It was fast, and they might not even have shut the door.

It was fast, and she could feel the blood from her ankle running down her leg, flung in the air.

His face pressed so hard against her, teeth clicking, heads knocking each other, the sound that came from him only sometimes, once in a great while, a pressure so overwhelming and a relief so immense that his body racked and fevered, and she felt herself in the center of something ugly and breathtaking.

Even as it was happening, she knew that in the morning she wouldn't remember what they had done and if it had been different than ever before. All she'd remember was that she felt a shiver, a cold hush all through. And later, an unbearable heat that shamed her.

Married a long time, you think there will never be any surprises again, at least not those kinds. But you are wrong.

She pulled the sheets up over herself. Her chest was making a funny noise, and she couldn't get anything in her lungs.

Inhaling, exhaling, her palm on her chest.

She hadn't even felt him pull away, sit up.

Turning her head, her neck still throbbing, her legs still shaking, she saw he was already sitting up on the edge of the bed. Looking out the window into the pitch-black backyard, the garage's graying gable.

"I'm just trying to protect her from all this," he said. "From all these distractions."

"A boy died," she started, her voice almost like a chant, "a boy died."

"Ryan," he said, not turning around. "Ryan. I know you love to talk about Ryan."

"What?" Rubbing her face, trying to think. "Love to talk about—"

"That kid," he said. "That kid, the way everyone looked at him."

He turned around and faced her, leaning toward her.

"The way you looked at him," he said.

"What?" Katie said, wondering if this was really happening, the whiskey soaking through her.

"Fuck that kid," he said. "Fuck that kid and his beautiful face. That's Teddy's problem. And that psychotic niece of his, that's his problem too. Fuck that kid. Who cares about that kid?"

A coldness dropped through her.

"You know who cares?" She took a breath and said it. "Your daughter." It excited her to say it. "Your daughter loved that boy. Your daughter was sleeping with that boy."

"What?" he said, so quiet she barely heard him. "What did you say?"

"I said they were sleeping together. Hailey must have found out. They were sleeping together and that started all this."

He wouldn't look at her, turning back to the window, to the yard's depths, the open maw of the garage. The excitement in her chest twisted into something else.

"Eric," she said, "did you know about them?"

He spun around slowly and looked at her like he had no idea what she was talking about.

"No," he said, shaking his head. "No, Katie. I swear."

That's when she knew he was lying.

And she said, "You either tell me everything or you leave now."

And then he was gone.

"Katie, why are you calling me? It's two o'clock in the morning."

But Gwen sounded awake. She probably never slept at all, like a bullfrog or a shark.

"Go wake up my daughter, Gwen. She's not answering her phone. Wake her up and tell her I'm coming to get her."

"You need to settle down, Katie. There's no reason—"

"Get her up. She's coming home now."

Grabbing for her sneakers, one eye on Drew's open bedroom door, Katie could hear him breathing deeply, his hanging solar system tilting above him. Styrofoam planets, Saturn's rings coated in dust.

"Katie," Gwen was saying, "have you been drinking?"

"I know what you've been doing with my daughter. Have her waiting on your front steps."

There was a brief pause.

"Five minutes," Gwen said, and hung up.

The lights at the Weaver house all seemed to come on at once, the instant Katie's car touched the foot of the long drive.

At the glowing rectangle of the front door, Devon stood, poised.

"Mom," she called out, duffel bag in one hand and backpack in the other, both swinging, whipping around her as she skidded down the long slope, hair flying, flip-flops and her sleep shorts, a sweatshirt yanked over her bolt-tight frame, Thoroughbred legs gripping the blue carpet of the lawn.

"I can't talk about anything now."

They were still in the car, in the garage, and Katie's voice was louder than she'd ever known it, louder than Coach T.'s, her own clamorous mother's, anyone's.

"We are going to talk about it right now. You will tell me. About you and Ryan Beck."

"I don't know what—"

"Stop it. I know. His mother told me, Devon. Ryan's mother told me."

"She's lying," Devon said. "I don't even know her. She's lying."

Oh, to see her daughter look at her, her face so composed, and lie so easily.

"I saw your leotard, Devon."

"I don't know what you're talking about, Mom. I don't."

"Stop lying, Devon. Stop." Her hand reaching out, grabbing Devon's chin so tightly, clenching her fingers around her jaw. *"Stop."*

Like a pin pulled out, Devon's face seemed to collapse, her whole body sinking into itself.

"Devon. Devon."

She covered her face with one hand, turning away.

It all felt unfair. There'd been no ramp-up to it. Her little girl, so unflappable, so self-possessed, never talked about boys, never seemed to look at a boy, and now, like a mask torn away in an instant.

"I loved him, Mom. I loved him so much."

The words just like Hailey had said, her fist covered in ice, *I got so mad I punched my own wall. I love him so much.* But Katie recognized the feeling too. The unbearable push of feelings at that age. How she'd looked at Eric and would have done anything at all to have him forever, her own body feeling like it was spinning from her, unstoppable.

You make me crazy, baby. You make me crazy. "I loved him," Devon repeated, her body so still, her voice so small, "and he's dead and what if it's my fault?"

"It's not your fault, Devon," Katie said. It seemed like she'd said it a hundred times in recent days.

Devon's hand fell from her face, a pale smudge in the dark of the garage. There was a long pause, like before a vault sometimes, that strange dead-eyed look, her breath slowed to silence. *Breathing throws off your alignment*, Teddy always told her. *Don't breathe.*

"Devon," she said, "what is it? You know you can tell me."

But Devon couldn't seem to speak, her hand on her chest, a nervous gesture Katie recognized as her own. It was as if something had been undone. All that talking, the saying of things out loud, made them real. When you say it aloud, it becomes real in fresh and horrible ways.

"Devon—"

"He knows, Mom," she blurted, eyes panicked.

"Who knows?"

"Dad."

Katie took a breath, the heat of Devon, and the closeness of the car, the smell of exhaust and chemicals. "Tell me."

"It was a few weeks ago," Devon said. Her hand on Katie's arm, she was ready now. "We were driving home from practice. He made me get out of the car. He sat down with me and he was so upset, Mom. He said that he knew, and it didn't matter how. He said I was throwing my life away."

Katie watched her daughter, watched her mouth moving, words coming out, but it was like Devon herself couldn't believe each sentence until she'd uttered it. Her own words terrifying her.

"And he said I needed to know the biggest mistake you can make in life is giving in to sex."

"He said that to you?" Katie pressed her fingers to her temples as if trying to hold her head in place.

"I told him it was just for now," Devon kept going. "That it wouldn't change anything. And he said, 'All the things you do at your age seem like they're just for now. But they're all forever. You live with those mistakes forever.'"

She looked at Katie, her voice relentless, her eyes growing wider and wider.

"And then he said, 'Devon, there's a hundred ways sex can ruin you.'"

A bursting in Katie's eyes, making her dizzy, her mouth thick with alcohol and exhaust.

There's a hundred ways sex can ruin you.

Had he really said that? And all she could think was *What did that mean, to him?*

"Devon. Devon, what else?" Because she knew there was more. And she had to get it, all of it.

And then Devon was talking again. Devon wasn't done at all.

"The day of the funeral, Mom," she said. "Dad showed up at practice even though I had a ride. And when we were in the car, he . . . he said this awful thing. I can't get it out of my head."

Katie took another breath. She was thinking of him, his hands on her thighs not an hour ago, and wondering what was wrong with her.

"What did he say, baby? Tell me."

Her head bobbing slightly, Devon turned, and Katie watched as her eyes fixed on the door from the garage into the house. She couldn't tell what Devon was looking at, Drew's two-liter bottle, Eric's Gore-Tex jacket slung there on a hook, dark and swelling.

"He said Ryan got what was coming to him," Devon whispered, so close to Katie the words vibrated on her skin. "That's what he said. And he said, 'What made that kid think he had any right?'"

They locked eyes with each other.

"Devon," Katie said. "Look at me."

But Devon couldn't, and Katie found herself getting lost in

her head too. It was as though the garage were this haunted place, the empty spot where Eric's car usually sat like a stain beside them, like a black pit with no bottom.

"Devon," she said, forcing the words out, "do you think your father might have done something?"

With unbearable slowness Devon turned.

"Mom...I don't know what he did," she said, her face assembling into something grave and hopeless. "Do you?"

One hand on her stomach, Katie felt something pierce her, everything spilling out. She couldn't answer.

Devon was saying, "Mom, I can't go inside and see him. I can't."

And here Katie was, still drunk on his whiskey, still feeling his hands on her, back to the mattress—what was wrong with her?—a red daub spreading across her collarbone where his hand had pressed, other things she wouldn't let herself think about at all.

Who was that man? Did she even know? You were mysterious to him and he was mysterious to you.

She put a hand on either side of Devon's face.

"He's gone," she promised. "And you're with me. And everything's going to be okay."

Devon looked at her, jaw shaking between Katie's fingers.

"Mom," she said, eyes filled with bright tears, "you always give me everything."

Three a.m., four, sleep never came, not really, her heart pounding, cymbals crashing inside.

The photo on the bedside table, she and Eric in matching BelStars tracksuits, searing red, Eric smiling at the camera, Katie smiling up at him.

Before she knew it, she was dragging her wedding album out from the closet, behind the boxes of baby clothes, Devon's old leotards. The pictures, fading already, those disposable cameras people used to use, all the blurred, frantic shots that captured the feeling of life better than anything else.

The small catering hall, a raucous and joyous crowd of forty, kegs of summer ale, the DJ with rainbow sunglasses, everyone dancing, their faces glazed with sweat—three of Eric's old girl-friends came, one by one introducing themselves to Katie. *He's the greatest guy*, they all said. *The one that got away.* A gentleman, a sweetheart, a knight in shining armor. *And you did it, you got him, how did you?*

And she never knew, not really. Because yes, she was three months along by then, but that wasn't the reason. She'd already gone for her consultation at the Options Women's Center, lis-tened to them describe how they would insert a tube, "a suction device that will gently empty your uterus." But then Eric showed up the night before her appointment, saying he'd been driving around for hours and had come to important decisions about the things that mattered to him and it turned out that the life inside of her, which they'd created, was the Thing Itself, and he'd torn the pull tab from the Schlitz can and promised her everything, always and forever. *This must be how life really happens*, he'd said, *you don't know what you're supposed to do, what your purpose is, and suddenly life tells you.*

The wedding night, she wasn't supposed to drink at all, but she'd had three glasses of champagne, and Eric three times that, plus tequila and Mexican cigars, and they both smelled of sweat and crushed flowers and ended up having sex in the backseat of Eric's car in the hotel parking structure, neither able to remem-ber what they'd done with the key card and not wanting to wait one more second, his arm under her dress up to his shoulder and everything frenzied and luscious.

And the truth was, arm hooked in his, tight, she did think:

I've got him now.

Now he is mine.

Chapter Sixteen

Just before five, in the purple dawn, she crept down the hall and checked on Devon sleeping, her head a dark mass on the pillow.

Finally, she fell asleep herself.

Now it was nearly seven, the clock radio droning with weather, traffic, weather, traffic, her face muffled in pillows. Drifting in and out. The tug of forgetting.

The phone ringing. The landline again.

"Did you hear?"

"Hear what?" Katie said, her voice sleep-frogged. "Who is this?"

"It's Helen Beck. The police called late last night to tell me about the paint chips. I can't stop thinking about it."

"What? Wait. Helen." Sitting up now, her stomach churning with last night's liquor.

"They found some paint chips in Ryan's clothes. Car paint. And guess what? They're not purple."

"Oh," Katie said, biting down on her finger, trying to wake herself.

"They found just a few. Very tiny."

"What color, Helen?"

"So I guess that witness was wrong."

"What color, Helen?" Katie said, head throbbing with the knowing.

"Silver, they said. Or metallic gray."

"Silver," Katie repeated.

"I know. Doesn't narrow things down much. The detective told me there's more than six thousand silver or gray cars in this county alone."

"I see them everywhere," Katie said, her mouth dry.

Silver to match your eyes, she'd said when Eric first drove it home a half a dozen years ago. And he'd grinned. *My eyes are gray*. But the yellow ring around the center always made them glitter.

"So what does this mean?" Katie asked. "What comes next?"

"The state crime lab maybe can identify the make and model of the car from the samples. Sometimes they can do that."

"Make and model, that limits it a little, but—"

"I'm optimistic. I have to be. He's my boy," she said. There was a pause, Katie already on her feet, the cord, wreathed with dust, tangling up her legs.

"Katie, I bet we're both sorry now about the other day." Helen kept talking. "Mothers, you know. When they're born, we grow a new set of teeth. What's that line, 'There ought to be a law against a mother like that'?"

"I have to go, Helen."

"I guess I'm glad to know it wasn't his girlfriend," she said, taking a breath. "It was just some random monster."

★

Stumbling into the bathroom, Katie ducked her head under the sink faucet, gulping hungrily.

Silver, gray, metallic, her head clunking and clanking from one image to the next, like coins jangling against each other.

Silver, gray, metallic, like coins. Melted coins.

Drew's fever-streaked palm open before as they stood in the garage, and the three silver specks stippled in the center.

She stood in the garage, barefoot and wearing only Eric's old BelStars Booster T-shirt, eyes on the greasy blot where his car was usually parked.

Kneeling, one hand holding back the bowing handle of the rusting lawn mower, its wheels turning, she used the light from her phone to look.

Down on her knees, now, fingers spreading, she searched. Even in the crease between the concrete and the garage wall.

There was nothing glinting.

The greasy blot, though—she crawled over to it. At night, it had looked like a pit. Now she could smell something. Motor oil, and something else.

"I saved them."

"Show me," she said.

He pointed to his window, to a piece of Scotch tape, a few inches long, sealed diagonally across the pane.

It was only when she walked right up to the sill that she could see them: three hard sparkles, one as large as a dime, the sun perforating the center.

Her arm stretched, she tore off the tape and crumpled it into her palm.

"It's not safe," she said. "There's lead in it."

He looked her.

"Like in the school basement?" he asked after a few seconds. "They used a big vacuum cleaner. They wore these white space suits and big masks."

"Are you sure you didn't dream that?" Katie said, rolling the tape tighter and tighter in her palm.

"You always think I dreamed things that were real. They came when we were at that meet after Halloween, the one far away. We didn't get back in time to empty out my cubby. The Parthenon got ruined."

"Oh, Drew, yes," Katie said. "That was rotten." Drew's prizewinning sugar-cube Parthenon—the same kind she'd made when she was in fourth grade more than a quarter century ago. Like his sister, he did everything with precision, until his hands were hard with glue.

The entire drive home after the meet, she and Eric kept promising they'd make it back in time. *We'll rescue the Parthenon, kiddo!* Eric said, pounding the gas.

But by the time they got home, the remediation workers had thrown it away, dumped it in a bin out behind the school.

"I'm sorry, honey," she said now. "We all felt really bad about it."

Drew didn't say anything, just looked back up at the window, the sticky streak where the tape had been.

"Drew," she said, looking at his digital clock, "where's Devon?"

"School," he said. "Mrs. Chu came and got her. She said you needed to sleep and to let you."

"Drew," she said, rolling the tape in her hand until it was fine as wire, "go watch TV. Watch anything you want. Mom has to work."

*   *   *

It was as if her body were moving on its own, pure muscle memory.

Later, she would wonder why she didn't even hesitate.

Standing over the sink, she tore every bit of the tape off her fingers, where it stuck, glue-thick, to her nails. The sound of her own breaths like an animal.

The garbage disposal hummed and grinded and then she wondered if it would be enough. Would the tape, like potato peels, celery string, grip and line the pipes, stay there forever?

Devon, you ok?

Yes, she texted back.

Have u heard from yr dad?

Dont want to talk abt dad

I'm coming to get you

Mom, no. I want to be here.

Everything will be ok, D

Ok mom

It was all adrenaline, blood. Breathe in, breathe out.

Back downstairs, turning on her laptop, nearly shaking it to life.

Eric had taken the car to the shop—which day had that been? Was it a tune-up? A cranking sound, the alternator again? There were always car problems, both their Fords gasping past a hundred thousand miles, countless out-of-state meets, the daily sojourns to and from gym, school, booster meetings.

She couldn't recall seeing his car the day they learned about Ryan. Katie had driven them all to practice in her old warhorse, Eric decamping to a nearby diner with his laptop.

All she could remember was his car was in the shop the day of Ryan's funeral, and when she came home after, she'd found Eric in the garage, the car returned.

And the garage—hadn't it smelled of something? Solvent, or aerosol.

Or was it paint?

She tried to log on to their credit-card sites, but she didn't know the passwords. Eric paid those bills.

She didn't know anything.

Click-clicking, palm wet and sticky, she tried to open his e-mail.

Incorrect password.

It had been Elite-D, for years. The only password they ever used, but now it didn't work.

One by one, she yanked open all the warping plywood drawers of the desk, paper wafting. Booster minutes, work orders, credit-card bills, mortgage statements, past-dues. One drawer glided free, landing on the floor, releasing something.

It fell to the carpet, tented there.

A creased Father's Day card from years before, an illustration of a card deck on the cover:

I was dealt to be your daughter.
You were dealt to be my dad.
No matter how the game turns out,
You're the best hand I ever had.

Bottom drawer, a fat stack of receipts—gym dues, meet fees, furnace maintenance, last week's dinner at the Wooden Nickel.

She sat down at the swivel chair, breathing. Then she bent

down to pick up the greeting card, her foot hitting something: the shredder bin under the desk.

She dragged the bin toward her and overturned it, knocking the cross-cut shredder onto the carpet. Over and over, she plunged her hands through the confettied shards, nicking her knuckles once, twice, until she found it: a pink paper corner, the staple trapped between the shredder blades: BRIGGINS' COLLISION.

It wasn't a place she knew, not the Firestone they usually went to.

BRIGGINS' COLLISION.

REARDON.

Reardon, which was forty-seven miles away.

It took her a long time to free the pink paper from the keen blades of the shredder, but she did.

QUARTER PANEL $400 +, another shard read. CASH.

She placed it in the center of the desk, bent her shoulders forward. As if her body had lost its bones, that's how it felt. One too many shocks to her shocked system, she could no longer tense, no longer charge forward, no longer do anything. Her body was sinking back into itself like a slime-thick snail. Hiding.

Seventeen years of knowing him—the particular softness of the inside of his wrists, the way he whistled whenever he walked into a bank, the precise choreography of his fingers when he wanted her to turn over in bed.

Devon, do you think your father might have done something?

I don't know what he did. Do you?

None of this, she said to herself, again and again, was Eric. This was not Eric.

Except there was this: He would always do anything for her, wouldn't he? For Devon.

Trampolines, second mortgages, booster president, Gwen,

the new equipment, the pit, the righteous e-mails he wrote to unfair judges but never sent, shouting down a heckler in the stands and again in the parking lot.

And yet sometimes he still seemed surprised by the power and weight of feelings she could stir in him, the anger when she was criticized, the awe when she performed.

I didn't hear him, Lacey had said, *but Devon kept saying, Dad, Dad, don't cry, don't.*

And: *What made that kid think he had any right?*

So many things you never think you'll do until you do them.

She stared into the shredder bin, the pink accordion snares of the receipt in her hands. If someone taped them together, they could still figure it all out, couldn't they? And surely Briggins' Collision had another copy, the original. And signs on the car, telltale clues, faint ridges that spoke of new paint. Patches, like the surface of an orange peel, like the time they'd had their bumper repaired.

Everything was there, if someone wanted to look.

She picked up the bin and thrust it under her arm, carried it to the sink and lit a kitchen match, watching the pink tatters burn. After, she turned on the faucet, the ashes sinking down the drain.

She thought about the piece of Scotch tape, the paint chips on it. She should have burned it too. There might be microscopic pieces left in the drain. You could never hide everything.

Lying on the bed, the lights off, the ceiling fan burring softly, she tried to make the pieces fit together.

(*Could you recall the details of a random night in your family life?* she wondered, as if there were a *you* to hear it.)

Time passed, hollowed out, and she tried to do something akin to meditation, self-hypnosis, a trance like at slumber parties as a kid. That night, the night Ryan died, everyone was tired and frantic. Everyone was always tired and frantic. Lacey's birthday invitation had threatened *Pedicures, pottery painting, and petits fours!* and Katie remembered hunting for wrapping paper, worrying over the gift—a desk lamp that looked like a gummy bear, a pair of glitter bracelets—because Gwen's daughter didn't want for anything, as long as Gwen wanted it too.

Devon, exhausted from the Flip into Spring Invitational, her face with that kind of numb glaze, could barely tie her tennis shoes.

I'm gonna walk, she said. *I don't need a ride. It's not that far.*

Okay, but call us when you're ready to leave. It'll be dark.

And Eric, most of his sleep lost that week getting Devon to practice by six a.m., was hunched over his laptop, headphones on, dark pouches under his eyes, old coffee on one side of him and a warming liter of diet soda on the other.

Katie had taken Drew to the mall for rock salt, right? And run into Kirsten Siefert in the parking lot, on her way to Lacey's.

In the backseat, barely visible behind the raffia and cellophane, her daughter Jordan held a colossal spa birthday basket suited for a Beverly Hills grand dame.

I hope the party goes long. Greg's taking me to Randello's for dinner, Kirsten had whispered in Katie's ear, her hair stiff with spray, an energy on her. *But you've seen the way he eats. We'll be home by nine. Eight if he starts ordering Jack and Coke.*

At home, she'd lost an hour or two helping Drew with his science project, the shrimp eggs and the salt, salvaging a two-liter from a neighbor's recycling bin, slicing the top off to serve as a hatchery, filling it with salt water. Standing on a kitchen chair,

Drew sprinkled the shrimp eggs—glossy little beads the size of pinheads—inside.

Did Devon call? Eric had asked, vague tang of beer on his breath.

Right. He'd had a beer at dinner, and another while he watched, standing at the kitchen counter, the Junior Olympics National Invitational on one of the ESPNs. He'd drunk it guiltily, greedily, looking tired, all the adrenaline from the meet, from Devon's win, from everything.

Or was he thinking of Devon and Ryan? Was he thinking of them constantly since he'd found out?

I thought she'd want me to pick her up by now, he'd said, watching Katie mop the briny water from the counter, the kitchen floor, the dining-room table, even the back of Drew's neck.

They have to sit for three days, Mom, Drew had said. *To see how many die.*

She told him to put the hatchery in the basement or the garage, or it'd get knocked over and she'd be cleaning up salt water for days.

Then she began gathering laundry, handwashing Devon's competition leotard in the sink.

But where was Eric? The TV on, everyone's computer humming. The blip of cell phones. Everyone in a different corner. He must have put Drew to bed. She didn't remember that.

There was a whole pocket of the evening she couldn't be sure Eric had been there at all.

The next time she looked at her watch it was nearly eleven, and she ran down the basement stairs to throw a clot of crusted dishrags in the washer, the final load.

And she'd finally heard the door from the garage slam, heard Devon pounding up the stairs, the shower turn on. She'd knocked on her bedroom door at one point. Said good night.

Night, Mom. Night.

She and Eric often didn't go to bed at the same time. They almost never did.

Then, the part she remembered, two a.m., a tunnel of sleep and Eric reaching over, pressing against the small of her back, his fingers digging into the base of her spine, then climbing under her T-shirt, urgent and insistent.

Her demon lover.

What had he just done?

She felt her stomach turn.

I promise im ok. Really, mom.

Katie sat on the edge of her bed, phone in hand. It wasn't yet nine o'clock in the morning and she was already so tired she couldn't imagine standing, or putting on clothes.

I'll get you after last period. DO NOT leave with anyone else. Ok.

"This is Mrs. Knox. I'm calling to make a special request. Devon's father—he's on medication. Back pain." It was so easy to lie. "He's not supposed to be driving, but he's very stubborn."

"Sounds like my husband," the school secretary said with a sigh.

"If he shows up, I don't want him to leave with Devon."

"Mr. Knox? Really?"

"He just doesn't seem to be able to take it easy," Katie said, forcing a wry tone. "It's strong stuff he's on. And he just can't be trusted right now."

"Of course, Mrs. Knox."

"He's not himself."

IV

But I sometimes wonder, to this day, if courage is just another word for desperation.

—Nadia Comaneci, *Letters to a Young Gymnast*

Chapter Seventeen

She didn't hear the car pull up the driveway.

She was on her hands and knees in the garage, looking for more paint chips, for glass.

All she could see was the long trail of rock salt from Drew's first, failed science project.

The garage door was open only a foot when she spotted the cuffs of a man's suit pants. A pair of scuffed wingtips.

The shoes paused a second, then kept walking.

A second later, the doorbell rang.

Katie looked down at herself, T shirt, her bare legs, knees covered in garage-floor grime. Dirt- and dust-flecked.

Through the frosted panel on one side of the front door, she saw the car in the driveway. A black Dodge.

Moving to the other panel, she spotted the two men on the porch, both in suits. One had a phone clipped to his belt.

Had they heard her in the garage, seen her feet?

The buzzer became a knock.

She could hear the crackle of a two-way radio through the door.

"Ma'am" a voice came. "Ma'am, I'm Detective Renton. This is Detective Furey. Can we speak to you?"

Three minutes later, after throwing on a pair of Devon's workout capris swiped from the laundry basket, streaking a dish towel up and down her arms, across her face even, she opened the door.

"I'm sorry," she said. "My son is very sick."

"We're sorry to bother you at home, Mrs. Knox," said the younger one, Detective Fury, or Furey—had that really been his name?

The detectives settled into the slow-sinking sofa across from Katie in the wing chair, which still seemed to bear the scent of Gwen from days before, tuberose and musk.

The chair she and Eric had once copulated on. That's the word that came into her soiled brain. *Copulated.* Animals.

But she needed to focus. She needed to—

"Is Mr. Knox here?" Detective Renton asked.

And there it was.

"He's at work."

The way they were watching her, she wondered how tight the capris were, how her face looked. Her hands went to her forehead, the slick of sweat there. Had she even brushed her teeth?

"What can I help you with?" she said. "What is it you want?"

"Mrs. Knox, are you okay?"

"Yes," she said. Breathing from the center, like Coach T. always told Devon to do. *Breathe, focus, let go. Breathe, believe, and battle.* "But my son has scarlet fever. You probably shouldn't be here."

"I'm sorry about your son, Mrs. Knox," Renton said. "But

don't worry about us. We're strong like bulls." He tried to smile, or do something with his face.

"This won't take long," said the young one, Furey, with the freshly shaved neck, pink and angry. But his voice was gentle. "We just have a few follow-up questions."

"Questions?"

"How's your daughter doing?"

The hover of relief in her throat made it hard to talk. The locker-room fight, of course. "She's fine," Katie said, folding her hands, resting them on her thighs, the slippery spandex of Devon's capris a half a foot too short for her. "As fine as can be expected."

"That's good news," said Furey, very earnest. He was just a boy, really. The Adam's apple, the razor marks on his neck. Officer Furey, Boy Detective

"I'm sure you heard," Detective Renton said. "Miss Belfour has been under twenty-four-hour psychiatric care since the incident."

"Yes. We were very glad."

"Well, it looks like she's going home today," he said, and then paused.

"Really?" she said. They both seemed to be watching her so closely, even leaning forward. Scrutinizing. Were there paint chips under her fingernails, maybe a ribbon of half-shredded evidence stuck to her foot bottom, pink slivers of the repair receipt clinging to her ankles? You could never hide it all.

"So we'll be talking to Miss Belfour again about what happened," Renton continued, watery eyes on her. "After the incident, she wasn't too coherent, and after her attorney arrived, well, she wasn't talking anymore."

"Wait," Katie said, her voice squeaking like the uneven bars, like Devon's hands gripping the fiberglass, body swinging, chalk spraying. "Wait. I don't understand. She's a criminal. She attacked my little girl. You're charging her, right?"

They both looked at her.

"There haven't been any charges yet," Renton said, voice even. "Before we submit our report to the DA, we need to follow up on a few things we've learned."

"What things?" Katie said. Why had they come here, anyway, instead of calling her to the station? And wasn't it odd that they'd just stopped by, unannounced? Renton with his gravelly voice and his worn skin like an old potato, right alongside Furey with his delicate boy face, and was one the good cop and one the bad?

The thought came to her. "What happened to Officer Crandall? He's the one we spoke to after my daughter was attacked. Wasn't this his case?"

The two men looked at her, Furey's forehead crinkling gently.

Then: the squawk of her phone upstairs, those stroking first beats of "Assassin's Tango."

"Excuse me." She leaped to her feet, moving quickly to the stairs.

"If that's your husband, Mrs. Knox," Renton called out, "we'd like to speak to him too. He works out of that studio over on Merricat Road, right?"

"Gwen," she whispered, shutting the upstairs bathroom door behind her, making sure no one could hear. "I can't talk now."

She never would have answered if it weren't for the detectives, their starchy blue shirts and thick-soled shoes. The squinting of their eyes and the leaning closer. She needed some space, some time. To think.

"Katie," Gwen was saying, already mid-harangue, "I'd like you to reconsider your position here. Even if you want Devon home that doesn't mean she can't continue her sessions at EmPower—"

"That's not going to happen. And I can't talk."

"—because in a month, your daughter will step out onto that competition floor and have what could be her last chance at qualifying for Elite after the catastrophe of two years ago."

"I'm not discussing this with you," Katie said, her hands on the sink, sticky from something—soap, last night's noxious whiskey. "This has nothing to do with you."

"Well, that's just false. I'm the treasurer of this entire operation. Devon's success or failure will have a major impact on the finances of this gym."

"I don't care about the gym's goddamn finances." Trying to keep her voice low. The silence from downstairs—those detectives, could they hear?

"The boosters have invested a great deal in Devon," Gwen continued. "And her fate affects our daughters too. Do you see what I'm saying?"

Leaning against the peeling vanity, Katie turned on the water so they couldn't hear. The old mold-thick vents might just muffle the telltale heart. Those detectives down there, surely Hailey had told them about Devon and Ryan? And if she hadn't told before, what would stop her from telling now? And then they would talk to Eric. And want to see Eric's car. And—

"Katie, do you see? Are you there? I can hear your anxious little breaths."

"I'm hanging up."

"Katie, were you an athlete?"

"No," she said, wanting to scream at Gwen and fearing the detectives could hear, imagining them both leaning forward, craning necks. *Who is she talking to? Is it her daughter? Her husband?*

"Of course you weren't. I don't know what you wanted at Devon's age, Katie, but I'd bet my daughter's college fund you couldn't name it then or now. But Devon is different. She knows what she wants. She's not like the rest of us, Katie."

"Who the hell do you think you are?" Katie whispered, her mouth pressed against the phone. "Slinking into our lives with your snakeskin shoes and your big checkbook and your—"

"You wanted that checkbook, didn't you?" she said icily.

Downstairs, Katie thought she heard footsteps. She thought about the door to the garage. About what else might be in there. Glass fragments, the microscopic residue of paint—flakes and chips too small for the eye to see. But they would see.

"This isn't about your maternal vanity," Gwen was saying. "It's about your daughter."

In her head, Katie was screaming.

The water running, she leaned down as close to the rush of it as she could and said through gritted teeth, "Go to hell. You go to hell."

But nothing ever touched Gwen.

"Because, Katie, there's nothing on God's green earth I wouldn't do for my child," Gwen said, the bastioned fortress in the center of an impassable moat. "That is something Eric and I agree on. Don't you? What kind of mother wouldn't?"

What kind of mother. To say that to Katie, who had given every waking hour and every sleeping hour to her daughter. Who sat in that gym every day, spent hundreds of hours in backless bleachers, elbows perpetually rubbed raw from all the bleacher leaning. Who drove as many as thirty hours a week, who spent hours hunting for lost grips or a favorite leotard, every leotard costing more than any item of clothing Katie had. Who hadn't had a professional haircut in four years, who'd never been on a trip alone with her husband at all, her only vacations consisting of free hours torn from tournament weekends, her shoulder bag filled with water bottles and ibuprofen and gluey hair gel and sharp bobby pins and lucky grips and the right kind of energy bars you could only get online and the right kind of athletic tape and the lucky socks and the lucky hairbrush and Devon's inhaler and her backup inhaler, her hands resting on Devon's weary shoulders as they tromped through the museum, the science center, the amusement park in the forty-five minutes they had before prac—

"I refuse to deprive my daughter of the opportunity to achieve her dreams," Gwen continued, unrelenting. "I will not give up on her. Will you give up on Devon?"

"You're lucky I didn't call the goddamned police," Katie said instead, jaw grinding. "You took my daughter."

"The police?" There was a brief pause, then Gwen's voice returned, grim and precise. "You don't want to call the police."

Something in her tone. Something with portent. Whatever it meant, Katie could not hear it now.

"I'll do whatever I need to do to protect my daughter," Katie said, and hung up.

Walking down the stairs, she dragged down the hems of the capris, smoothed her hair.

"I'm sorry," she said, returning to the living room, blood high and with new purpose, "but it's not a good time."

The detectives looked up at her, half rising, then sitting again.

"We get that a lot," Renton said, trying for a smile.

Instead of sitting, Katie rested her hands on the back of the wing chair, hiding her shaking legs behind it.

"We already told Officer Crandall everything we know. And we're a sick house."

We're a sick house. Her words sounded funny to her, but they seemed to have weight, impact. That big way of talking, she'd never tried it before. *Nothing on God's green earth I wouldn't do for my child.*

"Mrs. Knox," Furey said, his neck less pink now, expression oddly tender, "we do understand. We're here to help you."

She felt very tall, the detectives slunk so low on the ancient Sears sofa. She straightened her back. She would be ready this time.

"We reviewed security-camera footage of the gym lobby," Renton said. "And you can clearly see Miss Belfour following your daughter into the locker room."

"She was hunting her," Katie said, "like my daughter was some kind of animal."

"But you should know Miss Belfour's injuries far outweighed your daughter's," Renton added.

"My daughter's strong. She knows how to defend herself. Thank God."

Her spine tight and taut, nothing they said touched her. It was like the rival gym parents at the meets, the way they would talk, trying to diminish Devon's achievements, cast doubt. Noting the extra time Coach T. gave her, the special privileges. You had to be above all of that. Or trample it under your feet.

"And you," Furey said, lifting his pen in the air, pointing it in her direction. "You too, Mrs. Knox. You defended yourself. Are those from Miss Belfour too?"

She followed his pen to her forearm, bare. The brown serrations etching that fish-hook scratch, elbow to wrist. Conscious of the gaping armholes of Eric's shirt, air hitting skin, their eyes on her. Her marks.

"Of course they are. You see what Hailey's capable of, then," she said, discreetly displaying her forearm. Furey looked at it, noted it.

"Mrs. Knox," Renton said, "have your daughter and Miss Belfour been involved in any back-and-forth? A kind of feud? There was talk of texts exchanged. Girls can—"

"No. Absolutely not. And, by the way, Hailey's not a girl. She's the adult who attacked my child. A minor. That's what we're talking about, right?"

"Right."

"And she's the adult whose car was seen at the site of her boyfriend's deadly accident, correct?"

"That's a separate investigation, Mrs. Knox."

"And as for talking to my husband, he wasn't there when my daughter was assaulted. I was. And I will tell you again what you already know. What a dozen people saw."

She felt something stirring powerfully in her, and the words just came, her finger poking at them like Coach on the floor, *To stick it, you gotta grind those baby-girl heels of yours*, hand on the vault punching every word. *When it hurts you know you've landed it right.*

"That twenty-three-year-old woman, half a foot taller with at least thirty pounds on my child, a woman with a history of instability and juvenile delinquency, tackled her, pounded her head into the floor. Wrapped her hands around my baby's throat.

That's what matters. And that is why you're here, isn't it? Because we don't live in a place where adults are allowed to beat on children."

Watching her, Detective Renton jiggled a pen on his knee. One of their radios crackled.

It didn't matter that there'd been no head pounding, no hands to throat. Not like some of the fights she'd seen, long ago, waiting tables at the Magic Stick the summer after high school, or that woman who'd bushwhacked her mom in the parking lot for giving her phone number to her husband. Her keys had been between her fingers, ready to pounce.

With Hailey and Devon, it was more chaotic, all elbows and knees and squeaking sneaker soles. It was blood and nails and teeth. But Devon knew how to take hits, had been taking them most of her life, chin to beam, knee to mat. The red marks from Hailey's hoodie cord embedded in her palm were no worse than any day's gym rips, than anything that might happen to Devon, whose body was so constantly tested, battered, shocked.

"You should know that Hailey Belfour has always been jealous of my daughter," she went on, her voice gaining still more energy. Hands gripping the back of that ridiculous chair, still smelling of Gwen's tuberose. Gwen was everywhere. "Of Devon's talents, the attention she receives from Hailey's uncle, from everyone. You see, Hailey was never a real gymnast herself. She was too big, too graceless. Maybe she watched my daughter and saw what might have been ten years ago. If she'd been a less troubled girl. If she'd had the discipline but also the innate talent. The thing Devon has that makes her exceptional."

"Mrs. Knox, I—"

"A grown woman so jealous of a child that she physically attacks her. Can you imagine the rage inside? What do you think a woman like that is capable of?"

She looked at them, they looked at her.

"But this is something we've dealt with Devon's entire life. The envy of others."

Chapter Eighteen

The detectives were still standing in her driveway, talking.

She watched from the window, watched how closely they stood, and how near the garage. Furey was nodding at everything Renton was saying, his mouth moving ceaselessly.

Then she saw them looking across her lawn.

To Mr. Watts's fading ranch house. The driveway. Mr. Watts was there, the hood of his green Impala open, doing one of his endless repairs.

They walked over to him. They said something to him and he looked up, his old aviators flashing.

She imagined what he might say:

On the garage floor, Detective. The boy thought they were silverfish.
Yes, I showed them to Mrs. Knox.

Later I thought, Oh, paint from her husband's car. *Yes, it's that color exactly.*

She must've thought the same thing.

She watched as Mr. Watts shook his head, then shook it again.

Then they left.

*   *   *

"Mr. Watts," she said, her feet still bare, soles sunk in dew, "were they bothering you?"

"Nope," he said, wiping his hands with an oil-soft rag. "Were they bothering you?"

"But what did they ask you?"

He paused, looking at her, those aviators reflecting herself back in both mirrored teardrops.

"If I had a permit for my RV," he said. "What'd they ask you?"

"I'm sorry," she said. "Someone's been harassing Devon. It's very upsetting and I'm . . . very upset."

He nodded, folding his arms. "That is upsetting," he said. "I hope they're helping you. Your daughter's in the paper so much now. That brings out the crazy."

"Yes," Katie said, catching a glimpse of her drawn face in his sunglasses. "It does."

"I always try to keep an eye out for all of you. I still think about Devon's accident. Things like that can do bad things to a family."

Katie nodded. It had happened soon after they'd moved in, and they barely knew Mr. Watts. But he'd run over to help. Leaning down, he'd tried to talk to little Devon, *What's your favorite ice cream*, anything to distract her from the blood and chaos. The smell of gas, the shrieking lawn mower.

"I'll never forget seeing you at the screen door before it happened," he said now, pointing up the driveway. "I was out there in my garage and saw you watching her run out to her daddy."

"Standing at the door?" The way she remembered it, she went to the door only after hearing Devon's screech, like a cat caught in a hunting trap.

"What a thing," he said. "It was like you were frozen. Like ice."

*   *   *

The sexy, slashing violin thrusts.

Her phone again, those opening jabs of "Assassin's Tango."

That song, the one from the spring invitational, Devon performing her floor routine to its slinks and jabs, the day Ryan died.

The slippery magenta of her leotard, her buttocks high, those hard-hewn legs, muscles grooved and bronzed. Undulating under her leotard with every move. The staccato march of her colt legs, the sharpness of the foot flick, the haughtiness of the head snap. The slow glides.

There had been something different in it, in that performance. At the time, Katie hadn't been able to put her finger on it. Now it seemed so clear.

That hip swing, slow and mesmerizing. Then down on the mat, lolling and rolling, the straddle. Thump, thump, whip, snap, the purr of her feet. Earthy, carnal.

My God, how had she missed it? All the clues right there.

Before, Devon had always been so intent on her performance—the physics of it, the aerodynamic logic of it—it never even seemed like she heard the music at all.

But that day, Katie realized, it was as if Devon really heard it, moved with it and in it. And her body was no longer a machine, a tool, a weapon, but a body. Moving. Taking pleasure in itself, in its power. Seducing.

Had Eric seen it too? How could he not?

The exultation as she landed her last dizzying run, her feet bolting to the floor, face piped pink and exultant. Radiant under the fluorescent lights.

The look on her face as they all walked to the car after the meet had been a look Katie had never seen, nearly prurient. *I finally got it. That's what it's supposed to feel like.* It was almost too much for Katie. But Eric couldn't even look at his daughter, averting his eyes, dropping his keys, walking faster.

"Teddy, you just called?"

"Katie, I know you don't want to talk to me," he said, his voice scratchy like after a long coaching day.

But she did want to talk to him. She needed to. Before the detectives. She had to be first.

"I hope you heard about the paint chips." He sounded like he'd aged twenty years in a few days. "We knew the truth had to come out. That eyewitness was a liar or a fool. Here's a fella, been arrested twice for drinking Jack Daniel's while under the influence of driving. Nearly lost his commercial license. Get this—turns out he used to deliver for Gwen Weaver and she fired his sorry ass."

"Teddy, why did you call me?"

"Katie, we've brought Hailey home to us."

She bowed her head, trying to concentrate, to think it through.

"I see," she said carefully. "Because she's all better. Just like that."

He cleared his throat, a roar in her ear. "Katie, dear, we were hoping you and Eric might come over. That we all might talk."

"Eric's not here."

"I know Hailey has some things she'd like to say."

"Teddy," she said, "I don't want to hear anything she has to say."

"We'd really like you here," he said, his tone unreadable. "The silver paint changes everything. I think you'll both want to hear what we have to say. We'll be waiting."

Chapter Nineteen

"Drew, I have to go out for a little while."

In the den, her son's body was rooted deep into the springless furrows of the sofa, his pajama-clad arms swathed around a book.

"Okay," he said. "I wonder who won."

"Won what?" she said, tying her shoes briskly, thinking.

"The science fair," Drew said, a clicking from his throat as if it still pained him. "Last night."

The science fair. She felt a pang in her chest, like pliers squeezing.

"I'm sorry, Drew. It's rotten being sick, isn't it?"

"You can throw it all away," he said. "The shrimp must be all dead. Like I said."

"Honey," she said, "we'll get you back to school in a few days. There'll be another fair soon, right?"

But he just returned to his book.

She looked at him, his head bent, the rosy crook of his neck, the slightly damp curls pressed there, reminding herself the scarlet fever wasn't her fault, but it felt like her fault, everything did.

Kneeling down behind the sofa back, her fingers reaching for his shoulder, she leaned over, glanced at the sentence next to his thumb, pink from the pressure, which meant he loved the book: *"I'll tattoo you if it's the last thing I do! I'll do it for nothing!"*

"Is that the one Mr. Watts gave you?"

"Yeah. *The Melted Coins*," he said. "It smells funny, but it's good. A pirate named Needles Ned tries to tattoo Joe."

"Drew," she tried, "I need a favor."

Turning the page back, he began reading aloud: " 'Then he reached down and ripped open the boy's shirt. "Give me the needle, Lopez!" ' "

Katie heard her phone again. Ringing again.

" 'Joe felt a stab of pain,' " Drew continued, " 'as the tattoo artist crouched over him and the needle pricked the skin on his chest.' "

"Drew—"

" ' "First, I prick the design. Then comes the dye." ' " Drew flipped a page, found another highlight. " ' "The mark will stay with you for life," cried the pirate.' "

"Drew, honey, listen to me. I've got to go see Coach T. for a little while."

"Mom, the tattoo ruins your life," he said, looking up. "Once he puts it on you, you have bad luck forever."

She could ask Mr. Watts to watch him, but she didn't want to. (What had he meant, anyway? That she'd been standing at the screen door before the accident. That she—)

"You have a tattoo, Mom."

"I do," she said. "Not a pretty one." *Fight Like a Grrrl* on her left thigh. She'd done it stick-and-poke style, with a sewing needle and an ashes-vodka slurry when she was Devon's age.

Placing her hand on the top of his head softly, she said, "Pal, you think you'd be okay here for a few minutes by yourself?"

"I saw it when we went swimming that time."

"It was a long time ago," she said, "so the curse must be over." A funny hitch in her voice.

"And a pirate didn't give it to you."

"No," she said. "I gave it to myself."

Drew's always-sticky phone in her hand, checking the battery charge, she explained again how to reach her, as if he hadn't called her hundreds of times.

"It's only nine blocks," she said. "And Mr. Watts is next door if you need anything. Or if you just get lonely. But I'll only be gone a half hour. I'm just at Coach T.'s."

"Okay," he said, the book still between his fingers, his other hand scratching his temple, the rash peeling now, like an overripe plum.

"I'll be back before you know it," she said, opening the front door, car keys clutched in her hand. "It's just nine blocks."

"I think this is going to be my favorite book," he said.

"That's good. It's nice to have a favorite book."

"Ryan had a favorite book," he said. "He kept it in his back pocket all the time."

"Did he?" She looked outside, at the quiet street. No sign of Mr. Watts or anyone at all.

"You know he did," he said.

She turned and, for the first time ever, he looked at her like he knew she was lying. Which she was, though she wasn't sure why. But in that look, his eyes dark and sad, she knew something had ended, that great parental loss, the moment they realize you're not perfect, and maybe even a little worse.

"In his back pocket," he added, watching her, squinting. "You know it."

*   *   *

She sat in her car for a minute, staring up at the sprawling house, bright yellow with white trim, like a slab of coconut cake, layers piled high.

The new cedar deck stretched twice the length of the entire first floor of the Knox house.

No sign of the detectives' unmarked black Dodge.

Katie smelled her shampoo first. Like Love's Baby Soft.

Then, walking across the softly carpeted living room, she saw her.

Knees together, hands folded, Hailey posed. Swimmer's shoulders hidden in a blush-pink oxford shirt, her face was paler than her usual golden-girl glow, but she was meticulously groomed. Katie pictured Tina leaning over her niece, brushes and wands and implements, incanting some kind of brisk Southern sorority-girl magic. Jerking Hailey's curls into a long ponytail that looked as shiny as a girl's favorite doll, soft and staticky and overtended so Katie could see every brush mark.

But something was wrong. One sandy spiral hung down, a forelock that didn't belong. *A big hank of her hair got torn out.* Artfully positioned to cover a bare patch, pink puckered. *Her scalp opened up where she hit the floor.*

"Okay," Katie said. "Why am I here?"

All three of them, sentried together on the sofa, heavily upholstered in bold plaid, her uncle and aunt didn't look at Hailey, and she didn't look at them.

They all looked only at Katie, their eyes clear and inscrutable.

"Eric wouldn't come?" Teddy asked.

"I told you he's at work. You're going to have to deal with me."

Teddy nodded, then Tina too, watching Katie closely, with twinkling eyes.

"Katie, we are thanking the heavens that Hailey's name has been cleared."

"Has it, Tina?" Katie said, straightening herself. Readying herself. "Because my daughter's battered body suggests otherwise."

Teddy's head bobbed in dramatic assent. "I know that none of this takes away what Hailey did, laying her hand in anger on our Devon," he said, pointing at his niece as though she were set in a pillory, face winsome and pleading. "But Katie, can I ask you, do you know, truly, how you might behave if you lost the person who mattered most to you?"

"And you were the one blamed?" Tina burst in. "That you not only lose your true love in a horrific accident, but on top of it you face this smear campaign—suspicion, rumors, dirty digs—"

Teddy raised his arm in front of Tina like spotting the girls on the bars, and her mouth closed briskly.

"Grief can drive you mad, Katie," he said, taking a different tack. "That wasn't our Hailey in the locker room with Devon. That was grief."

"Well," Katie said, looking over at Hailey, unable to stop herself, "it sure looked like Hailey when I pulled her off my four-foot-ten, ninety-two-pound little girl."

Turning her head slowly, Hailey met Katie's gaze. Composed, enigmatic. Katie had never seen her like this—a young woman whose face had always been like soft taffy, stretched into smiles, laughter, *C'mon, gymmies, let's show 'em what we got.* But maybe that had been a composition too, a mask. You never really knew anybody.

"Katie," Teddy said, clearing his throat, leaning forward. "I understand there've been some issues between Devon and Hailey."

He turned, for the first time, to Hailey.

"But Hailey was wrong about some things."

Katie looked over at Hailey, her stillness.

"And"—Teddy was still talking, his dulcet tones and bent brow, that mesmer-coach thing he could do—"I need you to know she has not shared with the police any of the wrong things she once believed. About your daughter."

"Ron wouldn't let her, thank God!" Tina jumped in. "He said it would only have made things worse for her. It would have made her look . . . a certain way. That's what Ron—"

Teddy's arm came up once more.

"And she will not be telling them now, or ever," he said. "None of us will."

Teddy and Tina looked earnestly, meaningfully at Katie. Their matching pearly hair, their tanned skin and finely laundered sportswear.

Beside them, Hailey. All three of them, their honeyed tans blurring together, the crispness of their shirts. All three becoming as one. A united front. Confederates. That's what families were, weren't they? The strong ones, the ones that last. Not supporters or enablers so much as collaborators, accomplices, coconspirators.

Hailey looked at her uncle, face benumbed, and nodded. A stuttering nod, like a record skipping.

"Yes, Mrs. Knox," Hailey said, nodding and nodding. "I was wrong. I was wrong about everything. I behaved wrongly and I believed false things."

*   *   *

There was a mysterious interlude, the passing around of footed glasses, the pouring of Tina's ambered sun tea, the entrance of Nadia and Nastia, Tina's snapping terriers, nipping and licking at Katie's feet.

Katie felt confused, light-headed in a way she couldn't recall since she was a child when the dentist put that glorious sucking mask over her face, what he used to call "happy hour."

Now, the talk was of the warming weather, the ragweed, the problems with their new deck, wood already splitting in the vertical posts, and did they need to sue the contractor. It was always something with these contractors, the workers they hired.

Somewhere, in all of it, Hailey disappeared into the kitchen, for napkins, for sugar, and never returned.

"Where did she go?" Katie asked, head jerking backward.

The temporary looseness in Teddy's bisque-colored jowls tightened and he leaned toward her again, setting his glass on the table.

"Katie, don't you worry about Hailey. She had her come-to-Jesus moment locked in that unholy facility. That is over. And I get why Eric wouldn't come with you today. But maybe you can talk to him. About his plans for Devon, and BelStars."

Tina sprang forward, past Teddy's block this time.

"John Ehlers is a fraud!" she shouted. "He's tried to poach from us before. He's tried many times. The stories I could tell you about him. About how he's boarding one of his gymnasts. A sixteen-year-old. He says it's all proper, but she's posting pictures of herself on his water bed—"

Teddy's hand landed firmly on Tina's linen-shod knee and her mouth shut again.

He looked at Katie, those misty eyes he used to such strong effect during his pre-meet speeches.

"Katie, gymnasts—all gymnasts but especially the exceptional ones—thrive on routine, on fair winds and following seas. And I can't apologize enough for our role in disrupting those waters for Devon. But we want things to go back." His eyes glowing wetly, Katie feeling her chest swelling out of habit. "We want to return to those bright days when all our hearts and minds were directed toward Elite Qualifiers. We want what you want: for Devon to realize her deepest promise, at last."

On his feet now, lifting Katie to her feet too, holding her hands in his, between his.

"With your say-so, we start over, now. We refocus all our efforts. Forget all this confusion, leave it in the darkness. Remove any obstacles from our champion's way. Return to our path, the one we mapped out together, all those years ago, all of us together, right here in this house, at that table in there."

Katie looked through the arched entry into the dining room. She could see it. Eric and herself leaning forward nervously, watching Teddy with his Sharpie, his flow chart. Deciding Devon's future.

She felt something turn inside her. A phantom kick to the ribs.

At that moment, a sharp thwack vibrated from the ceiling. And something else, almost like an animal scratching a carpet on the floor above them.

"You say the word, and the minute you leave," Teddy said, as if he hadn't noticed. *Could he really not notice?* "Bang goes the starter pistol. We are back."

Tina was on her feet now too, her hand on Katie's shoulder, the hard pebble of her engagement ring pressed there, talking loudly into Katie's ear, loudly over the thudding of a door over and over again upstairs.

"Practice at two forty-five sharp, as ever," Tina said. "Devon back where she belongs."

Upstairs, a brief lull came, before the ceiling itself seemed to shake from a fathoms-deep, from-the-bellows sobbing.

"And I promise you this," Teddy intoned, moving closer to her, all their bodies nearly touching, as if in prayer. "I will devote every fiber of my being, every cell in this aging body, every drop of my heart's blood to making Devon a Senior Elite in one month's time. She will have it. I leave it in your hands."

What could she say? What else could she possibly say?

This is how it is, Katie thought, sitting in the parked car, not ready to turn the key. *Our shared effort, the things we all do to keep following that Sharpied arrow.*

It made her think of something from months back. She'd come upon Eric and Teddy in the living room, watching footage from Devon's failed bid for Junior Elite two years ago. Their faces lit by the screen, Eric's hand on the remote, pausing on every frame of the vault. Hurtling down the runway, round-off, feet slapping board, rocketing backward, hands hitting table, body rising, left arm down, right elbow lifted, and then twisting, arms close to chest, spinning madly like a lathe.

Then landing, legs fused, on the mat.

Again and again, the frame palsied on that landing, that slightest of ankle rolls, the half step at most. A decade of work, an inch, two, of blue foam.

"That's always been her Achilles' heel," Teddy had said. "That foot. It makes her work the other one too hard. It's like she can't bear how wrong that foot is."

"The foot's not wrong," Eric had replied, eyes on the screen. "The foot's everything."

Still sitting in her car, from the corner of her eye, she saw a blond blur speeding past the Belfours' side deck, the one she'd stood on after Ryan's funeral.

Pound, pound, pound across the deck, the sharp twang of the small dive board.

A swelling plunge, a splash from the chemical depths of the Belfour pool.

Exiting the car, Katie walked quickly up the lawn and through the arbor.

Just then, Hailey emerged from the water and climbed, shirt and jeans drenched, up the ladder.

"Hey!" Katie said. "I need to ask you something."

Sweeping her hair back with her hands, the pectoral fins of a slender dolphin, she looked over at Katie, chin trembling. Katie could see the stippled spot on the scalp where the hair was gone, the purple under her eye where Devon's teeth had been.

"They'll see you," Hailey hissed, eyes darting toward the house. "They see everything."

Her pink shirt stuck to her brown skin, Hailey sat, dripping, in Katie's passenger seat.

"Mrs. Knox, I can't talk to you," she said, the wetness like a presence, a third thing in the car. "I made promises. I made my promises and I'm taking the pills and I'm moving back home with them. I'm getting my act together."

"Maybe you've convinced them," Katie said, "but I'm not convinced. How do I know you're not going to wake up tomorrow and call those detectives or come after my daughter again?"

Hailey shook her head, water scattering across Katie's arm. "I'm not saying a word. I'm never saying anything. What would it get me, Mrs. Knox?"

Katie said nothing for a second, watching Hailey, her eyes pinned, her hands tucked under her soaked jeans. She looked like a teenage girl gone wrong, caught and cowed.

"Mrs. Knox, I don't know what happened to Ryan," Hailey said, eyes flitting up the slope to her uncle's house.

"I didn't ask—"

"But I do know about Ryan and your daughter, and I'm not talking about it. Not ever. So can I leave now? Can I?"

"But why?" Katie knew she shouldn't ask. She couldn't stop herself. "Why would you do that?"

"They took care of me," Hailey said. "Uncle Teddy and Aunt Tina. When I was Devon's age, younger, I... You know how babies, when they first come out, you swaddle them? To keep them from scratching themselves, from scaring themselves? That's what it was like."

Katie felt her phone vibrating under her hand but didn't dare look. Instead, she focused on the browning half-moon under Hailey's eyes. Had Devon really bitten her?

"And they're still here, looking after me, even after everything the last week." Then a funny look passed over her face, a shadow, something. "I should've listened to Aunt Tina. She never trusted Ryan. A whistling girl and a crowing hen always come to some bad end, she said."

She looked over at Katie, a smile lurking, rueful and sharp-toothed.

"The night it happened, I thought he was going to propose. I thought that's why he'd picked the nice restaurant. But he'd picked it so I wouldn't make a scene when he broke up with me."

"Wait. Wait."

"I spent the rest of the night sobbing my heart out, then I find out he's dead. And I want to die from how bad it hurts." She shook her head, the scattering of droplets, her eyes chlorine red. "Then, the day of the funeral, I get this call. From Ahee Jewelers. They saw my name in the death notice and called me up. Ryan had ordered something but hadn't picked it up. So I got there and you can guess what I'm expecting."

Katie took a breath. "A ring."

"Sure. And what do I find instead?" She reached into the nearly sealed wet pocket of her jeans. Yanking something out, she then slapped it in her other palm. "I can't seem to stop carrying it around."

It was a necklace, gold plate. It was cheap, a girl's mall necklace. A pendant dangling at the end, a tiger figurine.

A tiger like the poster in Devon's room. A tiger like her lucky stuffed animal, plush and matted.

A tiger for Devon. Its haunches spreading, its legs poised, as if about to vault.

Small as a peanut, Ryan had said to Katie that time, about Devon, *but strong as a tiger.*

"Eye of the goddamned tiger, just like her stupid routine," Hailey said, staring at the necklace. "I slammed my fist on Ahee's glass counter and cracked it. They said I had to leave."

"You're lying," Katie said, shaking her head. "You knew about them before he died. You'd been sending her texts. You sent her texts the night he died."

She looked at Katie, head tilted, still holding the necklace, the tiger spinning in the air between them.

"No. I found out when I went to the jeweler. The day of the funeral."

"That's not true," Katie said, thoughts churning. Remembering Ryan's funeral reception, Hailey thumping on the glass, demanding things.

"I never sent her any texts, Mrs. Knox. I had no idea about Devon. That's how dumb I was. I should've known. Everything's always about Devon, for all of us. Right? My uncle, my boyfriend, those booster parasites. It's all about Devon and that fierce little body of hers, and that deformed foot. Everything depends on it."

"You're a pathetic girl," Katie blurted. "You're a pathetic little girl."

"Isn't it something," Hailey said, her gaze returning to the tiger necklace, her breathing harder now, "the things we do for our family?"

Reaching out, Katie grabbed for the necklace so forcefully Hailey flinched.

"Jesus," Hailey said, holding her wrist. "Jesus."

But Katie had the necklace, and held it. Just like the leotard, she would not let it go.

"Keep it," Hailey said. "I don't want it. It disgusts me. Maybe it's made me lose my mind this last week. Maybe now it'll stop."

"I think you should go back inside," Katie said. "Now."

A look of revelation appeared on Hailey's face. A knowing look that made Katie crazy.

"I was so mad when I was younger," she said. "And then you grow up and you think you're not that girl anymore. The girl you were at fifteen, sixteen. Angry and nasty. Hungry for love—"

"—I guess some girls are like that," Katie said, coolly.

"But the thing is, you're always that girl," Hailey said, stepping out of the car. "She never goes away. She's inside you all the time. That girl is forever."

Hailey touched the violet half-circle under her eye, the bite mark. It was like Devon's mouth was there, screaming.

"Get out of here," Katie said, turning the key in the ignition.

On her lap, she saw it: Missed call. Eric.

A prickling feeling around her temples, spreading hotly through her skull.

"Mrs. Knox, one last thing," Hailey was saying from the curb, hand still on the open door. "You know what I kept thinking when I saw you at the funeral?"

"I don't care, Hailey."

"I was thinking, I had it all wrong. That night after regionals in January. The tiki party. Remember?"

"Yes," Katie said, hand on the gear shift, a queasy feeling. Of course she remembered, all the women hoping to dance with Ryan, the air in the catering hall muzzy with mom perfume, rum, promise.

"I had it all wrong," Hailey said, fingers wrapped around the window edge. "I thought it was you I had to worry about. The way you danced with Ryan, your skirt inching up so he could see your tattoo. Sharing cigarettes in the back hallway, whispering in his ear."

"What? What?" Her face burning, her chest so hot, the heat in the car suddenly everywhere. "I don't know what you're talking about."

"But it turned out it was Devon, your little slut of a daughter. It wasn't you he chose. It was Devon."

Katie looked at her, breathing, breathing.

"It was never you," said Hailey.

And Katie lifted her foot from the brake.

Hailey jolting backward, stumbling on the pavement, Katie said, the words from some deep well, and unstoppable:

"You come near my daughter again, I'll break your neck."

That tiki party, again.

Always telescoping back to that night, months ago.

An evening of heat and pleasures for all of them. For everyone.

Everyone with their stolen moments, playful ones.

Teddy, Kirsten, and Bobby V. flicking bottle caps for cash in the back alley. Molly and Jim Chu making out like teenagers.

She'd seen Eric with his hand on the small of Gwen Weaver's back.

So what had been wrong about dancing with Ryan?

And enjoying it, the feeling, the sureness with which she could feel his heart beating behind the laundry-worn cotton of his shirt.

It wasn't like Hailey said, none of it.

Pulling over, she picked up her phone. Clicked.

The BelStars Facebook page shimmered. Finger to screen, she scrolled through all the pictures, every meet, pool party, pancake breakfast. And, yes, the tiki party.

The flare of the torches, Teddy limboing with Molly Chu, Devon beaming under a blaze of paper lanterns, under Eric's proud gaze.

Now that everyone had a camera in the palm of their hand, there were photos of everything. There were photos even when you thought no one else was there. Like the blurred one of the dance floor, Becca Plonski and Jim Chu leading some kind of conga line.

Crouching over the phone, pushing her face close, she spotted Ryan and a woman in the background. In the hall by the restrooms. Such a grin on the woman's face. No, on her own face.

Oh, yes, *that*.

She might not have remembered, ever, but for the photograph.

But still, such a small thing.

She had just been waiting for the restroom. And Ryan had been sneaking a smoke, the back door propped open. She hadn't even known he smoked, but everyone was smoking that night.

Can I have one? she'd asked, which meant she was drunk. She hadn't smoked in twenty years.

He'd smiled, nodded.

It was so meaningless, she'd mostly forgotten all about it.

She couldn't recall how they'd started talking about the book in his pocket, the one with the soft cover, pages curled. But suddenly it was in Katie's hand.

Then he told her the same thing he'd told her before, about never reading as a kid and reading now, and how he loved the book so much and he didn't know why.

It made her sad, a little, that he didn't remember telling her before.

Let me show you, he said, moving close behind her, leaning over her, cracking the book's many-cracked spine, forcing its pages open. They smelled like smoke.

So much taller, his forearm thrust in front of her, nearly grazing her collarbone, or beneath it.

And she thought there could be nothing more private than the inside of the forearm, the tenderest of skin, the push and throb of one blue vein.

The way it arrowed to the soft center of his half-open palm.

Resting her fingers on that skin, helping him keep the book

open, she watched as he turned to the most dog-eared page, its corner folded down.

She leaned close. It was dark, the hall was dark, the light covered with old kitchen grease like Vaseline gave everything a glow.

On the page was a line drawing of a tombstone (*But I don't just like it because there's pictures,* he'd said, winking) with words printed on it. They said:

EVERYTHING WAS BEAUTIFUL AND NOTHING HURT.

What does it mean? she asked.

But he just kept grinning, his arms turned out, open, the book splayed.

Like your heart, inside out, splayed.

Like he was saying, *I'm giving you something. I'm giving you* this.

But instead he said, *Your hands are hot.*

And she realized she was still touching both his arms, her fingertips resting on them, and she should have been embarrassed but wasn't and didn't know why.

But it was just a moment. It was just a moment. That was all.

And no one saw.

(Could Devon have seen?)

Later, as she was leaving, she spotted him one more time. He'd found Devon's lei in the parking lot. She wanted to take it, but her arms were full of party favors.

I know, he said.

Nearly slipping on the glassy pavement, he draped it over Katie's head.

Everything was beautiful and nothing hurt.

That was it, she realized now. She hadn't put it together before, the contexts so distinct. The same words Katie had seen in Devon's diary a month later. Like you write a boy's favorite song lyric. The kind of thing you do in the first heat of infatuation. Or love. Or something.

"Drew," she said into the phone. "I'm heading home now. I'll be there in less than a minute."

There was a noise on his end, like a seashell.

She remembered Drew explaining it to her once, that you're not just hearing air. Part of what you're hearing is yourself.

"Your blood even," he'd said. "You're hearing your own blood."

I'm hearing my blood, she thought now.

"Drew, are you there? What's all the noise? Are you outside?"

"Yeah," his voice came, "I can see you."

"What?" Her foot on the brakes, her eyes searched the road frantically.

"I can see you by the tall trees."

And there he was, tramping up the low hill in front of her, his hood pulled tight against his pink-thick face.

He was breathing hard into the phone, pressed so close.

I'm hearing my own blood, she thought, running out of the car. *It's roaring.*

"Don't be mad, Mom," he kept saying. "It's only nine blocks, just like you said."

"Drew, that doesn't matter," she said, hands on his arms, her chest jerking. "You could've been run over. You could—"

"But I had to tell you."

"Tell me what?"

"Dad called."

"Why couldn't you call or wait until I got back?"

"You were gone a long time."

"I wasn't gone a long time."

"You were gone for eighty minutes."

Eighty minutes. "Drew, something happened and—"

"And Dad called twice and said he was at Devon's school. He sounded really weird. I never heard him sound like that."

She looked at him.

"Drew, what did Dad say to you exactly?"

"He said they wouldn't let him take Devon out of school and that it was your fault. And he wanted to know where you were."

"Okay," she said. "Okay."

"I said you were in the shower. But then you were away so long I thought he might call back. Or something." He looked at her, a worried, almost paternal furrow in his brow. "So I thought I'd better find you."

She looked at him and thought her heart might burst.

"Mom," he said as she pulled him close, pressed him against her chest, the smell of Chloraseptic and panic, "are you okay?"

The corridors were empty, but all the classroom doors were open, the June heat filling the old high school and stray sounds wafting, the chant of French verb conjugations, the squeak of moving chairs, one student's lone protestation, *I'm so hot, Mr. Manear. Can we have class outside?*

Drew kept wandering from her, staring up at the display cabinets, the team banners, the signs—STAY STRONG, JAY CHONG! and SENIORS: TAKE THE PLEDGE TODAY!—all so mysterious to Katie, who hadn't been inside the school since parent-teacher conferences months ago.

"Devon," Drew said, and she turned quickly.

But he was only pointing to a bulletin board: TENTH-GRADE WRITING CONTEST: "DREAMS, WISHES, GOALS."

Beneath it were the top three essays, and Devon's was number one. Always number one.

Katie walked closer. She'd never seen the essay and Devon hadn't said anything about the contest.

She started reading it, her eyes moving so fast the words seemed to smear.

My Dream by Devon Emory Knox

I have never had any desire to be ordinary, or normal. But to be extraordinary, one must learn to conquer weakness.

I was three years old when I first set foot on the gymnastics beam.

"You were fearless," my parents tell me. They believed in me from the start.

I was seven when I got my first rip, a flap of skin the size of a nickel torn from the center of my palm. I knew what it was. All gymnasts get them, from the friction of your hands on the bars all day long.

And I rubbed chalk on it and went straight back to the bars.

Same with the jammed fingers, the wrist sprains, the hamstring that cost me a year.

All those years, all that work, I can't believe I never got broken.

Now I am almost sixteen and I have known fear, and failure.

Two years ago, I had my crisis point. I faced a difficult vault. No, I did not fall. But I did fail. And it was because I was afraid and I was weak. I didn't want it

enough. Or I was afraid to want something so completely, as completely as my coach did, my parents do.
They want everything for me.

So, for many months, I became a slave to my weakness. I was afraid of falling. Of landing on my neck, my
head. Of my bones breaking like wishbones. But most of
all, of failing.

I lived with that fear, saw it in the faces of others as
they watched how close I came. To falling. To losing.
The greatest of all fears and the one that can destroy you.

My dad tried to fix it. He built me a landing pit, and
he worked very hard to show me how important it was.

But the day the pit was finished, I was afraid again.
More afraid than ever.

"What if I don't want it enough?" I asked my dad.

He looked at me. "Devon, I promise you do. It's the
reason you're here. This," he said, pointing to the vault,
"is why you're here."

He was right. Because my vault was perfect, I was
fixed, and everyone loved me again.

I learned that day that I must trample fear and I must
own my desire. To be extraordinary.

It has been hard. I had to learn how to go inside myself. Places no one could touch, or see.

But I can say today that I am no longer afraid. I
have learned to make fear my slave. Whenever I confront my own weaknesses, I look in the mirror and
say, "You have taken things from me. You will take
nothing more."

Now it is only desire that rules me. Desire to win,
yes, but also to be the best. To be extraordinary.

It was like a picture of your life from an angle you'd never seen before. And Katie didn't know what to do with it, one hand pressing the paper, her other hand on her mouth.

Then she saw it. Across the bottom of the page, scrawled in giant diagonal letters and paper-tearing tugs, was a word:

Freak!!!!

Underneath, someone had drawn a cartoon, lurid and X-rated, a girl whose head dwarfed her little naked body, doing a split, her hairless crotch exposed.

"She's in her history class right now," said the principal, an earnest-jawed man named Mr. Waltham whom Katie had never met. "Room one twelve, if you'd like to check."

"I'm sorry about all this," Katie said. "My husband is having some medical issues."

"He seemed very upset," said the principal, who seemed upset himself. "He seemed to believe we were being deliberately obstructive."

His gaze falling, nervously, to Drew's pink, gummy face, the way he kept scratching at his scaly skin.

"It's the medication talking. I'm very grateful," Katie said, grabbing Drew's hand. "I won't bother you again."

"We don't see too much of you two here," Mr. Waltham said, hoisting a smile. "We'd been hoping to recruit Mr. Knox for the PTA, get him—both of you—involved more in school activities. I understand he's a very successful fund-raiser—"

"Absolutely, Mr. Waltham. I promise."

*   *   *

She moved with purpose through the musty halls, Drew's hand, his delicate peeling fingers, in hers past all the classrooms until she found the right one.

Seated in the far corner by the window was Devon. Pencil in hand, her warm-up jacket's sleeves creeping over her gnarled gymnast hands, as if she wanted to hide them. Hair pulled into a bun hard as a walnut.

It had been a while, more than a while, since she'd seen Devon among so many other girls her age. Non-gym girls. But, whether thick-bodied or willowy, with cat's-eye glasses and braces, or thickly eyelinered and greasy-foreheaded, or donning Day-Glo nail polish and a do-rag, they all looked so much more like one another than like Devon.

None of them looked anything like Devon.

When had they all developed these bodies, whether hard little tennis balls or absurdly luxuriant breasts stretched beneath straining T-shirts? And hips, hips that seemed to sway and undulate even when they shifted in their seats, stretching across revealing ample, fleshy waists and downy hair.

They were women, or close enough.

And a few feet apart from them, in her quiet corner, her pencil moving, her eyes on the teacher, on the whiteboard, on something, sat her tiny, herculean daughter, stallion thighs stretched against the denim of her jeans, her face wan and small. Her feet, misshapen and scarred, hidden in her softest pair of sneakers. Nearly sixteen. Fearless. Extraordinary. Like no one else. Only like herself. Whoever that was.

The bell rang, the door pushed open, and Katie retreated quickly into the crowd.

Book bag swung over her shoulder, all the boys, most of

the girls towering over her, Devon hurried out to her next class.

"Hey, Baby Gap," one jug-jawed boy called out, "can you carry my bag too?"

"But look at those thighs," another added, grinning, his teeth monstrous. "Wrap those thighs around my cock, Baby Gap."

"Watch out for her toes. They look like nutcrackers to me."

"I'd let her work my beam any day, but what do you hold on to except biceps?"

Devon walking, and walking, never turning her head.

Back in the car, Drew didn't ask what was going on with his dad, what had happened at the Belfours', why the police had come to the house.

It was as if he knew she wouldn't be able to answer, the noise in her head so loud.

They were driving on Sparrows Way when she noticed the turnoff, spotted the flutter of yellow tape through the trees. *Ash Road.*

"That's the spot," Drew said, as if reading her mind.

"Yes." She decided in an instant, turning the wheel hard, the gears gnashing. "It is."

But the minute her tires landed on Ash Road's soft asphalt she regretted it.

"Except the picture's from the other side," Drew said.

"What picture?" she asked, but something began sliding into place in her head.

"Ryan's picture."

Pulling the car onto the road shoulder, she stopped the engine, hand shaking on keys.

"The one on his refrigerator," she said, realizing it. The snapshot taped to Ryan's fridge door. A blur of greenery, the swampy colors of a cheap printer. "This is the place."

"Yeah," Drew said, almost a sigh.

Looking at him, a revelation felt close, just beyond her grasp.

The yellow tape twisted, held pockets of dew, rain.

"Drew, go back in the car, okay?"

Arrayed on the dirt road, spilling onto the shoulder, were a series of small fluorescent flags, mud-splattered, bending in the wind.

Each flag had a number, marking something. Maybe a gouge in the dirt, glass fragments, a heel print. They looked so festive, like miniature versions of the scoring flags judges flashed at meets, or the parade of flags at the Olympics.

A few cars sped by, jolting her as she walked along the shoulder, the dirt beneath her, dusting up the sides of her shoes. *Hairpin turn.* That's what everyone always said, but it was just a sharp one, and not blind at all.

Her sneakers, half untied like a sloppy teenager's, slid on the shoulder, the dirt sandy, almost like silk. The edge was so steep you could imagine at night, with streetlamps several spans away, getting turned around, getting lost inside yourself.

Off the shoulder, there was a drop, and a shallow ditch heavy with old rain, filmy pools of motor oil floating on top. One lone flag lay flat in the water, spinning like a propeller, like those whirlybird seeds that fell from the maples.

This was where Ryan fell. His body knocked, hurled, jettisoned.

There were no skid marks on the road, the reporter said. *Whoever the driver was, he never even set his foot on the brake.*

The silver car never stopped.

The shallow ravine looked scraped clean, long rake grooves thatched across, combed for evidence, for glass, for paint. As the slope cantered down, it was like the earth folded up upon itself, a green swoop, a pelt of foliage at its center.

Even though it was daylight, just shy of noon, it was the darkest place she'd ever seen, a cut in the earth.

I saw one of his shoes.

That was what Eric had said, nearly asleep and holding her arm, stroking it, the night after they heard the news, after he'd been to Ash Road.

She thought about Ryan's shoe tumbling down, one lace spinning like a whirligig.

I saw it, Eric had told her. His voice mournful, lost.

Now the words sounded different. Meant something different.

I saw it. Because he was there when it happened.

"Why did Ryan have a picture of the place he died right on his refrigerator?" Drew said, standing next to the car.

Katie didn't say anything for a moment.

"Maybe it was his favorite place to walk," she tried, finally.

Drew looked around doubtfully.

"Maybe if you didn't want anyone to see you," Katie said, thinking.

"Maybe."

"Or something else."

A meeting place, a lovers' rendezvous point.

One that sentimental Ryan kept a photo of on his refrigerator door.

Now Katie could see it.

There's a hundred ways sex can ruin you. That was Eric's doomful warning to Devon.

Amid the balloons and banners of Lacey Weaver's party, had Devon gotten a call, a text, not from Hailey but from Ryan?

Meet me at the turn in Ash Road. You know the spot.

He must have. *There's a hundred ways sex can ruin you.* And he wouldn't let it, wouldn't let her. Did Eric find out?

"Why are you going down there, Mom?"

"Just to see."

She eased down into the shallow ravine.

Drew was looking down at her, eyes black under the overcast sky.

A wind glittered up glass and leaves as she eased down, as she saw.

Paint, glass; there were hundreds of chips, fragments, specks, shards.

And Ryan had fallen down here. And there were a million flecks of ephemera that could have pressed into the folds of his clothing, scattered through his hair.

She realized it in a flash: *The police will never know who hit him, not for sure.* Not with all this. So much glitter, a mad confetti. From a decade or more of bottles lobbed from car windows, from battered fenders, a car hood into a tree stump, teens stalking the woods, forties in hand, in pursuit of magic and mayhem.

Like the time she and Eric, that first wild summer, got caught trespassing in the woods behind the church. Running from the security guard, laughing and huffing in cold air, then Eric trying to boost her over a wire fence and her sandal caught in one of the zig hooks. Trapped at the top, she couldn't shake it loose, her chest pressed against the chain mesh, laughing so hard and crying so hard she couldn't move.

The fence left diamonds on her chest for days.

The most brilliant of tattoos—a lifetime of good luck, Eric promised. Diamonds are forever, right?

Like hog rings, her mother said when she saw them, shaking her head. *And that guy's never going to marry you.*

But then he did. He did.

Devon inside her already, waiting. He did.

At the end of the summer she told herself she loved him so much she would rather die than lose him. And she still felt it. Because there's a hundred ways sex can ruin you but there's no end to the ways love can.

Walking back up the slope, she heard something, a branch cracking, and she could feel her ankle turning, her body starting to pitch forward, and suddenly Drew appeared, his hand grabbing for her, trying to hold on to her.

"Mom!"

She caught herself, dug her heel hard into the mud, steadied them both.

"Thanks, sweetie," she said. "I'm okay."

But there was a look on Drew's face she'd never seen, his hands gripping her impossibly hard, as if she were still falling.

"Mom, I want to go home," Drew whispered. "I wanted to for the longest time."

Chapter Twenty

He didn't say anything during the short drive, but when she pulled into the garage, Drew grabbed her arm, the seat belt straining.

"Mom, why did you leave me by myself?"

She unfastened her belt, turned and faced him.

"Drew, I'm sorry. I had to see Teddy. A lot is happening now. Things I need to take care of."

"Why do you always leave me by myself?" He said it louder, with startling firmness.

"Honey, I don't. And I'm sor—"

"I'm always by myself."

She looked at him, those coffee-bean eyes, and put her hand to his forehead.

"Did you get spooked, honey?"

"I thought maybe I'd get in trouble. For leaving. But I had to. Because Dad was so weird."

"No," she said. "You're not in trouble. And I'm so sorry."

He nodded, vaguely. That was when she noticed it, perched on the utility shelf: the two-liter bottle studded with rock salt, clouded pink. The remnants of Drew's science project, abandoned due to illness. The second failed attempt.

"Drew," she said. "The brine shrimp in the oil. What happened the first time?"

He paused, throat clicking.

"Remember? I had to throw them away."

"Why?"

"You know. They spilled. That's why I put them up higher this time. But then I got sick."

"How did they spill?" She only remembered Drew telling her. The night after they found out about Ryan. The night after Ryan died.

Drew looked at her, and Katie was alarmed to see his chin shaking.

"Maybe she didn't want me to win the science fair."

"What?"

"Maybe that's why she did it. She never won a science fair."

"Who?"

"Devon. You told me to put the container in the garage while they hatched. And she knocked it over with Dad's car. So they all died."

"What?" she said again, kept saying. Something throbbing in her head. "Devon doesn't drive by herself. She doesn't even have her license."

"I kept telling you she was. You said I was dreaming. I'd hear her in the garage at night. I told Dad."

Katie looked up at the garage ceiling, Drew's room right above it.

"I told him a long time ago. Like when it was Easter. I said Devon sometimes took his car after we all went to sleep. Or early, before the newspaper came."

"Drew."

Sneaking in the garage, sneaking the car out. The constant rumble and traffic of their home. The garage door open most of the time. Was it possible?

"I guess Dad finally caught her. I heard them in here. I went to check on the shrimp and I saw them through the door crack. She was crying. She was crying and he couldn't get her to come out of the car. And she kept holding the wheel except the car wasn't on anymore. She was holding it tight like you are now."

Katie looked down at her hands, shaking.

"He kept telling her she needed to be quiet," Drew said. "That Mom would hear."

Katie nodded.

"She was crying and she wouldn't stop. She sounded funny. I never saw her cry. And then Dad stopped yelling. He told her he would fix things."

"Drew," she said, looking down at him, "this was a week ago Saturday, wasn't it? The night Ryan died."

He didn't say anything, breathing softly.

"Drew."

He nodded.

As if in some silent agreement, they both opened their car doors, stepped out.

When she tried to reach for him, he moved away, pointing down at the floor. Not looking at her.

"I went in after," he said. "The plastic bottle was stuck under the tire. I couldn't pull it loose. She knocked all the water out and all the eggs too. They died before they were real."

"They weren't real yet, Drew. I promise."

"But they were going to die anyway," he said. "Once I

292

put the oil in." He paused. "Maybe Devon didn't want me to win."

"Drew." Taking a breath, Katie reached for his arm. "You know this is about more than your experiment, don't you?"

He paused and in that pause Katie saw his little face age ten years.

Then he nodded.

"Oh, Drew," she said, her hand on his arm tighter now, "why didn't you tell me?"

He didn't say anything, plucking at the peeling skin on his temple.

"You know what you're telling me, right? About your sister?"

He nodded.

"You've known all along."

He looked at her, eyes glassy and bottomless, and said, "Yeah, Mom."

Rummaging through the recycling, she couldn't find an empty two-liter. Three doors down, she lifted the lid on the biggest bin on the block and took two.

She had decided it was to be their lost hour.

An amnesia. An hour free from everything else that had happened, was happening.

Maybe it was a kind of madness, but it was the least she owed him.

Drew rinsed the bottles, then she took the bread knife and sliced off the tops. Together, they filled them with water and salt. They marked the waterline with a Sharpie to monitor evaporation, and then Drew sprinkled the eggs inside.

Katie cleared everything from the highest shelf in the TV room. All of Devon's trophies, three BelStars albums. She dumped them on the sofa, dust gusting.

"It'll be safe here," she said, setting the two-liters down on the swollen wood.

"Yeah." Drew nodded.

"They hatch in two days?"

"Then we add the motor oil. And check under the microscope every ten minutes for an hour. To see if they're still kicking."

"Okay."

Drew looked up at the plastic containers, the cloudy water, the shrimp far too small to see.

"I don't want to add it, really," he said. "It seems mean."

"It's not mean," she said. "It's nature."

The phone call came just as they finished.

"Devon," Katie answered, her voice shaking. "Devon."

"Mom!" Devon's voice, like a claw over Katie's heart. "Guess what? Everything's back. Coach T. is holding practice today. Can you believe it? Mrs. Chu's here at school. She's going to drive me and Cheyenne."

She sounded so buoyant, as buoyant as Katie had heard her in months.

"Devon, no," she said. "I'm coming to get you right now. I'm taking you home. We need to talk."

"I can't hear you, Mom," she said, Cheyenne's squeals in the background, the sound of doors slamming, an engine starting, and Molly Chu's excitable voice, *Hurry up, girls. There's bound to be traf—*

"Devon, wait!" she said, but Devon didn't hear.

When Katie tried to call back, she got voice mail. When she called Molly, she got voice mail. As she set the phone down, it rang again.

"Kirsten."

"Did you hear? Coach T. is back. That sly dog, he must've known his days were numbered. Listen, can you take Jordan? I'm at work and——"

"Devon's on her way with Molly."

"Goddamn it," Kirsten said. "Goddamn it."

"So she misses today."

"I bet you'd like that."

"Excuse me?"

"I'm sorry," Kirsten said quickly. Then she sighed, her voice wobbly. "But I have a career——"

"We all work," Katie said. "All of us."

"——I have clients. Sometimes I think I'm just working to keep Jordan in those goddamned two-hundred-dollar leotards. Don't you ever get tired?"

"I'm tired all the time," Katie replied, her hand covering her face, the smell of the salt under her fingernails. "Kirsten, I have to go——"

"You and Eric just never miss a beat. The gym in the basement, the library of Olympics DVDs. When Devon's down on the floor, you and Eric in your matching BelStars shirts doing the counts with her, moving when she moves. God, I just don't have that kind of time," Kirsten said, sighing. "And Jordan blames me for it. I know she does."

"Kirsten," Katie said, a voice coming from somewhere, a voice hard and cool. "I know you wish Jordan were half the athlete Devon is. And I know you wish that the difference was just a matter of you having more time to devote to her. And it's not because you don't commit like we commit. It's because Jordan isn't that good. She's ordinary."

"Jesus, Katie——"

"And when you have an extraordinary child," Katie said, a heat under her eyes, "you'll do anything for her."

"This is the last time, Mr. Watts," she said, opening the screen door for him. "I promise."

The hush the antibiotics brought on, Drew was sound asleep in his bed, his hands still sticky from salt too.

"I just have to get Devon. And I'll be back."

"You don't have to explain," Mr. Watts said, stepping inside. "You never did."

Three miles into the twenty-eight-mile drive to BelStars, she caught sight of the original Weaver's Wagon, the only one where the wheels on the sign really turned. Where Ryan had been a line cook, and where Gwen had her office, her fancy leather-bound checkbook binder, her sterling-silver check-signing pen.

The truck in front of her slowed and turned into its lot.

Night Owl Distributors
Beer ◆ Fine Wine ◆ Distilled Spirits

Its orange logo was a pair of owl eyes, one winking tipsily. It looked familiar. Where had she seen it before?

Then it came to her. Just a few days ago, the doodle on Eric's notepad as he talked to Gwen. A pair of slanty eyes, a *V* between them, like a cartoon owl.

Behind the wheel, the driver wore a cap with the same logo.

He looked familiar too.

She watched as he drove through the lot to the restaurant's loading area.

And she followed.

Iced coffee in hand, Gwen stood on the loading dock as the men emptied the Night Owl truck and another one, a side of beef painted blistering pink on the side, pulled up.

The driver walked over to her, clipboard outstretched. Squinting, Katie watched him, his dewlapped face and the ambling way he moved.

Tugging at his cap, he looked just like he had when Katie had first seen him at the police station, holding the door for Helen Beck, tipping his brim at her.

Did you see his hat? Drew had asked Katie when they spotted him in the parking lot of the police station. *It had two eyes on it. And one was droopy. It made his face look droopy.*

He held Gwen's coffee while she signed the form. Rocking foot to foot just like Uncle Don.

Here's a fella, been arrested twice for drinking Jack Daniel's while under the influence of driving . . . Used to deliver for Gwen Weaver and she fired his sorry ass.

Gwen handed him the clipboard and he saluted her and climbed leisurely into the truck's cab.

Lifting her coffee, she seemed to salute him back.

Slamming her car door, Katie bolted across the parking lot toward Gwen. She didn't know what she was doing, but she was doing it.

"Who is he?" she shouted, jabbing her finger at the truck. "Who is he? You know him, don't you?"

Gwen's mouth twitched slightly, but she covered it with her coffee, then smiled.

"Paul? Sure. I own six restaurants, three with liquor licenses. I know all the Night Owl guys."

"I saw him, Gwen. At the police station. He's the witness, isn't he? The trucker who said he saw a purple car?"

Gwen beckoned her inside, through the kitchen, with its squall of clanging pots, chugging machines, through the swinging double doors, into the empty quiet of the dining area, lunch service cleared save one remaining tub of dishes slithering with grease.

"Katie," she said quietly, looking down into the bin for a moment, "I don't know what you're talking about. You seem upset. You seem upset a lot lately. Very dramatic and interesting. What is it today? Diphtheria? Smoke inhalation? I heard you conducted a little Olympic torch ritual in your backyard."

"How did you know about—goddamn it, Gwen," Katie said. "I talked to the Belfours. That guy's the witness who claimed he saw Hailey, right? The one who got it all wrong. And he used to work for you. And now he does again."

She squinted at Katie, cocked her head. "I'm a firm believer in second chances," she said, just as she'd said about Ryan. "It's the American way."

"Gwen, what is this? Did you pay him off?" Katie asked. "Did you pay him to lie? Do you want me to tell Teddy that?"

Gwen paused, then let out a sigh. She never had been patient. She didn't know how.

"I didn't tell him to say it was a purple car," she said, shaking her head. "In fact, I think I suggested blue. Generic. Purple was Paul's embroidery. Turned out he doesn't like Hailey. She was a careless driver. Ran into one of his hand trucks in our lot once. I wasn't going to pay for the four cases of Old Grand-Dad, so he had to. Anyway, he happens to have some debt—"

"Gwen, I don't care—"

"Debt really runs this country, doesn't it? Maybe you know something about that. Everyone wants more than they can pay for. Can you blame them? He needed money, he needed my business. He was willing to do something to get it."

It was so bold, so stark. Katie nearly leaned back from it, the bald admission.

"For BelStars?"

"For all of us."

"And you would have just let that train keep going? Let Hailey go to prison?"

"I doubt it would have come to that. But it gave us time. And would you have preferred the alternative?" Gwen said, tilting her head and squinting at her. "Is that what you want, Katie? The police looking elsewhere? Finding suspects, motives? What exactly do you want here? You'd better be sure this is a conversation you really want to have."

Katie looked down at the table, its bleach-streaked whorls. She thought of Eric on the phone with her. The two of them plotting together. It was like finding him in bed with her, with anyone. Naked and ugly. It was worse. Why it was worse, she didn't know. It was.

"I don't want you near my daughter again," she said. "Or my husband."

Gwen smiled dimly, leaning against one of the booths.

"You can make me the bad guy if you want," she said. "The tiger mom, the rich bitch. The husband stealer—that one's flattering. But I never got my kicks that way. I know where I want my energies invested. And Eric does too."

She looked at Katie, eyes narrow and crackling.

"You don't know anything about him," Katie said, tight and

low but every word like a scream in her ear. "He brought you in for your sacks of cash. He works to keep you here for them."

Gwen's face loosened a split second, a jolt of surprise, or hurt. "Look at you," she said. "Well, I may not know everything about Eric, but I know about you. You've always wanted to play the selfless mom, the good sport, the one with the kid whose talents just fell in your lap. Like she was born a gold medalist and you just stood on the sidelines and clapped. But we both know it isn't like that."

"Stay out of my daughter's business. You have——"

"What I have are resources. As you kindly pointed out, that's why you brought me on. That's why that smart, ambitious husband of yours found me, courted me, won my favor. So I could pull out my checkbook and make sure that racehorse of ours keeps running."

"My daughter's not your goddamned horse. She's not anyone's horse."

Gwen smiled, leaning back farther, resting her hand on the banquette behind her.

"But none of it works without a Devon," she said. "A Devon lifts up the gym, raises everyone's game. Gives all those parents the delusion that they too could produce a Devon."

A hot gust blew from the swinging kitchen doors, but Katie felt herself shiver.

"She's not 'a Devon.' She's my Devon. And she's not there to serve anyone else's fantasies."

Gwen lifted an eyebrow, blond and precise.

"And this isn't a problem to solve, like a failing coach, bad equipment," Katie continued. "A boy died. A boy we all knew."

Gwen sighed, her eyes returning to the ketchup-slicked dish bin beside them.

"A boy died, yes. A pretty boy who made us all feel prettier."
She paused a moment, then looked back at Katie. Looked at
her like she'd look at Lacey, and Lacey would tighten her braids.
"And, from what Ron Wrigley tells me, the police stop investi-
gating these hit-and-run cases in a few days. I mean, a few paint
chips, what do they mean?"

They locked eyes for a moment. A moment that seemed to
crackle and buzz between them. What they both knew and neither would say.

Finally, Gwen opened that perfectly painted mouth of hers.
"You haven't asked me, but I really don't know what happened
to poor Ryan Beck that night. It's not my business. All I know is
it was my daughter's birthday."

"What does that have to do with anything?"

"Lacey was so glad Devon came to the party. It meant a lot."

"Gwen—"

"It's a shame she had to leave before we even got to the
presents. Though Devon's gift was very nice. Lacey wears those
glitter bracelets constantly, even if they make her wrists itch."

"Devon doesn't enjoy parties," Katie said, the words coming
automatically, not liking the feeling, the sound, the prickly edge
of this. "She never stays for long."

"She got a call right before she left. She sounded very anxious on the phone. But she promised she'd find a way out. That's
what she said. I guess she did. Find a way out."

The bad feeling, it was growing.

"You just follow my daughter around, do you? That's all any
of you do. Do you think Devon has time for your little-girl
parties?"

Hearing herself, her tone, the thickness of everything, Katie
felt queasy.

"I saw her through the front window. Charging down the lawn like it was the vault runway," Gwen continued. "I called after her. It didn't seem safe, at night. But she's very fast, as you know. Lacey should sprint with half her power."

A loud crash from the kitchen, the sounds of bottles rolling, breaking.

"Luckily, you don't live very far. She was moving with great purpose. As if she had someplace she needed to be. I was the only one who saw her." She paused, looking at Katie. "But no one will ever hear it from me."

"There's nothing to hear," Katie said, but in her head she was picturing it all. Her daughter dashing through the night, those soundless sneakers, all stealth and speed.

Gwen nodded as if she could hear Katie's thoughts.

"Katie, don't mistake me. I know my horse in this race," she said. "We all do."

"My daughter," Katie repeated, "is not a fucking horse."

"What I'm saying is don't worry, Katie. I'm taking care of it. That's what I'm here for."

"To protect your investment."

"Isn't that what parents do?" Gwen said, smiling. "When we're young, we don't know what we want. We're blobs. We need shaping."

"She's shaping herself," Katie said. No one ever understood.

Gwen shook her head. "They think they want things. Tits, sexy boyfriends, McGriddles every weekend. But they don't really know what these things mean. That's why we've got to want things for them, Katie. The right things."

"I'm not like you," Katie said. "I'm nothing like you."

Gwen just smiled.

"It's funny. Teddy always says girl gymnasts are like horses, high-strung," she said. "I was never a gymnast, couldn't even do a cartwheel. But horses. Well, I rode horses from the time I was five. Every day for years."

"And here you are, still trying to ride horses."

"My dad loved them," Gwen said, not seeming to have heard. "He used to take me to the stables every day. My whole world was saddles, hay, bridles, and bits. Chantilly—that was my first horse, a ravishing OTTB mare."

As she spoke, her face turned younger, softer.

"When I got her, she was lame on the right. Dad showed me how to use a rasp on her. File the flaring, nip the crack. After that, she never put a foot wrong. I rode her all the way to the Jubilee. My dad was so nervous he bit the tip of his tongue clean off when I won."

She looked at Katie, shaking herself from the reverie, or trying to.

"It's important that we do that," she said. "*That's* important, Katie."

"Do what? Gwen, you're—"

"Whenever I doubted myself, my dad would say, 'Grab that dream by the hands, Gwennie. Clutch until the knuckles go white.'"

"Whose dream?"

"It doesn't matter whose dream it is," she said. "Just that it's a dream."

Katie stared down at her hands, the rock salt still under her nails. There were many things she wanted to say, like that she'd never had a dream for Devon, had only followed her daughter's desires. But then her thoughts snagged on that word, *desire*. That word that was all over Devon's essay. Desire, desire. *Now it is only desire that rules me.* Whatever desire meant to Devon. Whatever it had done to her.

"Gwen, you're wrong," Katie said. "About everything. And this gym, you boosters, all of this—it's poison. It's poisoned everything. I'm going to BelStars now and I'm taking my daughter away from all the poison of that poisonous place."

"And you and Eric were delicate virgins when you arrived at BelStars all those years ago, right? Katie, that just doesn't fly with me. Eric *made* the boosters. The two of you *are* BelStars."

"Not anymore," Katie said. "You'll see how little we need you."

The bell over the front door rang, and Gwen's gaze turned to it, the older couple walking inside.

"And Gwen," Katie said. "I'm sorry your daughter's second-rate, second-string. I'm sorry she'll never be your elite, your Thoroughbred. Her legs aren't strong enough and soon practice won't matter anymore."

It was as if Gwen didn't hear, and, the customers arriving at the hostess station, Gwen's eyes landed instead on the dish tub with the ketchup lapped up one side. She shook her head.

"Heather! Jeff!" she shouted, so loud and so sudden, Katie nearly jumped. "Come get the fucking tub. Get the fucking tub now."

"I'm nothing like you," Katie said again, wanting to say it a hundred times.

Gwen turned, looking at Katie.

"No," she said, a grim tug to her mouth. "You're much better."

"I changed my mind," Katie said. "I want him with me."

Mr. Watts nodded as if it made some kind of sense, helping Katie rouse Drew from his sickly slumber, tug on his coat.

"Where we going, Mom?"

"The gym."

"Okay."

Mr. Watts followed her outside, Drew lagging behind, resting on the porch steps, tying his shoes.

"Are you okay?" Mr. Watts looked at her. She had no idea what he saw.

"Thanks for watching him."

"I like him. I don't need any thanks."

"Mr. Watts," she said, looking at Drew on the front steps, pulling at the tongue on his sneakers, "you said something before. About the day Devon got hurt. The mower."

"I did."

"That you saw me. You said you saw me."

"Standing at the screen door. You had your hands over your ears because of the mower. You were watching her run to her daddy. You always loved to watch her run."

"You're remembering it wrong," she said. "I wasn't at the door. I was in the kitchen and I heard her scream. Then I ran to the door. It was over by the time I got there. So you had it wrong."

He looked at her. Her keys jingling in her hand, her body fixed and tight. She didn't move.

"Well," he said, blinking slowly, "my memory isn't what it used to be."

"No."

"Memory can be a funny thing," he added softly.

"You ready, Drew?" she called out, voice rasping.

He rose, and then began running toward her.

"Safe drive, Mrs. Knox," Mr. Watts said as she hurried Drew to the car. "You be safe, okay?"

*　　*　　*

On the ride, she let Drew sit beside her in the front seat.

She was thinking of the first time she'd ever visited BelStars. Walking into that hallowed space. Seeing all those girls, the older ones, impossibly strong and fresh-faced, practice their floor routines. The music echoing from the old boom box Teddy used to use. Russian folk songs, high opera, tragic arias, erotic tangos. Bouncing, running, diving, propelling themselves into the air to music grim, dramatic, melancholic, carnal.

At the time, she'd thought how strange it was, all these little girls performing to such adult songs. Songs about things they couldn't possibly understand—songs of desire, longing, sorrow, passion, loss. What did they know of such feelings, the big emotions of life?

Slowly, Katie and Drew walked up the stands, to their usual spot, 13-J.

She didn't look at the other parents, the boosters, but she could hear them behind her, whispering excitedly, pointing and churring and chattering and pant-hooting, about the new beam coach, how three of her girls earned top spots on beam at the last qualifier and how Teddy must've poached her from EmPower, what a coup.

On the floor, bodies were moving—bounding, swooping, flicking, spinning. Girls on the ropes, climbing with ferocity. Girls on the bars, swinging layout flyaways, straddle backs, baby giants. As if nothing had happened. As if the last ten days had been a fever dream.

"Do I see sickled feet, missy?" a familiar voice rumbled. "Because those are deductions, my dear. The ugliest kind."

Coach T., feet planted on a stack of orange mats, face red, mouth open.

Just a few hours before, he had been sitting across from her, pleading his case, pledging his troth. And now here he was, along with Amelise and Bobby V. and two new coaches, both with necks as thick as tree stumps, their log arms flipping girl after girl, their voices low and steady and constant.

"Swing! Swing! C'mon, strong. Strong."

"C'mon, fivers! That's sad juice. Garbage in, garbage out."

"Work your arms in the double lay, Cheyenne. Work straight. Head up, head up."

All the shouts and grunts and squeaks, hands slamming on beam, feet punching the mat, the hiccup of the vault, the squeeze of the springs.

"Big smiles, no mistakes, Li'l Miss Weaver."

"Come on, Jordan. Arms, arms, arms. Sell, girl, sell, perform."

"Don't let me see it hurt. Remember: everything's beautiful, nothing hurts."

Everything was beautiful and nothing hurt. Katie felt the words shiver through her, and it was that moment that she saw Devon taking the beam, Teddy on the floor, approaching her.

Devon leaning down, hands on her knees, listening to him, nodding.

That's my daughter, she thought. *Look at her. Look at that fawn-eyed little girl. She would never harm anyone. She would never do any of these things.*

It's not possible, she thought. *Drew's wrong. Gwen's wrong. Everyone's wrong.*

She knew he'd arrived the minute she saw Devon straighten her spine, lengthen her form, shift her center ever so slightly to the rear of the gym.

Katie turned, and there Eric was, standing just inside the doors on the far end of the stands.

Face gaunt, hollow, eyes russet-ringed, he was watching Devon, hands shoved in his jeans pockets, the same jeans from last night, the knees darkened with dust.

The ground beneath the two of them was gone, and might be gone forever. The eternal aerial, the falling-forever.

Abruptly, he looked up into the stands. Catching his gaze, she couldn't remember how she was supposed to feel or understand any of it.

That's the awfulness of love, her mom once said to her, peeling off last night's eyelashes, resting them on the table beside her coffee. *Every feeling, all at once, all the time. That's when you know it's real. And by then it's too late.*

Her head darting between the two, Katie's eyes unfocused, and husband and daughter blurred, the same dark hair, the same hooded eyes, the same fixed jaw, mouths like bruises. They were like twins. Or the same thing.

She knew she should be thinking, *Look what they've done. Look what she's done (and why?) and look what he's done in hiding it, hiding her.*

But instead, all she could think was *Why didn't you tell me? Why didn't you share it with me? Either of you. It's always been we three. Collaborators. Conspirators. We three against the world.*

We four, she corrected herself.

Drew beside her, head down in his book. Hardy Boys again. *The Secret of the Caves.*

On the floor, all the girls, all the coaches had stopped, mid-drill. Devon was at the vault.

"C'mon, missy, let's see that double-twist Yurchenko," Teddy said, clapping his hands. "You've done that one in your sleep before. No going backward here."

On the runway, Devon bobbed from foot to foot, clenching and unclenching her hands.

"She nearly took a header on it last week," murmured Jim Chu, Molly shushing him.

Shaking her fingers at her sides now, Devon was talking to herself, staring at the springboard eighty feet away.

Then, as if she'd heard something, Devon lifted her head and looked over at her dad, locked eyes with him. And just like that, everything changed. As far away as Katie was, she could feel the change, Devon's chest filling, her body battening itself.

Her head turning again, Devon looked up at Katie.

Like a foot to the rib cage, it was. Katie nearly lost her breath from the pain and power of it. *My girl*.

The minute Devon exploded into her run, Katie closed her eyes.

"Look at her go," someone said behind her. Kirsten Siefert, her body inching forward. "Would you look."

Hearing the thunk of the springboard. Opening her eyes. Seeing it. Springing what looked like a hundred feet in the air, then landing, both heels thumping the mat with such force that, sixteen rows up, Katie could feel the shock up her spine.

You can't understand what it's like until you see your child do something you could never do. No one could ever do.

This is what fearlessness looks like, Katie thought. *What desire can do.*

"God," Jim Chu muttered. "She's like a machine. A perfect machine. Do you ever want to open up that head of hers and see what kind of wiring she has?"

"My daughter's not a machine," Katie said. "She's extraordinary."

*   *   *

"Where'd Dad go?" Drew whispered.

Touching her ribs, the phantom bruise from Devon's phantom kick, she peered out to the double doors, but Eric was gone.

Back down on the floor, Devon was waving up at her, her face streaked white, those dark eyes. A face ghostly and exultant.

Mom, she seemed to be calling out. *Mom, I did it!*

She was smiling.

"Twenty-seven years ago, when Tina and I opened BelStars," Teddy began, assembling everyone at practice's close, "it was basically a garage. We had to drag big fans across the concrete to keep the girls from fainting. Well, to keep *me* from fainting. Eventually, we moved to a church basement with a swamp cooler, then an old ballroom with warped wood, three floors in a warehouse. All before finally breaking ground a decade ago on what is now a state-of-the-art facility. And you may have noticed something about this facility. Look up."

All eyes lifted upward, to the suspended light banks and timber beams and far beyond.

"You may think you see a ceiling," Teddy said. "But your eyes deceive you, my friends. There is no ceiling. BelStars has no ceiling. No ceiling, no roof, no limits. Your dreams are ours. Our only limits are the skies. The heavens. Am I right?"

The applause came fast and loud, ebullient, a hundred ripped palms slapping, a hundred pounding parent feet in the stands.

"And look at us today," he continued, turning toward Devon, beckoning her over. "Despite recent distractions—or perhaps because of them, as we return from them stronger, more committed—we are on a miraculous path. Because, after all, to-day we are in the presence of a future Olympian."

Head dazed and wobbling like a drunken sailor, Devon walked over to him, his bear arm encircling around her, usurping her, tucking her in his chest's deep pocket.

The claps and cheers and raised hands, they were everywhere, parents rising, draped jackets slipping from their arms, hats off, cheering and shouts, the girls on the floor yelling, twirling grip tape, unfurling wild streamers of it in the air, Jordan Siefert and Dominique Plonski bent down and hoisted arms full of foam cubes from the pit, hurling them in the air, a ticker-tape jubilee.

That pit, that pit, which had brought Ryan into their world—

And finally, the frenzy nearly at its peak, parents stomping in the stands till they shook, Lacey Weaver ran to the chalk bowl, plunging arms in, lifting them toward Devon, the chalk atomizing.

Covering Devon like confetti, like snow.

Screaming now, all of them crowding her, their hands white, their bodies too. Surrounding her, crushing her. Swallowing her whole.

A panic in Devon's eyes, Katie was sure she saw it before the swarm of arms and ponytails blocked her view.

Devon, Devon, Devon.

Devon, do it for us. Devon, we're counting on you. Devon, do it.

Chapter Twenty-One

It was nearly nine o'clock when practice ended. Everyone else, all the boosters, all the girls, were decamping for a chili dinner at Teddy's house. To mark his triumphant return.

"Aren't you coming?" Cheyenne Chu shouted at Devon from across the parking lot.

"We're going home," Katie said, grabbing Devon's shoulder. "Right away."

Devon looked at her, her face darkening.

"What about Dad?"

"Why isn't Dad here?" Drew said when they got home, drive-through tacos seeping onto the kitchen table.

"He's not coming home," Katie said, looking at Devon. They locked in a long, complicated gaze.

"I'm not hungry," Devon said, running up the stairs before Katie could stop her. "I'm taking a shower."

"Is it because of what I told you?" Drew asked. "Because Devon's here. She's allowed to be here. Because—"

"No. That's not why."

"Mom," he said, "I'll never tell again. I promise."

The graveness in his face: someone who'd witnessed horrors and miracles and knew how to endure them.

"Drew," Katie said, "I'm sorry."

"For what?"

"For everything."

Everything before, everything to come.

She knew Devon was talking to Eric on her phone. Katie could hear her through the bathroom door. She was in there a long time and Katie could hear her pacing, her voice high and inaudible.

Finally, she came out.

"Mom," she said, her face marked where the phone had been. Like a stamp, a seal. "You don't understand. You've got it wrong. About Dad. Whatever you think you're wrong."

Katie looked at her, waited for more.

Devon's mouth was open, but she couldn't seem to make the words come.

As if to say it would mean she would turn to stone.

Maybe they all would.

We're a sick house, Katie had warned the police. *I have a sick house.*

"We'll talk in the morning," Katie said. Because she needed to think.

Drew was lying flat on his bed, staring at the ceiling, the peeling nearly gone from his face. The new face was sneaking in, making its presence known.

A different face, an older face.

She gave him his antibiotics, with juice.

"Good night, Mom," he said, swallowing the pills, reaching for *The Secret of the Caves*. "I think I'll be done tomorrow."

In the dream, she was sitting in the bleachers, and her stomach hurt. Eric's hands were on it, rubbing it. But the pain got worse and worse. Pressing down, she could feel something inside, just beneath her navel.

Eric's head to her belly, he told her he heard something. A grunt. A snarl.

And that's when she felt a sharp tugging, like teeth. A tail flapping.

Looking down, between her legs, she saw it.

Tawny fur, black stripe. A tiger's paw, claws unsheathed.

Katie's own voice woke her, a strangled cry. Her head jerking up, her body lifting, running from itself.

There's something in the bed.

There's something in me.

Turning, she saw Devon standing in the doorway.

"Mom." Stepping inside the bedroom.

Katie turned away. In the dark, her daughter's face was like a black hood.

Behind her, she heard the footfalls on the carpet, a shush of bedcovers lifting, Devon sliding in bed beside her, next to her, breathing quickly, her body shuddering as if with heat and horrors.

"Have you ever done something so awful?" Devon asked.

"Devon."

A moment passed, Katie listening to her breath, waiting.

Finally: "I have to tell you, Mom."

"Tell me," Katie said. "Just tell me."

314

*   *   *

She did love him, maybe. But she wasn't sure what that meant, and did anyone ever know?

She'd never had a boy even talk to her before.

It was after a bad practice. Coach had yelled at her, everyone saw. She couldn't make her body do the things it was supposed to do. Everything felt like it was falling apart. Ryan saw her hiding under the bleachers. He said, *If you ever need someone to talk to*. And explained he'd been a basketball player in high school, a good one. Everyone told him he'd get a scholarship. He didn't. He liked pot, liked to party. He went to juvie instead. *It's hard*, he told her, *when everyone wants it so much but you're the one who has to do it*.

The first time it happened was in the back of the restaurant, on the slumped sofa in the manager's office. The huff of the oven, blazing from twelve hours of use, the spray and gush of the dishwasher, the hot-red blink of a voice mail on the manager's phone.

("Mom," she said now, "everyone tells you how much it'll hurt. But it didn't hurt at all.")

She was so focused on her own body, on what she was doing, on what was happening to every muscle, every nerve, that she nearly missed the look on his face, the flush that came over him, his shoulders shaking.

("Mom, it was so exciting," Devon said now, clutching her mom's arm. "All of it."

"I know," Katie said.)

After, he covered his face in his hands. She thought he might be crying. He said he wasn't, and turned away.

She'd seen many men cry—Coach T. after a very good meet

or a very bad one; a dozen dads, including Jim Chu, who'd cried when Cheyenne landed on her head during a tumbling run— even Bobby V., when he'd moved the uneven bars an inch without telling anyone and two girls fell.

(And your dad, Katie thought. On the freshly sheared grass of the yard. But Devon couldn't possibly remember.)

It's not because I'm sorry, Ryan said. *It's because I'm not.*

The next time Devon saw a man cry was six weeks later when her dad told her he'd found out. He wouldn't say how he knew, but he said it was his job to warn her that she was throwing everything away.

That Teddy would never forgive her, that everything would change.

That the biggest mistake you can make in life is giving in to sex.

All the things you do when you're young seem temporary, but they're all forever, he told her. And there's a hundred ways sex can ruin you.

That became the thought she couldn't get out of her head.

("I felt sick all the time," Devon said to Katie. "What Dad said made it seem different, feel different. Like I'd maybe ruined everything already. And qualifiers were coming.")

She had nightmares he was chasing her through thick woods. She could hear him breathing behind her, panting after her. He had long teeth like a vampire and wanted to drain her of all her blood.

She dreamed he was choking her. She woke up panting for air.

But she couldn't figure out how to end things.

("I thought maybe I'd be in love like Hailey," she said. "Like the girls at school. But it wasn't ever like that. It was just a thing I was trying.")

The call came while she was at Lacey's party, pedicures under way, rows of girls with their toes turned in, red and crackled and deformed.

Skip the party, he'd said. *Can you sneak the car out again?*

She'd said she couldn't. She didn't want to do that anymore. *My dad knows*, she kept telling him. *I have to stop.*

It's important, he said, and Devon crept into one of the Weaver bedrooms, Lacey's party-favor wrappers strewn across the floor. It was hard to hear him because he was outside, he was walking on the road. *I need to see you.*

And he told her he'd just broken up with Hailey. It wasn't fair to her, what they were doing.

It's someone else, Hailey had said, and she was very angry and very loud.

He'd told her no, but he didn't think she believed him. He'd driven her home in her car, and now he was walking and he wondered if it was time to tell her the truth, tell everyone.

That he and Devon were in love, and it was real, and they weren't ashamed. (*But I don't love you*, she thought, *and it's not real, and I am ashamed.*) And that neither of them cared about the consequences.

The panic in her chest, like a bird trapped there, flapping.

But he said she was just scared and not to worry.

Pick me up at our spot. Ash Road.

A spot that mattered to him, the spot he'd seen her running that time and given her a ride. *It's dangerous here*, he'd said. *Jesus, you could die.*

Meet me, he said. *It'll all be okay.*

It was like his hands were closing around her neck.

Everyone would know. Coach T. would never forgive her. Everything would be over.

*   *   *

Slipping out of the Weaver house, past the laughing girls, half of them singing, voices lifting to the rafters, their feet tapping under tables, the pink pulsating karaoke machine humming at their painted feet, she was gone.

She was gone, and no one saw.

Running the mile home, her chest tight and punishing, she couldn't get there fast enough.

Except Drew was in the garage, doing something with his science project. And he was always trying to catch her.

Hiding behind the tool bench, she waited until he left, then grabbed Dad's keys on the hook just inside the kitchen door. She'd only done it three times before, and once she'd had to stop to figure out how to turn on the headlights.

She wasn't thinking as she drove there. She couldn't make her brain stop whirring long enough to think.

The sign seemed to jump out at her: Ash Road.

They were both sitting up now, Devon taking little breaths.

"Mom, it happened so fast," she finally said, her voice small as when she was a child having a nightmare. The kind when even after Katie thought she'd wakened her she could tell Devon was still seeing it, her eyes dancing under her lids.

"You can tell me," Katie said, grabbing for her hand.

"It was darker than it had ever been before," Devon said, shaking her head. "I couldn't tell where the road ended and the rest began. I didn't know how to make the lights go bright enough."

"Oh, honey," Katie said.

Devon leaned against her arm, her mouth inches from her mother's ear.

"Suddenly, he was there," Devon said. "And I didn't turn the wheel fast enough."

A rush of feelings came, every feeling all at once, Katie's stomach turning.

"My foot never...it was so fast and then it was too late," Devon said. "I don't even remember getting home."

"Oh, Devon."

"Mom, I swear, it was darker than it had ever been."

They didn't say anything, or even move, for what felt like a long time.

"You were lying, then," Katie said, finally. "About Hailey's texts, her calls, the things she said. You let me believe your dad..."

"I'm a murderer," Devon said, the words so big neither of them could speak for a moment.

Katie couldn't order her thoughts. None of it seemed real, the comforter bunching in her hands. But she knew whatever she said next would decide the course of everything.

"You're not a murderer," she said, the words soft in her mouth. "That's not what it is."

"Mom, I am. I just kept going. I didn't stop, I didn't do any-thing. I froze. I—"

"No," Katie said, a growing force in her voice. "It was an accident. It was a terrible accident. There are accidents, and we can't always stop them, and it's no one's fault."

"It is my fault. I'm a monster," she said, turning, her face so old Katie didn't recognize it. Small and stretched and old. "Because I'm not sorry enough. I missed him, but I'm free. He might have taken it all away. I—"

"That's not true," Katie interrupted. "I know it's compli-cated, but you really don't—"

"You never want to hear what it's like being me," she whispered.

"What?" Katie asked. "What do you mean?"

But Devon didn't seem to be listening, her face in her hands now.

They sat for a second, a draft nudging the door open. Katie could hear Drew's deep, throaty breathing down the hall, the walls humming with it.

And she looked back at Devon, cross-legged on the bed, and reached out to touch her cheek. As she did, Devon's face seemed immediately to unlash itself, to grow tender and young and unruined. It was the face of a little girl sprawled on her bed, or the back lawn, her foot caught beneath her.

"I'm a monster," she repeated. "I am."

"No, Devon," Katie said, pulling her close, her hands on her hair, smoothing it, "you're my girl, you're our girl. You're mine."

There were so many things she and Eric had tried to buffer Devon from, the shocks and trauma of the world. Anything that might distract her, hurt her.

The gym and her home were both siloed tight, the floors padded, all the noises of the world sucked out.

All so Devon could stand—beam, runway, corner of mat— and only hear the sound of her own breath, her own heart beating, only see the air, the ground, the air and ground again. Only worry about herself.

Which is what all parents want to do for their children, after all.

All of Devon's life she'd been nestled in that amniotic swirl, the swirl she inhaled and exhaled. Nestled, smothered, choked. By her parents. Wasn't that right?

And the minute she'd forced her way out, kicking spastically at all corners, been sucked out by the grappling hands of that handsome boy, she hadn't known what to do, how to live in this world. Everything had been too much.

She hadn't learned, no one had taught her—Katie and Eric hadn't taught her—that the things you want, you never get them. And if you do, they're not what you thought they'd be. But you'd still do anything to keep them. Because you'd wanted them for so long.

V

I could hear thousands of eyes watching us.

—Nadia Comaneci, *Letters to a Young Gymnast*

Chapter Twenty-Two

There were three things Devon would never tell her mother.

The first was what Mrs. Weaver had said before she left Lacey's birthday party that night. Sneaking out of one of the half dozen bedrooms, Devon felt a hand on her shoulder. There was Mrs. Weaver, and Devon knew she'd heard her on the phone with Ryan. Had heard everything.

For a second, Devon thought it was all over, and in some way she was relieved. That everyone would know and it wouldn't be hers anymore.

But instead, Mrs. Weaver just shook her head and said, in the iciest of voices, "I hope your mother never has to know this."

The second thing she'd never tell her mother was what happened after, when she saw Ryan on Ash Road that night.

Driving, hardly breathing at all but almost flying, she thought: *My life is ending, my life is over.*

Once Ryan had asked her if she ever thought about him when she was on the floor, the beam. Of course she never did, and never would. It was a place she would never let him in. (*Single-mindedness*, Coach T. always told her, *is the greatest of your great gifts.*) But that was when she'd known she'd never feel for him what he felt for her.

There was not enough space in her heart.

Her heart was different.

She was different.

This is what she knew: you win or lose everything with a flick of the wrist, a turn of the ankle, not enough lift, a slipped hand on the beam.

And everything changes, everything goes dark, and is gone.

What if we just tell everyone, won't it be wonderful, he'd said, even as he knew she was pulling away. Because he knew she was pulling away.

She'd turned on the high beams.

All the dust and sand and road salt glittering up into the air.

The hot yellow of the center line, like an arrow straight to him.

Headlight-struck, face like blasted marble and eyes filled with love.

He was the most beautiful thing she'd ever seen.

Her hands on the wheel, for a second she thought, *Forget what Dad said, what Mrs. Weaver said, what anyone thinks.* He was so beautiful. What did anything else matter?

Strange that it was in that moment that she did it.

The moment she made the turn and saw him waiting for her, waving to her, seeing him so rapturously handsome, lit by her headlights, that great golden flame of a face.

Standing at the fog line, his feet planted on the shoulder.

Waving to her, slowly waving, his arm swaying.

That *that* was the moment she—

You must be in control of your landing, that's what Coach always said.

Bounding down the vault runway, feet hit springboard, hands hit table, the push—

—flying through the air, soaring, a spinning weightlessness, arrowing down, the surge of feet to ground, body electric.

Thump, thwack, smack, and she felt it, down there:

The ancient throb in her foot, *that* foot, blood surging, pressing down on the gas.

There's a hundred ways sex can ruin you. The words came to her in that moment, a thunderclap in her head.

Her mouth made a funny noise, and she felt a twinge over her heart. But not enough to stop her. At least not in time.

Her arms jerked, the wheel seized, he was there in front of her, waving and smiling.

For a second, the white tail of his shirt, like a bird flying, and she shut her eyes.

Her right foot throbbing, she plunged it downward onto the pedal.

He was there, and then he was gone.

Then there was the third thing she'd never tell.

Which is how it really began, with Ryan. What had started it, for her.

It was back in January, the night after regionals, a big booster party. Tiki torches. Some of the girls sneaking sips of coconut rum from white bottles smooth as milk.

Her head doing starbursts when she closed her eyes.

Air, air, air, she thought.

I am, I am, I am. Which is what she always said when she was on the vault runway. It cleared her.

The flowers tickled her neck and smelled like the inside of Mrs. Weaver's car.

The all-around gold medal beneath it, cold against her hot chest, her hand pressed there.

You made us so proud, her dad told her. *But you always do,* kissing the top of her head.

And a song came on through the popping speakers, something about a girl with a blister on her hand, that felt like it was just for her.

It will be like this forever, she was saying in her head, *I will feel this way forever.*

That's when she saw it. The dance floor crushed and impossible and in a far corner, by the swinging doors to the kitchen, a ponytailed woman with her hand on a man's hip.

She blinked once, then twice, because it had to be the coconut rum swirling. Except it wasn't, because the woman with the ponytail was Mom and the man was Ryan Beck, Hailey's boyfriend.

Ryan, the one all the girls always talked about. And she'd never really looked at him. Even the time he found her retainer, held it right in his hand. She'd never looked because it felt like she shouldn't, like staring into the sun.

Her mom did, sometimes. At the booster events, at Weaver's Wagon, where he worked. The night they'd all stayed at the Ramada, the way she'd watched him down at the pool.

"Oh my God," her mom was saying now, her eyes wide, her hand jumping to her mouth, "I thought you were my husband."

Ryan Beck's smile, easy and loose, and open.

"I bet that's what they all say to you," her mom said, and then both of them were laughing and it didn't seem like her mom at all, one strap on her dress slipping down her shoulder, golden under the grease-slicked light fixture, a glass bowl glowing over their heads.

Her mom looked so young, which was strange, because she wasn't.

Something—and not just the mai tais because she'd seen her mom like that before—was making her cheeks look brighter, making her body move differently, fluidly, fleshily. Everything different from the ordered, slunk-shouldered, hank-haired mother she was. That something was in her mom.

Was it the thing she saw in the girls at school? The ones who showed off mesh bras and metallic thongs, whispering to one another of feelings and mysteries, belt buckles under blankets and the tastes of things and that look on their faces, and when they saw the boy from the night before, or the one who just might be that night.

It felt like a secret kept from her her whole life. Like: *You're adopted. You have a brother you've never met. Your father isn't dead, he's in prison.*

How come no one told me?

Your mom, secretly, at night, turns into this. And so do other women, other girls. Just not you. All of them except you.

How come everyone hid it from me? How come Mom did?

She watched them.

Their faces pressed close because of the swinging door behind them or because of this thing, this conspicuous energy, practically glowing, and she could have sworn that, when her mother was laughing and leaning close, her mouth pushed against Ryan Beck's cheek, even his tanned neck, and the kitchen door swinging and pressing them close.

And then her mom asking for a cigarette, but she never smoked, not ever, and as he went to light it for her, her hand leaped out, grabbing for something, the paperback with the red cover shoved in his back pocket.

Ryan's eyes went wide with surprise. A grin there.

Devon couldn't believe she'd seen it. *Her mom's hand in his pocket!*

And both of them laughing and the song ending and then she saw her mom leap back, as if touching a flame.

Oh! Covering her mouth again. Repeating, with a wink this time, *I thought you were my husband.*

In the ladies' room, Dominique Plonski heaved coconut pudding, slippery tongues of guava, spattering Devon's brand-new metallic open-toe pumps for which her dad had paid forty dollars.

I don't know what happened, Dominique kept saying, her little body shaking from it.

You can't eat food like that, Devon said, looking down at her silver shoes, ruined. *Your body doesn't know how.*

After, leaning against the dumpster behind the restaurant, a wet paper towel in hand, she took off her shoes, her lei.

It was then she saw Ryan, ducked behind the dumpster, smiling at her and smoking a cigarette.

She decided she would talk to him, which she never had.

I didn't know you smoked, she said, her voice embarrassingly high.

I gave it up a hundred years ago, he said, *but we all have our secrets.*

But what should she say next?

Don't hide it, he said, catching her hiding her foot behind her other foot.

Her right foot, its lumpen side, the soft pad, its split thickness. (Her Frankenfoot, that's what her mom used to call it until her dad made her stop. Thank God, he made her stop. But her dad, sometimes it felt like he never stopped looking at it. Her foot, that foot, it was more theirs than hers.)

It's ugly, she said. *I hate it.*

I doubt that. He smiled.

You shouldn't smoke, she said. Then blurted: *And you should stay away from the moms.*

And he laughed, a loud bark, and nodded his head yes.

Okay, he said, and he looked down at her foot again, and it was like he could see it pulsing, like a second heart.

She knew he could. And he was right. It was beautiful.

Chapter Twenty-Three

Elite Qualifiers
One Month Later

The four of them walked into the conference center, the QUAL-
IFIERS DAY 1 OF 2—BALLROOM B sign rippling above them over
the bank of doors.

The four of them—Eric's hand squeezing Devon's shoulder,
Drew wheeling the mini-cooler, Katie hauling Devon's gym
bag—walked inside, and they were ready.

And Katie looked at her daughter, her hard, small little body,
her muscled neck. The blankness in her eyes. Shades drawn. No
one could peek through. No one.

"We'll take her from here," the blond official with the lanyard
said, clasping Devon by the shoulders.

There was no grandstand, no booming sound system, no grease-
lined concessions or foil balloon banks or sponsor banners. No

bleachers, even, just a set of risers clotted with parents, fists knotted with nerves.

It was just another convention center: dropped ceiling, thirty thousand feet of industrial floor divided into quadrants, long tables and metal folding chairs in the middle, between the beams and bars, judges seated there, Styrofoam coffee cups in hand, watching.

A few officials were milling around, and coaches walking their girls, hands to shoulders, patting their hard little backs, the shells of baby turtles. A tracksuited volunteer dragged a springboard across the floor as a girl hinged into a handstand, turning hypnotically on the beam, releasing a smattering of claps from the risers. In one corner, a purple-leotarded sylph slashed her legs through a floor routine as a boom box echoed wanly. On a tumbling strip, another rubbed her hands frantically, counting in her head.

The *smack-smack-smack* of the vault.

Farther down on the risers, an unshaven father, arms across his chest, looked like he might be praying.

The night before, all the booster parents had assembled at Gwen's house, their faces gray and hoary from four weeks of punishing driving schedules, the pit-foamed air of the gym, the precompetition hysteria of "gymjuries"—overworked girls jamming fingers, rolling ankles, popping knees. Molly Chu, twelve pounds thinner from nerves, her cheeks hollow, kept sliding antacids under her tongue. Becca Plonski's hands cradled her jaw, which ached from gum chewing, teeth grinding.

But there was something else on all their faces too: that feeling of being on the cusp, like generals on the brink of battle, bunkered deep in the Pentagon war room.

It was probably superstition, then, that no one wanted to talk about anything related to qualifiers, about their daughters least of all, their daughters who were all at home, bodies Gordian-knotted, hunchbacked over gym videos, soaking in blood-blooming bathtubs, their feet and hands shredded.

Instead, the parents gathered in one corner of Gwen's palatial living room, their minds fired and their bodies responding with beer-pounding, overeating, and listening to a long, dirty story from Jim Chu about the time his roommate supposedly slept with Mary Lou Retton.

It was Kirsten Siefert who brought out the joint, swiped from her son's backpack, and they shared it, even Molly, who said, red-faced, that pot made her "erotic."

Eyes twitching and nostrils flared, Gwen tried to talk shop, but no one would join her. (Katie herself had not said one word to her since their conversation at Weaver's Wagon. They glided past each other with the hooded eyes of those who'd shared a mortifying one-night stand.)

Finally, Gwen surrendered to the group, the gym-parent equivalent of a key party, returning from her kitchen brandishing a bottle of tequila in the shape of a skull, looking like she wanted to throw back the bottle and swallow the worm whole.

Who's feeling dangerous? she asked, in her tall boots, the kind you might ride in. *Where's the crop?* Jim Chu had laughed, and kept laughing even as his smile fell, Gwen's gaze on him.

The boots were magnificent, and worn, and when she walked in them, she looked taller, stronger, younger. Prettier.

A picture came into Katie's head, Gwen at fifteen or sixteen, smart cap and flowing hair, arms latched onto a sleek mare, hands following the bit. Body radiating. Cheeks flushed. Her face the face of someone lost in a dream. *Daddy, watch me. Watch me win.*

"Eric," Kirsten shouted, waving across the room, "the tequila yearns for you."

The only remaining outlier, Eric had yet to join the revels, sitting in the far corner nursing a beer, rubbing his face, eyes bloodshot, brow graven.

(*Katie,* he'd said to her just three weeks ago when she'd first let him back into the house, though not into her bed, *if Devon gets this* . . . But he never could finish the thought. One of a thousand half conversations, neither of them able to finish one.)

"Eric, it's your turn," Becca Plonski demanded, lifting the shot glass, wiggling in her seat.

Eric walked over, took a swig from the tequila, grinned boyishly, faking it, faking it, faking it, that sun-burnished face, and how he could make his eyes dance, who could do that, make their eyes dance?

Eric could.

A few more swigs, and he began talking freely, buoyantly, about Coach T.'s near laryngitis, about how Bobby V. accidentally ordered the team towels from a massage-parlor supplier, about anything at all. Everything he said made everyone laugh and slap knees. Becca Plonski even reached out to touch his arm, as if to say, *Oh, stop, Eric, but don't ever stop.*

Slipping off into the hallway, Katie spotted Lacey, that sex-doll face of hers, peeking through the rails of the staircase, watching them all, the manic chatter and gamesmanship, the way adults, parents, could talk forever and forever and without ceasing about nothing they cared about just to stop the worries churning in their hot brains.

(The next day, Lacey would fall during one of her qualifier routines, her heels catching one of the uneven bars and her body folding in upon itself. Everyone would watch her crumpled on the floor, face blue, Coach T. crying out. One fractured vertebra, another dislocated, and this would be the last time she'd ever compete. But none of them knew it now, except maybe Lacey.)

"Katie!" Molly said, finding her in the hallway, grabbing her by the arm. "I'm so happy for Devon. For what's going to happen tomorrow. Her life will change forever. All of yours will. I always wanted to do it like you did."

Molly was nearly crying, holding Katie's hands, swinging them.

"How did I do it?" Katie said. "What did I do?"

What did I do.

Around ten, Katie found Eric in the kitchen, talking on the phone, asking Drew about something he was watching on television, a show about a woman who'd died of yellow fever and whose body had turned into soap.

As he talked ("She was wearing kneesocks? For real, buddy?"), his face relaxed for the first time in months. It reminded her of some things, and erased other things.

Watching him, she knew she would let him back in their bed later that night. She knew she would press against his back, burying her face in his thick hair, listening to his heart beat.

What would he be thinking, though, when he slipped under the covers?

Would he be thinking of what his daughter had done? What he'd done to conceal it?

Or might he be thinking of how she'd trapped him seventeen years ago, turned his youthful fling with a concessions girl into marriage, family, mortgage, second mortgage, days sardined with school, practice drop-off, dry cleaner, grocery store, practice pickup, homework, overturned fishbowl, torn cereal boxes oozing flakes and Os on the top of the refrigerator, booster e-mails, dinner, laundry, collapse?

Maybe he'd be thinking he'd found a way to happiness, even if he hadn't expected it. The life they'd created, or built—from their wayward romance or from the bloody back lawn where Devon was, in some ways, born—was far greater than the both of them. It was a beautiful, an extraordinary thing.

But, deep down, Katie knew Eric wouldn't be thinking any of this.

Instead, he'd be thinking, *Please, for Devon, tomorrow and the next day, let her hit all her spots, let her keep that right leg high, let her stun with her double-twist Yurchenko, let her show them everything that she can do, everything that she is. Let her make it.*

So Katie left the kitchen and took the passed joint and drank long tugs from the beers that became margaritas later, at Casa Pepi's down the road, a marimba trio playing raucously, a song called "I Already Have a Husband," and Molly jumping up, starting to dance.

The musicians applauded, one of them handing her his mallet, and Molly grabbed it.

Laughing, she started twirling it over her head, just as she had at the tiki party.

And they could all see it, or Katie could, watching all that joy.

As everyone cheered, Molly twirled like she'd twirled that silver-sprayed pipe stolen from her father's tool bench twenty-five years ago or more. It had looked like a pinwheel in the sun.

Remember that kind of wanting? she'd said that night of the tiki party. *That kind that's just for yourself? And you don't even have to feel guilty about it? You wouldn't know to.*

*   *   *

And now it was all happening, up there on the creaking risers at qualifiers.

Amid the roaming judges, black blazers and appraising eyes, and the metallic leotards, hologram swirls, mesh, spandex foil, the girls like jewel bugs hopping, flipping.

Beside her, Drew, the fever long gone, skin peeled away revealing a face that was not the same face, was new.

Curling him close, she looked into his eyes, and they weren't the same eyes. Suddenly, with great pain, she knew she couldn't see into them as she once could.

She had no idea what he was thinking at all. Eyes blank, blinds drawn.

"Mom, Devon's going to do it," he promised, patting her hand. "She's going to make it. I told her this morning. And she said she loved me."

"We all love you, Drew," she said, pulling him closer.

They had never talked about the role he'd played in any of this, and never again about what he'd seen in the garage. His father and his sister, their world flayed before them, both their hands covered in blood and gristle. His father and sister conspiring to form a lie to last forever. Fortress walls thirty feet thick. A surrounding moat a hundred yards deep.

Or maybe Eric had talked to him, taking him, of late, on long, meandering walks through the woods to look for sphinx moths as dusk fell.

The Knoxes—they were four, but they were one. Seated in the risers, backs arched in their matching BelStars tees, Katie, Eric, and Drew watched Devon, the matchless perfection with which she stormed through the compulsories on day one. The night in between, at the Best Western that smelled like carpet powder and pet hair, they shared both a watchful silence and the excitement of knowing that she would secure it on day two. And now here it was, the end of a triumphant day two, her last routine, her last vault run.

They had embarked on this epic journey long ago, centuries, it felt like, and it was unstoppable.

The force that through the green fuse drives the flower.

No one could stop it now. Not the police. Not Hailey Belfour, who'd followed her beloved uncle in lockstep. Not Gwen Weaver. Not a scattering of paint chips that never led anywhere. Another unsolved hit-and-run.

Not the envy of others, not all the people who'd misunderstood and judged them.

Not even the lobster claw at the end of Devon's ankle could stop them now.

Least of all a boy, a beautiful, ephemeral young man who'd floated up from the road like a feather.

No one could.

Was one meant to pay forever for a fleeting mistake? A turn of the wheel, a bobble of a foot, a pause that lasted seconds too long?

Because they had finally arrived at what it had all been leading to, since Devon first squirmed, a slippery minnow, in her womb. Promising Katie everything, beginning with Eric.

All forces had conspired for them at last, and it was time for the Knoxes, their hearts on the floor.

Katie watched, her breath even and sure, one hand in Eric's, the other tight on Drew's shoulder.

At the foot of the runway, Devon waited, her eyes on the gleaming leather of the vault table.

And from the stands, it was like her foot was glowing. It was glowing.

There she stood, Devon—her body, their body, one body—and all the exceptional talent contained within it.

Her body, a machine. A marvel. Her body was everything.

Her body was their heart.

Acknowledgments

There are not thank-yous enough to account for my debt to the extraordinary Reagan Arthur and her entire, astounding Little, Brown team, especially Michelle Aielli, Sabrina Callahan, Miriam Parker, Meghan Deans, Peggy Freudenthal, Tracy Roe, and Julianna Lee.

By the same token, I am so grateful to the marvelous Paul Baggeley, Kate Harvey, Emma Bravo, Francesca Main, and Ansa KhanKhattak at Picador for their brilliant efforts. And heartiest thanks are owed to Angharad Kowal, Maja Nikolic, and Taylor Templeton at Writers House and Sylvie Rabineau, Jill Gillett, and Julie Snider at RWSG.

Foremost gratitude to Dan Conaway, who makes all this happen.

And with special thanks to my infinitely supportive family: Phil and Patti Abbott, who inspire me regularly; Josh Abbott, Julie Nichols, and Kevin Abbott; and Jeff, Ruth, Steve, and Michelle Nase.

And to the dearest of friends: Alison Quinn, Darcy Lockman, and the notorious FLs.

I also owe a special thanks to Kat Howard—a wonderful writer and also a former gymnast—for her generous early read of this novel.

And lastly to what-would-I-do-without-you folks from Oxford, MS: Jack Pendarvis, Theresa Starkey, Ace and Angela Atkins (Angela, from whom I purloined a detail for this very book), Bill and Katie Boyle, and Jimmy Cajoleas. I could do nothing the rest of my life but sit and talk with all of you forever and count myself happy, and lucky.